The Man I Can't Forgive

BOOKS BY NOELLE HARRISON

The Island Girls
The Boatman's Wife
The Girl Across the Sea
The Last Summer in Ireland

The Gravity of Love
The Adulteress
The Secret Loves of Julia Caesar
I Remember
A Small Part Of Me
Beatrice

The Man I Can't Forgive

NOELLE HARRISON

bookouture

Published by Bookouture in 2024

An imprint of Storyfire Ltd.
Carmelite House
50 Victoria Embankment
London EC4Y 0DZ

www.bookouture.com

ISBN: 978-1-83525-076-1
eBook ISBN: 978-1-83525-075-4

For Bex
In gratitude for your gentle guidance, and the joy of dance.

LISTEN TO ME

I loved you more than anything but you did not love me enough back.

So that's why it happened. I wanted you to feel the same pain as me.

The shame of it.

I wanted you to know how it felt. To be broken. Fallen. Falling.

To mean nothing at all.

CHAPTER ONE

TWO DAYS AFTER, THURSDAY 4 APRIL 2019

He's gone. He really is this time. It has been two days now since Constance Garvey last saw her husband, Daniel.

Constance stands at her kitchen window, staring at the back of her neighbor's house. She sips her mug of tea as she watches the orange orb of the desert sun simmering behind the red roofs of the other buildings. The light is heavenly, and yet it only makes her feel depressed to look at it. Can she survive without her husband?

And yet is there not relief in the finality of it? The long agony of their breakup is over, and she can begin to grieve. Once, she said to Daniel she would rather he died than left her. It was an awful thing to say, but it was how she had felt at the time. That had been years ago though.

She finishes her mug of tea, immediately rinsing it out before putting it in the pristine dishwasher. She opens the cabinet above the dishwasher, surveying its spotless shelves, the glasses glistening with tiny reflections of her. She takes each wine glass out one by one. Lining them up on the countertop, she begins polishing them with a freshly laundered cloth.

Daniel chose his mistress over her. His wife of twenty years.

By not choosing Constance, she believes her husband has abandoned his teenage daughter too.

One of the glasses slips through her fingers yet she does nothing to stop it. It falls as if in slow motion and smashes onto the edge of the countertop, spraying the tiled floor with shards of glass.

Like a robot, Constance pulls a dustpan and brush out from under the sink, and begins to scoop up the broken glass. She pushes thoughts of Daniel out of her mind and focuses on her daughter instead.

Cathy is what matters most and she has become so secretive the past year. Constance never knows what her daughter is thinking anymore. She is either subjected to days of silence, or sudden furious outbursts over the slightest thing.

Just yesterday Cathy snapped at her for no reason whatsoever. They were sitting at the kitchen table. Constance had tried to please her daughter by making her a berry smoothie. Cathy had loved them when she was little. But Cathy complained it was too cold.

'It's giving me a headache,' she moaned, pressing her hand to her forehead.

'Sorry, love, I must have put too much ice in,' Constance said. 'It's so hot outside I thought you'd like it cold.'

'Yeah, but you have the place freezing with the air con,' Cathy said. 'You know it's bad for the environment.'

'So how's school?' Constance asked, changing the subject. She knew Cathy was right but she couldn't bear the heat in Arizona. Even at this time of year, before the full brunt of the summer hit.

Cathy shrugged.

'Fine.' She sipped her smoothie, outlining her lips in deep purple.

'So apart from Lisa, who else are you friends with?'

Cathy stared at her. How cold the blue of her eyes were. Just like her father's could be sometimes.

'What's with the interrogation?'

'I was just asking you about your friends, it's hardly an interrogation...'

'You're always asking me questions about who I'm hanging out with. Where I'm going. You're so controlling.'

Constance felt stung.

'I'm just interested in your life,' she said in a weak voice.

'Whatever.' Cathy got up, leaving her half-drunk smoothie on the table.

'It's too bitter,' she explained. 'I'm going out.'

'Where?' Constance asked before she could stop herself.

'See, there you go again,' her daughter said in exasperation.

'But you're not even sixteen, and this is America. I need to know you're safe.'

'I'm going to Lisa's, okay? We've a math test tomorrow. We're going to study together.'

'Shall I drive you?'

'Just leave me alone, will you?' Cathy stormed out the room.

One time, Constance followed Cathy all the way to Lisa's house. Creeping behind trees and fences, like some kind of stalker. But she had to make sure her daughter was going exactly where she said she was.

Constance tries her best not to question Cathy too much. She has to trust her. Because she remembers how much she resented the fact that her own mother had never trusted her when she was Cathy's age.

Still, no matter how patient Constance tries to be, it feels as if her very existence infuriates her fifteen-year-old daughter.

The best thing is not to push Cathy to talk. Constance read that in a magazine. She prays Cathy will come back to her as she gets older. She tries not to let it bother her, but it feels as if her daughter doesn't like her anymore. Blames Constance for the fact that Daniel has hardly ever been around the past few months.

She explained to Cathy that her father was busy in his new job as a realtor, working long hours for his brother, Liam. Trying to provide for them. But she had suspected otherwise. For a while she tried to ignore all the signs that Daniel was unfaithful because she hadn't wanted to acknowledge her marriage was over. All she wanted was her little girl back. To be a family again. But over the last couple of weeks, she's realized there is no hope of that now.

It is only three days ago since her suspicions were confirmed and she found out for certain her husband was having an affair. She hasn't slept since. Sitting up in bed, her body slick with sweat, unable to shake the dread in the pit of her belly. What if Cathy insists on living with Daniel and the other woman? Constance would be left all on her own. No husband, and no daughter. A lonely ex-wife in a place where she doesn't belong. The idea of it makes her feel wild with rage.

Constance takes a breath, tries to quell her trembling limbs. She dries her hands on a piece of kitchen roll. Opening the drawer, she takes out a plaster and seals a tiny cut with it. She has to keep on going. Stay busy for Cathy's sake. She picks up another glass, rolls its cold contours against her even colder cheeks. The motion soothes her. She stares across her backyard at the house on the other side and wills a light to go on, but it remains in darkness.

Constance steps back from the sink and leans against the wall, the small of her back, her palms, her heels pressed against its smooth chill. She tips her head back to look at the ceiling. It is perfectly white. Not one blemish or crack. She is hollow, emptied out. She does not feel human anymore. She needs to pull herself away from this wall, but she is flattened by terror. What will happen now?

CHAPTER TWO

TWO DAYS AFTER, THURSDAY

It's over. The words keep rolling over in her head as Maya grinds the bright red pigment. It has been two days since she was with Daniel. It feels so long ago and yet impossible to believe.

She dips her finger in the vermilion powder, examines its lethal shade.

'It's over,' she says aloud, the words making her tremble.

Deep down she has always known it was going to end badly one day.

She picks up a small bottle of oil, adding a few drops to the pigment and picks up her spatula. Slowly she mixes it into a soft crumbly paste. She doesn't know why she is making paint. It's all she can think to do to stop herself from falling apart. She can't believe what happened.

She gazes out of her studio window at the dark silhouettes of the trees against the early morning glow. She wills Daniel to appear among the greenery of the aspen trees. For him to walk back through the door. For them to make love on her old Navajo rug. No need for words, because everything would be as it was.

But of course, Daniel will never come to her house again.

She regrets the last words she remembers saying to him. Where had that anger come from?

Maya turns her back to the window, and begins scraping the paste into a jar. She is in no mood for the stickiness of oil paints. She goes to her sink and fills one of her ceramic bowls with water, and picks up her mixing plate of watercolors. She grabs one of her biggest soft brushes, and dips it into the bowl of water, splattering it onto the ceramic plate, and swirling it into all the colors. She brushes her wrist with wet paint, but the colors are so muted that it's merely faded into her dark skin. She needs to express her feelings because for Maya, this is never a choice.

She picks up a tube of crimson watercolor paint, and squeezes a long trail of it onto her painting plate. She plunges the brush back into the water, and plonks it right in the middle of the paint. It feels better to attack the color with such fervor.

Her eyes light upon one of her desert landscapes. Its delicate tones of pink and gold. The painting had been one of Daniel's favorites. She slaps the red paint onto the fragile watercolor. She covers the brush in swathes of red wash again, and sweeps it across the whole width of the watercolor painting. Again and again until the paper is buckling under the weight of water. She obliterates the whole picture under streaks of red.

When she is done, Maya wipes her hands on her jeans, but she can't get the paint off. Her fingers are stained red. She is the scarlet woman for all to see.

She surveys her red-splattered studio, the enactment of her sudden fury. She remembers how she had lost herself in such a maelstrom of emotion the last time she saw Daniel. Shouting at him. She remembers the shocked look on his face. But this is all she can remember. Nothing afterwards.

CHAPTER THREE

THREE DAYS AFTER, FRIDAY 5 APRIL 2019

This is the fourth time it's happened to Katarina in the Grand Canyon. Her first summer as a park ranger, she and Shane investigated a car driven off the rim. She remembered her dry throat, the battering of her heart against her ribs, as they approached the crushed vehicle. Shane had asked her if she was okay, and she said yes. But she knew that she probably hadn't looked it.

They had seen it all before. Not just in the Grand Canyon, but before that in Yosemite as well. Deaths that were impossible to tell whether they were accidental or not. Lots of folks died in the Grand Canyon. Fewer people have managed to hike the length of the Grand Canyon than scale Everest, and even fewer respect the dangers of hiking the canyon's unreliable terrain. It is not just the inexperienced who perish. She has known several seasoned hikers who have taken an unlucky step. Just one slab of rock needs to shift, and within a heartbeat you can plunge hundreds of feet. No one survives a fall like that.

Most deaths though are the result of dehydration or hyponatremia—when the hiker drinks too much water without any food.

Pure lack of preparation. The heat can be punishing in the middle of the summer. Sometimes when she is on patrol in the height of the season, she feels like she is literally being grilled under the blaze of the hard Arizona sun but as a ranger she has no choice. She has to get out on the trails every day and rescue the stupid people (usually city dwellers of course) who think they can trek through the Grand Canyon in their sneakers with no food or little water. As Shane was always saying, 'Folk come to the Grand Canyon, and they die. Our job is to deal with the fallout.'

That first time in the Grand Canyon, it was Shane who had seen the body before her. He had held his hand up to warn her not to approach. She could have turned away, waited for the helicopter to arrive, but something in her needed to see. The car had clearly landed on its roof, and bounced upright again. The interior was caved in. She had bent down, peered inside its dark cavernous interior, seen a crumpled body. At first, she wondered if it was a doll, some kind of joke, but the look on Shane's face told her otherwise. He had looked stern, but calm, although she could see his leg jigging up and down with the adrenaline rush.

Although she'd seen dead bodies before in Yosemite, she had been unable to stop thinking about the fallen man in the Grand Canyon for weeks. Maybe it was because it had been her first suicide. She kept imagining the moment the soon-to-be divorced man (as they had later found out) pressed his foot down on the accelerator and sped towards the rim. Had he changed his mind once the car had flown off the edge? Was it terror or elation that flooded his body moments before he crashed into the rocks below?

Night after night she had woken up shaking and parched. Shane would find her drinking glass after glass of water in the dark.

'What is it, baby?' he had asked her.

She had let him take her in his arms, kiss the top of her head.

'Just a bad dream,' she mumbled into his chest. She did not tell him that she had felt cursed by the sight of that dead man in the car.

All her mother's old superstitions—the part of herself Katarina worked so hard to suppress—surface at night, when the Moon hangs in the black outside their window like a skull, gloaming, and eyeless.

It has been a while since anyone has managed to drive a car off the rim of the Grand Canyon. But there are other jumpers. Some people they never even manage to identify. It makes her think of all the holes in all the families in America. Someone is missing, and they will never be found.

Today on her trek, she was on her own. It's her favorite time of year. April. The season only just begun. The land still felt fresh, the air scented with wild flowers. The Colorado River rolled wild, and swollen. Winter was well and truly over. And yet each step she took felt shadowed by foreboding. She thought she heard whispering. Echoes through the chasms of rock. Someone calling her name. *Katarina.*

She even called out.

'Who's there?'

Of course there was no answer. Just her own voice reverberating around her. She had taken the tube of hand cream from her pocket and squirted some onto the palms of her hands although the skin wasn't dry. Rubbed them together. Her hands had twisted in and out of each other, again and again. She had stared at them. For too long. She had smelled them. The coconut and vanilla calmed her nerves.

She took a breath and continued because she had to follow the trail all the way. Keep looking, stay vigilant.

Katarina didn't feel alone but there was no one else near her, of course. Merely the light bouncing off the rocks, bleached as bone. The space between the boulders almost skeletal in its form. She thought of her mother's devotion to Santa Muerte, Our Lady of Holy Death. The skeleton in the woman's robes. *Señora de las Sombras,* her mother called her. Lady of the Shadows. She who could work miracles.

She knew before she even saw him that there was something bad up ahead. She felt the breath of Santa Muerte upon her cheek. And in her heart, she does believe in the power of death. How it has the ability to make all men, and all women, equal in the end.

LISTEN TO ME

Let me tell you about my first memory. I was standing at the window by my bed looking at trees. Big trees. The girth of their trunks so wide I believed little people must live inside them. Their bark was gnarled, twisted into ancient knots, and they reached up high. Far higher than my house. These trees looked solid and safe. I dreamed of climbing them. Pushing through the canopy of leaves and hiding.

They would never find me there.

Once they had noticed that I was gone—a fact that might well take at least the length of one day—they would begin to search my room. Under the bed. In the closet. Places I had hidden before. They would do a sweep of the whole house. It was only then, after calling my name for hours, that they would begin to look outside. At first, they would be angry, then frustrated, and finally worried, but I would wait. I would eat berries and fruit from my lofty bower, and lick the morning dew from the leaves. I would last up there in the protection of my tree, until my disappearance united them. They would forget that they hated each other. And when I saw my father put his arm around my mother, I would call to them and make them promise to stop fighting. Only then would I come down.

My second memory is the sound of breaking glass. Her jagged accusations, his roaring. It is night, and I am in bed. I cannot stop shaking. The door pushes open, and I hear the pad of paws, sense the comfort of Rosie's presence. My dog springs onto the end of the bed, and I reach down for her. Feel her hot licks of solidarity on my hands.

You could say that mine was a normal childhood. I had a mother and a father. He went out to work, and she stayed at home. We lived in a regular family home, in a respectable community. My father made sure we had all the things every middle-class family has: a decent car, TV, washing machine, a swing in the garden for me, a family pet and plenty of flourishing houseplants. We had everything apart from love.

I grew up in a house of hate. This is what I told you.

And you said, *But of course, two can never be one. You are a fool if you think so.*

I did not want to believe it but I knew you were right.

Always there will be someone else to break
up a family. A stranger, an intruder, another
rival.

CHAPTER FOUR

ONE YEAR BEFORE, 5 APRIL 2018

Rain sweeps in across the Atlantic Ocean and the wind batters her car as Constance drives home from the gallery. It has been an exhilarating day, hanging a new exhibition in preparation for the opening tomorrow and the bad weather does little to dampen her spirits. She still can't believe her luck in finding her dream job here in Galway, but she's now been working at Frances' gallery for nearly two years.

Constance has never been good at making friends. When she was at college in Cork she had spent every weekend travelling to see Daniel in Galway, and there had never been any time to hang out with girlfriends. Since they got married and Cathy was born she has retreated even more. Things hadn't improved when Cathy started school either, despite Daniel's encouragement to make friends with the mothers of Cathy's playmates. Constance dreads the boisterous camaraderie of the other mothers at the school gate so much that she will always arrive late to avoid them.

But two years ago, she had been picking Cathy up one afternoon, late as usual, when she noticed another late mother at the gate.

'So you're Cathy's mam, late like me so,' the woman said to her. 'I'm Frances.'

Constance immediately warmed to the smiling face, the outstretched hand.

'I come late because the other mothers give me a vibe. I've no husband.' Frances rolled her eyes. 'God love them, they think I'm a threat. It's so stupid, as if I'd have any interest in their thick husbands!'

After a few weeks, Constance found herself looking forward to her chats with Frances. Sometimes they would take their girls for toasted sandwiches in a café after school. Once Frances showed Constance the art gallery she ran all on her own. Constance was in awe of Frances. She was older than her, from Dublin, and just so different from all the local women. She made Constance feel as if there were possibilities in her life. When Constance revealed that she had a first in History of Art and was passionate about art, Frances asked her to help out at her gallery.

Constance loves every part of her job—meeting the artists and learning about their work, talking to the clients, and experiencing the thrill of a sale. Her confidence has grown as Frances gives her positive encouragement. Most of all Constance feels of value. In Frances' art gallery she is more than a housewife, even if it is only for three days a week. By being around paintings, she can imagine herself outside the confines of being a mother and a wife. Art is a world where she can be herself, for no one else but herself.

Constance turns into their drive, her good mood sinking as she sees Daniel's car parked in front of the house. He has an interview for a new job this afternoon, in which case he shouldn't be home for at least another hour. Three months ago Daniel had come home from work with the shocking news he had been made redundant. She hadn't been too worried at first. Daniel is so charismatic and clever, she believed he would get another job easily. But as the weeks wore on, no matter how hard he looked, Daniel couldn't seem to find any position. He is over-qualified for service industry jobs, and not experienced enough for management positions. She has tried her best to be sympathetic but he's in such a bad mood all the time that she dreads evenings with him.

Constance sits for a moment in her car, engine off, as the rain buckets down. She takes a breath, preparing herself for the tense atmosphere once she walks through the front door. As she runs from her car to their stone cottage, she sees the flashing lights of the TV on in the front room, already setting her on edge. Sure enough, as she walks into the hallway, the house is in the same state as she left it this morning. Daniel hasn't even hung up his coat but left it hanging at an awkward angle at the end of the bannisters with his shoes kicked off and in her way. Her husband is slouched on the couch, eating crisps in front of an episode of *Judge Judy*.

'Hey, how did it go?' she asks him.

He doesn't look up at her but continues to munch on his crisps.

'Where's Cathy?' She tries a different tack. 'Did she get dropped off?'

'Yeah, she's with Darren O'Reilly, they're upstairs studying,' he says, picking up the remote and flicking through channels.

Constance struggles to suppress her irritation.

'So how did it go?' she asks again.

'Well I think it's pretty obvious it didn't go at all now did it?' Daniel snaps, looking at her at last. His eyes are dark and angry and the expression on his face makes her flinch. She reminds herself he isn't angry at her, but the situation he is in. He's always worked since he was a teenager. It must be so hard for him to be without a job.

'What happened?' she asks in a small voice.

'They cancelled the interview; the position was already filled,' he says, settling on an old episode of *Top Gear*.

'That's really shit,' she says, 'they could have told you before—'

'Yeah well that's what it's like out there in the real world,' Daniel interrupts her.

'Have you anything else lined up?' she asks.

'Christ,' he says, 'I'm only just in the door!'

'Sorry,' she says.

The tension stretches between them against the sound of racing cars on the TV.

'No, I'm sorry,' Daniel says after a minute, looking up at her sorrowfully. 'I didn't mean to snap. It's just really tough. What am I going to do?'

She sits down opposite him, trying to ignore the crushed crisps all over the couch, which she had hoovered yesterday.

'What about I work instead?' she suggests. 'Frances has offered me a full-time position in the gallery. Let me be the breadwinner and you can take your time, you know, look after Cathy, and work out what you want to do.'

'Are you mad?' Daniel looks at her incredulously. 'I need a career.'

'But what if I want one too?'

'The gallery's just a hobby, you know that. It doesn't pay enough to cover everything. I mean we need to start saving for Cathy going to college.'

He is right. Even if Frances gave her a raise, she probably wouldn't make near enough money to provide for the family. But still his words infuriate her.

'Why is what you want more important?' she complains. 'You've no interest in what I want, no understanding of what art means to me.'

'You're being ridiculous, your little art gallery hobby isn't a proper job,' he says. 'Have you any idea how much it costs to support this family?'

'We could cut back—'

'Get real.' His tone is condescending. 'Instead of whining on about how much art means to you, think about the fact I don't have the luxury to waft around artists for the love of *art*. I need a proper job in the real world. And rather than moan on, you could be more supportive.'

'How dare you?' she cries out.

All she has done the past few weeks is be supportive. Listen to Daniel's endless ranting about how unfair his situation is, type up his CV again and again and hunt the internet for agencies and positions. She has been cheerleading him every day telling him that he deserves a good job, that he is worth it, and yet all he does is put her down.

'Keep your voice down, Cathy will hear,' he hisses at her.

But his warning only infuriates her further. A part of her is desperately trying to stay calm, and rise above her reaction to his words, and yet another part of her wants to let go and tell him exactly what she thinks of him. She is turning into her mother, bitter at the disappointment of her husband.

'All you think about is yourself, you're so selfish,' she screeches.

His eyes harden and she recognizes the look. He will not take the bait.

'Do you even care what I might want to do with my life? Am I just here to serve you both?' she continues, her voice getting even louder.

Daniel gets up suddenly, and thrusts his face close to hers.

'Well fuck off then,' he hisses before turning on his heel and slamming out of the house.

His words feel like a stab to the belly, and her anger curdles around it. She gasps breathless with the shock of his cold hatred. She might feel like her mother in this moment, but

Daniel is not like her father, who always shouted back. The two of them locked in verbal dispute for hours which would eventually resolve. No, Daniel always walks out. Has the last word, storms off and leaves her fuming. But worse, when he returns he might not talk to her for days. Once it was two weeks. Which of course always prompts her to flip out again just to get a reaction.

She flicks the television off; the room reverberates with her furious words, and her husband's harsh reprise. Does he really want her to go? But how can she fuck off? She has hardly any money of her own, certainly not enough to support her and Cathy.

Constance tries to convince herself everything will be okay. They're arguing more because Daniel can't get work. He's depressed and frustrated, but as soon as he gets a job, they'll be okay again. She tries to ignore the little voice inside her head, telling her they haven't been okay for a long time, years even, before this happened.

CHAPTER FIVE

THREE DAYS AFTER, FRIDAY 5 APRIL 2019

Maya watches the sun filtering peachy light behind the red boulders of Sedona and presses her red fingers to her forehead as she faces another day without Daniel.

She had said she didn't want to break up his family, but it isn't true. She wanted Daniel for herself, whatever it took. She had reasoned it was for his own sake.

'You may as well be dead than stuck in a loveless marriage,' she told him.

Maya drops her head in shame. What has happened to her?

The first time she met Daniel was when he came into the gallery in Sedona. He was looking for a picture for his wife's birthday present. So there it is. Maya knew he was taken in the very first sentence he said to her. Their initial conversation was about the color his wife liked best.

'Green. Any shade of green,' he told her.

He said he wanted to buy his wife a painting with the colors of home.

'And where is home?' Maya asked.

'Ireland,' he told her.

'Of course, your accent,' she said. 'I love the way you speak.'

He actually blushed. She detected a rare shyness in this man. Her ex, Joe, was a musician used to the adoration of women. Confident of his own charm. In fact, all the men Maya had ever dated had been that way.

His face looked young, his cheeks almost rosy, and he possessed clean blue eyes. Yet deep laughter lines revealed his maturity. His red hair was a penetrating shade that she had since tried time and again to mix upon her palette. He looked like a pure Celt. She could see the powerful definition of his body through his clothes, and she began to wonder what he might look like if he took off those blue jeans, and white shirt. How pale was the skin beneath?

'Are you on holidays?' she asked him.

'No, we moved to Arizona a couple of months ago,' he told her.

'So where do you live?'

She continued to question him, noting how his blushing cheeks were fading into a pale pink blur.

'Flagstaff.'

He was looking at her. She was glad she had ditched her old jeans that morning, in favor of a dress. It was green. His wife's favorite color.

'And what about you? You're not from the States are you?'

'I grew up in England, but my father's Indian, from Goa, and my mother's American. I came to study art here. I never left.'

'We're not so different,' he commented. 'Both mixed heritage. My father was from New York, but I grew up in Ireland.'

'How do you like it in Arizona?'

She expected him to complain about how much he missed home. All the Irish men she had ever known would get nostalgic over Ireland, moaning about the heat in Arizona in the summer. Great as the States was, it just wasn't home. And yet this

Irishman raised his eyes to her. They flashed a brilliance and she could see through their blue right into his inner landscape.

'I love it,' he said with vehemence. It sounded as if he had been defending himself a long time.

Nothing happened that day. She admired him; that was all. She wondered about his wife. Even her name intimidated her. Constance. It was dignified, and solid. It gave her the image of a wife as permanent as rock. A constant Constance.

'Constance would love this.'

He held up one of Maya's small watercolors of the coastal plains of Texas. His hand brushed against hers as he put the picture back down. She had not been sure if it was accidental. It had to be.

Daniel walked to the other end of the gallery. Hands in his pockets, he stared up at the series of landscapes she had painted in the Brazos Bend State Park.

'I can see why she likes your paintings,' he said. 'All the green, just like Ireland.'

Daniel pointed to a small watercolor of the gallery forests that edged along the Big Creek's banks. It was a simple composition of the sparse corridor of trees, sycamore, cottonwood, and willows, all trailing into the water covered by green algae and aquatic plants so that everything merged into green apart from glimmers of the rich black soil.

'This is beautiful,' he said. 'How much is it?'

He turned to look at her, hands still in his pockets.

'It's sold,' Maya replied quickly, not knowing why she was lying.

'Oh.' He looked disappointed. 'But there's no red sticker by it.'

'I can paint another one just like it,' she offered.

She wanted him to come back, though she could not reason why.

'Her birthday is this weekend,' he told her.

'That's okay, it's a small watercolor. I paint those fast.'

'That would be great. It's so hard to find her something she likes.' He sighed. 'She's very difficult to please.'

Maya regarded Daniel in silence, for he had offered up a tiny chip of his marital discontent. There was an edge to his voice when he said *she*. He hadn't wandered into her gallery motivated by his own desire to find something his wife might like. He was fulfilling a demand.

'Constance asked for one of your pictures,' he clarified.

He pushed his hand through his thick red hair, a gesture Maya came to recognize as a nervous habit.

'I'm very flattered,' she said, taking a step back.

Was his skin crawling like hers? The heat was building in her body: between her breasts, at the nape of her neck, down on the very small of her back like pools of damp desire. Her fingers were aching to touch that startling hair.

'I'm not really into art,' he confessed. 'But I have to say I think Constance is right.'

He left then, but she knew it already, deep down in her subconscious. She knew what she might do.

Now, in this moment of clarity, the irony is not lost on her. It was his wife who had first sent him to her.

CHAPTER SIX

ELEVEN MONTHS BEFORE, 5 MAY 2018

Daniel is waiting for her. He's shaved and put on a clean shirt, which he has even ironed. He smiles at Constance as she comes in the front door and she wonders if he really is pleased to see her. Since their big row just under a month ago, there has been an uneasy peace. Neither of them have mentioned it, and Constance is too tired to bring it all back up again. Along with working more hours at the gallery, she's still doing all the cooking, cleaning, and laundry, as well as making sure Cathy stays on track with schoolwork. Meanwhile, Daniel is still out of work.

'Well, get ready quick, our reservation is in half an hour,' Daniel says.

'Are you sure we can afford this?' she asks.

'It's our wedding anniversary!'

Reluctantly she goes upstairs, and hunts through her wardrobe to find something she still fits into. Looking in the mirror, her expression is defeated. She slaps on some makeup, cajoling herself. Daniel is making an effort for her. She should be happy.

They go to the Chinese, which is Daniel's favorite restaurant, and Constance doesn't have the heart to tell him that she doesn't like Chinese food. Surely he knows this by now? Daniel is telling her about a new job he's applied for managing a furniture store.

'Aren't you overqualified for that?' she ventures.

'Well what do *you* think, that I have a choice?' he asks, his tone sarcastic, and she says no more. The last thing she wants is an argument in public. They continue to eat in silence, and Constance sees them from the outside. Another discontented middle-aged couple with nothing left to say to each other. She rushes through her food, keen to get the meal over and go home.

But as they leave the restaurant, Daniel surprises her by linking his arm through hers.

'Let's go for a pint at McGinty's,' he says.

'But we told Cathy we wouldn't be late.'

'She's fourteen years old; well able to look after herself. We can call her.'

'No she's not old enough to be left alone for so long,' she protests.

Daniel turns to look at her. She can see he knows it's an excuse. Constance has never enjoyed the pub. All the fake chitchat, and slagging. But Daniel likes going out. He's gregarious, and has never understood how torturous it is for her to socialize. She always feels so awkward in company, and used to hate going to parties together when they were younger. Every time, she imagined Daniel was flirting with one of the other women. But she knew in her heart that it was all in her head. Her husband was just being friendly. He had a smiley face, that's why people warmed to him. What she was really jealous of was that people liked Daniel whereas she was viewed as stuck up, and aloof.

'Come on, Constance, it's Saturday night,' he says. 'I can't bear to stay in one more night.'

'We can't leave Cathy—'

'Fine,' he snaps, pulling away from her. 'If you want to be so boring, go on home. I'll see you later.' He flags down a taxi for her, and before she can change her mind, struts off down the round towards McGinty's. She bites back the tears in the taxi. Why hadn't she told her husband the truth? That she hates pubs and wants to go home to bed, with him. That she was enjoying his touch upon her arm, the scent of him so close to her. That it had been so long since they had made love. But he wants to go for a pint with his pals, rather than go home and be with her. That much is clear. Even on their wedding anniversary.

Constance is not sure when Daniel gets home. She wakes once in the night, and he is still not back, though her phone tells her it's three a.m. She resists the temptation to call him, and turns over on her side. The next thing she knows, Daniel is not only home but waking her up, with a steaming mug of tea.

'Good morning, darling,' he says, kissing her on the forehead, and she gets a whiff of beer and cigarettes off him, although his hair is wet and he has clearly just had a shower. 'I'm sorry about last night.'

Disarmed, she cradles the tea in her hands, blowing on its surface to cool it. 'It's okay,' she tells him. Although it isn't, not really, but she doesn't want him to know that she cried herself to sleep.

'I wish I had come home with you.' He flops on the bed next to her. He is wearing his boxers and a clean T-shirt, his skin still damp from the shower.

'Who was there?' she asks.

'Just some of the lads, no one you know,' he says, before taking her mug out of her hands and placing it on the bedside table. 'I really am sorry,' he says again. 'Let me make it up to you.'

She doesn't resist because it feels good to have her husband kissing her so tenderly. Her hurt from the night before is swept away by his need for her, as she shimmies out of her pajamas and opens the covers for him. He sheds his T-shirt and boxers, staring intently into her eyes. She senses he wants to tell her something, but she doesn't want to hear anything he has to say right now. She wants to feel him inside her, know that he is hers, feel the rhythm of their bodies together, a pattern ingrained within them for years. He comes quickly, closing his eyes and gasping and she grips his back, willing him to stay inside her so that she too can experience what he is feeling. But he withdraws too soon, and she is left sticky, and worried they haven't used contraception. The last thing she needs is to get pregnant again.

Rather than falling asleep, Daniel surprises her by getting up again, and pulling on his jeans.

'Are you hungry?' he asks her.

She wants him to stay in bed with her, to fall back asleep in his arms, but already he is out the door, and calling to Cathy to help him make breakfast. She can't understand the sudden change of mood, when he has been so irritable for weeks, but it gives her hope.

Daniel and Cathy make pancakes for her and it almost brings tears to her eyes to see the two of them joking around in the kitchen together. There'll be a big mess for her to clean up after they are done, but right now she doesn't care. They are a family eating Sunday breakfast together and that's all that counts.

'Are you sure you've made enough?' she jokes as Cathy presents her with a stack of pancakes.

'You can never have too many pancakes, Mam,' Cathy says, her cheeks flushed, as she drowns her plate in maple syrup.

Daniel's phone starts ringing, and he picks it up but doesn't answer it.

'Who's that?' she asks.

'Just one of the lads from last night,' he says, not looking at her as he helps himself to another pancake.

And she knows, he's lying to her, but not why.

Over the next few days Daniel's phone keeps ringing at random times. Once waking them up in the middle of the night. Every time Daniel picks it up and looks at the caller I.D. he ignores it.

'Why don't you answer your phone, it could be a job.'

'No, it's not,' he says every time. 'Just a sales call. I recognize the number.'

She wonders again why he is lying to her. The answer is obvious, but despite the fighting between them, she trusts Daniel. Other husbands cheat on their wives, not hers.

The following Saturday afternoon, she is on her own at home. Daniel and Cathy have gone to the cinema together to see a horror movie called *It* but she declined. Her husband and daughter love horror, but she hates it. Though she asks Daniel not to fill Cathy's head with such dark stuff, he ignores her.

In the morning, she collected bluebells in the woods and their stone cottage is now filled with their purple haze. She shouldn't have picked so many. It is greedy of her, but there are so many bluebells in the woods. A vast carpet that spreads forever. She wants to bring some of spring inside her home. She has just finished arranging the last jug of bluebells, and is placing it on their pine kitchen table when the landline rings.

'Mrs. Garvey?' A woman's voice, brittle and accusing.

'Yes, who is this?'

'Your husband is a dirty whore!'

The woman is gone, but her voice is ringing in Constance's head. It doesn't need explaining. She knows what the woman's accusation means.

Constance runs into the bathroom and throws up. Wiping her mouth with toilet paper, she gets up unsteadily and walks back into the kitchen. The sight of all the bluebells in her home sicken her even more. Who is she fooling with her blooms of hope? Their marriage is broken. Daniel had sex with another woman, and then came straight home and had sex with her. She runs to the kitchen sink and spits into it, anger and hurt coursing through her.

When Daniel and Cathy get home, Constance manages to control herself while they eat dinner, but as soon as Cathy goes up to her room, she turns on Daniel.

'Have you cheated on me, Daniel?' she asks him.

Her husband starts at the directness of her question.

'What do you mean? Why are you asking me this?' he stutters.

Her heart sinks. What tiny piece of faith she had in him is gone. The guilt brims in his eyes.

'Answer my question,' she says in a low voice. 'Did you fuck another woman the night of our wedding anniversary?' She is surprised by how calm she sounds because inside she is screaming.

He says nothing for moment, staring at her, and to her astonishment his eyes fill with tears.

'It meant nothing, I was drunk,' he whispers.

To hear him confess, so easily, as if it was nothing enrages her.

'How could you?' she screams.

'Please, listen to me, it was a mistake, I was upset with you for going home—'

'So, it's my fault?'

'No, of course not, I was really drunk, and she took advantage of me...'

'And who is she?'

'Bridget Kearney. She keeps ringing. I keep telling her it was a one-off but she's been harassing me ever since.'

She is aghast because she's known Bridget Kearney for years. She's one of the other school mothers. How could he do this to her? Who else is Bridget going to tell? What about Bridget's husband?

'I'm so sorry, Constance,' Daniel says, tears trailing his cheeks. 'I've felt so worthless and now I've made things worse.'

'But you came home, and you made love to me, how could you?' she says, her voice breaking.

'Please forgive me, please.' Daniel grabs her hands and pulls her to him. 'I love you, I don't want to lose you.'

She begins to cry as confusion and hurt overcomes her. Daniel has broken their wedding vows, and yet most husbands slip up once at least, don't they? That is what her mother told her long ago.

'I promise I will make things right,' Daniel says, kissing her feverishly. She sinks into his arms, defeated, but also strangely elated. He is desperate not to lose her, and Cathy.

'I can't tell you until things are certain, but it looks like I've a job, and I'm going to fix everything. We'll have a fresh start.'

Relief sweeps through her, and she realizes it's more important to her that Daniel is happy than that he has cheated on her. But she doesn't know yet that their fresh start will make things worse. So much worse.

CHAPTER SEVEN

THREE DAYS AFTER, FRIDAY 5 APRIL 2019

After she calls it in, Katarina sits down on a rock and waits for the chopper to arrive. Her heart is hammering inside her chest, and she feels sick at the thought of what happened to this man. She takes out her hand cream, squirts it liberally over her hands, so that they are slick with it. She laces her fingers together, the cream oozing through the cracks. She rubs her hands together, again and again, turns her back on the body, and looks up at the sky. There is not a strand of cloud, the surrounding woods are still and unusually quiet, the sky steady blue. The long winter is finally departing the South Rim. April is the best time of year in the Grand Canyon.

It was in April that she and Shane got married. Two years ago now. All the others said they were the perfect match. Two rangers, who were park hoppers, attracted to the slow and simple pace of life in the Parks. They had met in Yosemite on internships while still at college. Friends at first. Until she had got drunk on the last night of the internship and tried to kiss him. At the time, Shane had turned her down. Told her he just wanted to be friends with her. She remembered his words.

'I like you too much to date you, Kat,' he had said, as she had buried her burning face in her hands.

She hadn't seen him for a couple of years after that, until he had turned up a few weeks after she had started working in Yosemite Valley again. They had lived in such a remote place that they ended up spending a lot of time together. Katarina had been shocked to discover that she still had feelings for Shane, but she was careful never to show them to him. Sometimes he might take off for weeks at a time but he was so good at what he did, the Parks always took him back. He was one of the best climbers, a reliable backcountry ranger, and did countless search and rescues.

When Katarina got her dream position based on the South Rim of the Grand Canyon, it was Shane who had followed her just one year later. When he invited her to share his trailer, she hadn't thought twice about saying yes. She was sick of her roommate, Elsbeth, a snobby interpretive ranger from Florida, who talked down to Katarina because she considered she had more education than her. She knew that Elsbeth judged her for her looks. Katarina's heritage was mixed—Polish, Norwegian, and Mexican—but it was the Mexican side that dominated. She possessed the same thick eyebrows as her mother, and long black hair. Outside of the park, she had encountered plenty of hostility when folk thought she was Mexican. It had made Shane so mad, but she was used to it now.

When Katarina moved into the trailer with Shane she thought it was as roommates. It wasn't until he had shown her the one bed that they were to share that she began to understand what he had really been asking her. She had felt confused because he had never hit on her before.

'Let's get hitched,' he said to her.

'But I thought we were just friends,' she protested.

'You've won me over, Kat.'

He had taken her hat off, stroked her tangles of black hair

away from her face, and looked into her eyes. She had felt a swell of emotion, as if a dam had collapsed on her feelings. And yet when she looked into his eyes, it was as if they were staring past her, into some kind of dream.

'I don't understand...'

'Let's just do it,' he insisted, pulling her to him, and kissing her urgently. She had known it was crazy, but how could she refuse his request? She had always wanted him.

Katarina tilts her head to the sky, listens out for the chopper blades, but the air is thick with silence and solitude. She misses Shane. Dreads going back to their trailer tonight. Especially after this.

She moves to the other side of her boulder, and looks at the body again. It is all twisted this way and that, the right leg bent back, the shin and foot sticking out at an unnatural angle. He had fallen badly. What broke first? The neck, the spine, or the leg?

Katarina takes out her phone. She wants to call Shane, tell him what happened, but there's no cell phone service in this remote spot.

She gets up, and approaches the body. He is lying on his back, and his eyes are open. Staring right at her. She should say a prayer for this man's soul, but that is not her job. Only Shane could understand why she is so calm. She is first and foremost a park ranger. Her role is to protect the park. Enforce the rules.

If she'd chosen not to follow the rules, she might not have called the dispatcher on her radio and told them about the body. She could have just left this man here, in the dense under-growth, and after a while, his body would have returned to nature—where it belonged after all. The bones would have been picked clean by the wildlife, and as the seasons turned, they would have been washed away by the summer storms into the river. His essence drifted down to its muddy bottom. No one would ever know where this man had gone to. Maybe that would be kinder for his family? They would get to avoid the whole media circus when a body is discovered in the Grand Canyon. Tragic accident or suicide?

She gets up and takes a step towards the dead man. Rousing herself, she realizes she should look for I.D. She scans the ground around his twisted form, takes another step forward so that she is standing over him. She feels pity for him now. He is better off in the next world.

She bends over him, and gingerly tugs at his jacket, slips her greasy hands into the inside pockets but they are empty. No wallet. Just a few quarters, and crumpled tissues in the outside pockets. She steps back. She is feeling a little dizzy. She should leave him alone. Wait.

She closes her eyes, and as she does so she hears the chopper. She watches as the pilot lands on a patch of flat red rock. She has been correct in her estimation that there is enough space for the chopper to land.

It's Special Agent Lopez, who comes running under the blades towards her, with his medical packs. Her heart sinks a little. She was hoping it would be one of the other investigators. There is something about Lopez that always puts her on edge.

'Is he gone?' Lopez asks, strands of black hair blowing loose from his baseball cap as he looks past her at the body.

'Yeah, no hope.'

'Any idea who he is?' Lopez asks, walking towards the body.

'No I.D.,' she says, following him.

'Hey, what's this then?' Lopez kneels down by the boulder she was sitting on. Tucked into the grass at its base is a leather wallet, black and shiny as raven feathers. How could she not have noticed it?

'Are you okay?' Lopez asks her. 'You look like shit. Tough morning for you, Ranger.'

She nods, but can't meet his eye. She feels sick in the pit of her belly.

Lopez opens the wallet, pulls out an international driver's license, and shows it to her. The face is the same. No mistaking.

'Daniel Garvey, the poor bastard,' Lopez says. 'Irish.'

Katarina knows Lopez is about to say, *Like your Shane*, but he doesn't. The special agent has asked her enough times over the past week when Shane is coming back. She told him in a few days, when Shane's father is better and he doesn't need his help on the ranch back home in Montana, but the truth is Katarina just can't answer that question. Not yet.

CHAPTER EIGHT

THREE DAYS AFTER, FRIDAY

Constance had been afraid. That was why she'd stayed with Daniel all these years.

This was what she had been afraid of:

1. Her daughter, Cathy, hating her for breaking up the family.
2. The shame because her marriage had failed.
3. Survival. How could she fend for herself and Cathy, even more so in the States? She had no job, and no money of her own, but worse than that, she had no confidence. She is no good with people.
4. Being alone forever. Constance is forty-one. She got married when she was twenty. She has no idea how to meet another man. As far as she could tell, all the men her own age want younger women.

But now Constance wonders why she is so afraid of being on her own: she is already lonely. She has felt more alone since she came to live in Arizona than she ever felt in her whole life.

Daniel is the only man she has ever loved. They were not

much older than Cathy when they first got together. They had grown up in the same townland, and their mothers had been best friends. It had been only natural that Daniel escorted Constance to her Debs. That night so many years ago now, she had fallen in love. She had been so nervous of this big social event. She had not wanted to go, but her mother had made her. She didn't have any close friends at her convent school. *Not a team player*, the teachers told her parents. Constance found anything involving her peers stressful. Even standing up in front of class to give a presentation gave her heart palpitations and her voice shook as she spoke.

'Daniel will look after you,' her mother had reassured her, as she brushed Constance's blond hair so hard it brought tears to her eyes. 'Let him talk for you.'

He had done just that. It was as if he had known how frightened she was, and he had spoken for Constance, guided her through the crowd with a protective hand on her arm. She had actually begun to relax. He was funny too. After being so polite to people's faces, he would make her giggle with witty little asides. As they swirled around the dance floor—Constance in a long green dress with a sequined bodice, and Daniel looking older in his brother's tux—they only had eyes for each other. She could not believe that this confident, good-looking boy was interested in her. But it seemed he was.

'You're different from all the other girls,' he had told her that first night.

'In what way?' she asked him, squirming with pleasure.

'You're still shy,' he said, giving her a charming smile. 'I like that.'

Constance lost her virginity to Daniel, and yet he has never given her an orgasm in all their years together. This is something she has only ever managed to give herself in her night-time trysts with her own imagination.

Long gone is the pretty blond girl in the green Debs dress.

Constance feels so unattractive. Her body has changed so much since she had Cathy. Just before they left Ireland, Daniel told her she was voluptuous. Constance got angry with him.

'That's just another way of calling me fat,' she accused him.

He shrugged, walked out the bedroom. It hurt her that he didn't work harder to make her believe she was sexy.

Tomorrow is Cathy's sixteenth birthday.

Constance planned a special day with her husband and daughter in Phoenix because she feared it might be the last time they would do something together as a family. She wanted them to go shopping in the big Fashion Square mall in Scottsdale, eat a sumptuous dinner in a good restaurant, and stay overnight in a hotel in Phoenix. It was a fantasy. Even if Cathy agrees to go with her now, it will just be the two of them. They will never be a family ever again. It is all because of the other woman.

Constance begins to feel cold with fury again. It gives her courage. She snatches the car keys up from the hall table, and marches out the front door before she changes her mind. As soon as she is out in the blazing sunshine, panic accelerates her heart. Is anyone watching her? Gossiping behind closed doors? Have her neighbors noticed Daniel is missing?

She opens the garage doors, and slips inside its cool shade with relief. She takes a deep breath, unlocks her car, and slides onto the driver's seat. It still smells new. Not something that belongs to her. Just like her life in America. She turns on the ignition, and looks in the rear view mirror. As she reverses out of the garage she sees a familiar figure in black, walking along the sidewalk towards the house. She brakes, pulling up the hand-brake before hopping out of the car.

'Cathy!' she calls out to her daughter.

Cathy turns towards her. A cross flick of long red hair, the whitest skin, hunched shoulders in a large black T-shirt. Her daughter says nothing, just pulls the straps of her book bag higher onto her shoulder, her expression hidden behind dark glasses. Constance can see the straining weight of the bag pulling down the whole of the right side of her daughter's slender frame. The tote bag is a copy of the classic book cover for Virginia Woolf's *A Room of One's Own* in horizontal bands of purple and white. The brilliance of its colors stand out even more against Cathy's somber clothes.

'I didn't expect you home so early,' Constance says to her.

'We got the afternoon off for study. Are you on your way out?' Cathy asks, nodding towards the SUV.

'Well, I was going to go somewhere.' Constance pauses. 'But I don't have to. I can stay. I'll make a salad or something if you're hungry.'

'Don't on my account,' Cathy says crisply. 'I'm heading out again. Meeting Lisa in the library downtown. I just need to pick up some things.'

'Okay,' Constance says, trying not to sound hurt. 'Well it looks like you need another bag. That one's about to burst.' She points at Cathy's Virginia Woolf tote. 'What have you got in there anyway?'

'None of your business,' Cathy snaps.

'Sorry, I was only asking—' she starts to say.

'It's just study stuff, okay,' Cathy interrupts, before pointing at her SUV. 'You've left the engine running, Mom. That's really bad. Either turn it off or go wherever you're going.'

Before she can say anything else, Cathy unlocks the front door, and stomps inside the house. Constance wants to follow her. But she knows that would make her daughter even more annoyed with her. She gets back into her SUV. Places her hand on the brake and slowly releases it.

The truth is Cathy doesn't want to spend time with her anymore. Nor does Daniel. Constance has hours to herself.

It is time she faced her husband's mistress.

CHAPTER NINE

THREE DAYS AFTER, FRIDAY

Maya should have stopped it from happening.

Daniel had driven to her studio at her cabin in Oak Creek Canyon, the very day after he commissioned the painting for his wife. He didn't need to. Maya told him the painting would be ready to collect in the gallery in Sedona on the Friday. Yet he had been standing on her threshold, the Wednesday sun spilling in behind him.

'Hi,' he simply said.

'Hi,' she said back, drawn to the flickering of his blue eyes.

A long moment. He licked his lips. She watched the tip of his tongue pass over their tenderness, and she could feel herself clench inside.

'I thought I should pay you first,' he said, producing a wallet from his back pocket.

'But there's no need,' she told him. 'Pay me when it's done.'

'Are you sure?'

'Yeah,' she said, looking into his eyes. 'I trust you. You shouldn't have driven all the way here.'

He was drinking her in. Maya could see it. He was fighting this attraction too.

'Right, okay,' he said, suddenly breaking away and opening the door again. 'I'll see you.'

After he left, she felt altered. The way he had looked at her. The heat in his gaze. Something was stoking between them and it was alarming.

Maya climbed the stairs to the cluttered space of her bedroom and stood looking out of the window. Her little house was situated in the heart of Oak Creek Canyon, surrounded by a dense wood, and framed by those red rock mountains of Sedona, containing her within their unearthly landscape. She watched the water tumbling down the creek, the sky blazing blue between the trees. The day was only halfway through, yet hot and tired. He was nowhere. Gone. She had not even heard him drive off.

No, she counselled herself. *Resist. Do not let this happen.*

She should have called him. Told him she couldn't paint the picture but she did not have his number. All she had was his name: Daniel Garvey. A country: Ireland. And the wife who loomed as large as the Sedona rocks. *Constant Constance.*

Daniel is her addiction. Maya knows it does her no good to give in to their love, and yet she can't stop craving it. Even now, as she follows the bobcat tracks on the trail up Bell Rock, she shivers when she thinks about Daniel's touch. She tries to tap into the power of all the nature around her but all she can think about is her lover. He is a deep need and she doesn't know if she can live without him.

She is a fool, because it's all just sex, isn't it? Self-indulgent and immoral pandering to the basest part of herself. She tempted Daniel to cheat on his wife. She destroyed his marriage.

It's not so simple. Nothing to do with love is ever black and white. Daniel's marriage was over long before they met. That much was obvious. At the beginning, Maya tried to stop the affair, but it was as if some kind of force was bringing them together.

Besides, he kissed her first.

Maya remembers that moment. The sun had been setting, filling her studio with a sultry red light. They had stood in its glow, side by side, as Daniel looked at the miniature landscape she painted for his wife. Its dripping green tones. Its watery world infused by the burnt-out Sedona sun. It gave the painting an otherworldly quality. A picture of a place that was more than just a memory. A painting of shadows and secrets.

'It looks like home.' Daniel's voice had been distant, as if he were in a dream.

'So you like it?' she asked him.

'Yes, it's perfect,' he said, suddenly turning his attention to her. 'This painting looks just like a place I know, not far from where I grew up.'

'And where is that?' she asked, counting the freckles faint upon his pale cheeks.

'It's this secret place,' he said, 'on this old estate in the west of Ireland, all rundown and abandoned. It's so lush, all this green spilling into the river. Like a place fairies would live.'

He paused, giving Maya the benefit of his brilliant blue gaze.

'And when it rains it is even more beautiful. The water dripping off the leaves. You can smell the earth's richness.'

She stared at him in wonder. No American guy had ever talked to her like that.

'Where is your most beautiful place?'

He was looking at her, really looking as if for the first time.

'It has to be the Grand Canyon,' she answered without hesitation. 'The immensity of it always takes my breath away. And the colors in the strata of rock. Ochres, burnt siennas, sizzling crimsons...'

'Have you painted it?'

'Oh yes, many times.'

'I'd like to see those pictures,' he said softly.

'It's better to view the canyon itself.'

'I've never been.'

Maya looked at him in astonishment.

'But you live in Flagstaff? How could you not have visited the Grand Canyon?'

He blushed, and she had wanted to cup his flaming cheeks in her cool hands.

'I know, it's pathetic, but you see I'm afraid of heights.' He coughed with embarrassment. 'Actually terrified.'

'Well we have to rectify that,' she said boldly. 'You *must* experience the Grand Canyon.'

He said nothing in reply. It was her turn to feel embarrassed. She had been too forward.

'I love all this space in northern Arizona,' she babbled. 'No high-rises, no light pollution. At night the skies are so clear you can see right up into the heavens.'

'So you like star gazing?' he asked her.

They were so close. She knew she should step back, break the spell, but instead she was diving into the blue of his eyes. His cheeks flared again. That blush was deceptive. He was not so shy.

Daniel had taken her by surprise. Leaning over, he touched her cheek with the tip of his finger.

'You have some paint on your face,' he explained.

She had let him rub the speck off her cheek. To feel his finger upon her skin was sending tremors through her.

'What color paint?' she whispered.

'Blue.' He leaned in closer. 'Midnight blue.'

He kissed her. She didn't resist him. She reveled in the sensation of the tip of his tongue against her lips. He put his hands on either side of her waist. She moved in closer. It felt so good to have the weight of his hands resting upon her hips. His fingers pressing into the denim of her jeans. Their kiss deepened. He knew she would not reject him.

He walked her backwards across her studio floor. All the way to the end of the space where Maya stored her paintings. He backed her through the rows of stacked canvases. The sun was sinking fast, and with no lights on, a glimmer of red sun bled into the studio. Neither of them could stop, nor even speak. They began to undress each other with urgency for if they slowed down reality might stop them.

His pale naked body shimmering in the dark room turned her liquid. Daniel took her in his arms again and they merged, pressed against the pure white walls of her studio. They had been a composition of passion. Daniel lifted one of her legs and she wrapped it around his back. He pushed inside of her, delicately tipping her, and with such ease, such exquisite care she drew him into her.

It had not been just sex.

Their eyes were wide open, searching each other in the gathering darkness. *What is this? What is happening to us?*

What had she been thinking that night?

Maya sees an image of her mother standing in front of her on the trail, with her arms crossed, her lips pursed, shaking her head.

You should have pushed him away when he kissed you, slapped his face and made him leave. How could you, a daughter of mine, betray another woman? What were you thinking?

Maya stops walking, takes a breath. Eight months ago, she had been so light of load. Now she is heavy with the guilt. But she hasn't forgotten what she felt that night Daniel and she first made love in her studio. At the time, she viewed it as just one more adventure in her life. A free-spirited action that would have appalled her mother.

She thought she could call a halt to anything between them

the next day. All she wanted was one night of passion. Daniel and she would flare just the once, brightly but briefly. But she could not have been more wrong.

Maya takes out her water bottle and drinks deeply. The water nourishes her, washing away her fatigue. She will get to the top of Bell Rock, and as she surveys the rough rocks, the twisted juniper trees, and spiky cacti around her, as she looks towards the ancient silhouette of Cathedral Rock, and over at the bulk of Courthouse Butte, she will try to draw courage from this landscape. She will not hide from the consequences of her and Daniel's love any longer. He is gone, and it is all her fault.

There's a strange noise behind her on the trail but Maya refuses to succumb to paranoia, for she loves her lonesome walks in nature, her hikes on her own. It's most likely a small creature. A jackrabbit or a squirrel. Or the rustle of a dry tight breeze among the juniper, a whisper of wind through the steps of rock above her. Sometimes she can hear nature sigh, especially here in her beloved Sedona.

Maya turns around. Sure enough, the trail behind her is empty. She thinks of Daniel again. Begs for a miracle. She wants to tell him that they can work it out. Somehow. She wants to say sorry but she cannot fix what happened. He wanted them to take a break but it was for too long, and she told him to get lost. Forever.

She keeps on walking, away from the red heap of Bell Rock, not even glancing towards the monumental Courthouse Butte beside it, as she clenches her fists.

Daniel lied to her. In the end, he had less courage than her own cheating father. He hadn't followed his heart. He had given up on them.

She can still hear the fury in her voice.

'You promised me. You said we'd be together. Soon.'

'I know, I'm sorry, but can't you see I've no choice?' Daniel pleaded with her, reaching out.

She had pushed him away, her whole body vibrating with betrayal.

'You're pathetic,' she raged. 'I hate you!'

They had been at Shoshone Point on the South Rim. There was no one around to witness her break down.

'I'll never forgive you!' Her pain echoed across the vastness of the Grand Canyon.

'Maya, I'm sorry.'

She remembers how confused he looked. Where was the chilled-out, sexy young woman he'd fallen for? Who was this raving, demented creature beating her fists on his chest?

She had been unable to contain her fury. It was as if all those years she thought she'd worked it out had blown into the wind. The numerous therapy sessions, and yoga retreats for nothing. She had been mad, deep down in her core. At her father, and at Daniel. They both let her down, and she was so angry with them for it.

Maya's legs buckle and she drops to her knees on the rough ground of the trail. Not anymore. She doesn't hate Daniel now. She just wants him back.

CHAPTER TEN

NINE MONTHS BEFORE, 17 JULY 2018

Constance slides onto one of the red leather banquettes in the diner in downtown Flagstaff. The heat is bouncing off the streets outside, and though they only walked a few meters from their air-conditioned car to the air-conditioned diner, her shirt is damp with sweat. It's not even nine o'clock in the morning yet.

'Isn't this great?' Daniel enthuses as his eyes light upon an old cowboy, resplendent in cowboy boots, spurs and Stetson, sauntering into the diner. 'I feel like I'm in a movie.'

'God, Dad, you're so corny,' Cathy says, but she is smiling.

She had thought her daughter would hate Arizona as much as her, but Cathy seems to have settled well. They've only been here one month and Cathy already has a new friend called Lisa, whereas Constance is still struggling to leave their house on her own.

Daniel orders French toast with syrup and bacon, while Cathy goes for pancakes. He asks the waiter for coffee, which he has taken to drinking since they moved here. She always thought her husband a tea drinker.

'Sorry if I am a bit corny,' Daniel says, beaming at Cathy,

'but I always loved Westerns when I was a boy and now I am living in one!'

'Well, Dad, you know that's not cool because all of these lands have been stolen from the indigenous people,' Cathy says, though her tone is non-accusatory.

'I know, I know,' he says. 'But please just give me this moment.' He sits back, beaming at them. 'I still can't believe we made it here. Isn't it great? I mean the house is amazing right?'

She nods, trying to look happy for Cathy's sake, but inside she is raging with protest. She's been angry since the day he dropped the bombshell on them. It had only been a week after the incident with Bridget Kearney when she came home one Friday afternoon from her best day yet in the gallery. But she never got to share her excitement at selling two paintings. As soon as she was in the door Daniel announced that his brother, Liam, had offered him a job in his real estate business in Flagstaff in Arizona. They were going to emigrate to the States. Constance had felt like he was telling her they were flying to the Moon.

'But what about my job at the gallery?' she had protested.

'What are you talking about?' Daniel had looked confused as he poured a glass of bubbly for her. 'You can get a job in a gallery in Arizona if you want.'

He had looked so happy that Constance could not bring herself to tell him how she really felt. She did not want to leave her home or uproot Cathy. Their daughter was just fifteen. It was such a crucial age—when her friends were her whole world. Cathy had begun to dress in black all the time. Stay in her room for hours on end listening to loud music. When she told Daniel, he just said their daughter was a 'Goth' and it was all perfectly normal for someone of her age.

But there would be no Frances in Arizona. Constance would have no support, and she would be all alone.

Daniel saw no problems. This was his golden ticket out of Ireland, and unemployment. He had taken her hands in his and spun her.

'This is our fresh start, honey!'

Despite her resistance, Constance had found herself smiling at him. He hadn't called her honey in so long.

'A new beginning. We can leave all the bad things behind us.'

He stopped spinning her, hugged her tight.

'You know I will never forgive myself for what I put you through. It's going to be different in Arizona. I promise.'

Constance decided to believe him. She had been determined to try, if not for their marriage, then for Cathy. But she didn't expect to hate Arizona as much as she does. As her family tuck into their huge American breakfasts, she wishes they were back home jumping the waves on Spiddal Beach. The three of them huddling together afterwards on the windy beach, drinking hot tea from a thermos and munching slices of her homemade barmbrack.

'What's wrong with you now?' Daniel says, frowning at her.

'Nothing,' she mumbles into her plate of scrambled eggs.

'But you're crying!'

She brings the back of her hand up to her face in shock.

'She's always crying,' says Cathy, shoving a piece of pancake into her mouth.

'Jesus, what is it?'

'I just... please, I want to go home.'

'Back to the house?'

'No, Ireland. I want to go home to Ireland.'

'Well I don't want to go back,' says Cathy, emphatically glaring at her. 'It's so backward in Ireland.'

'Will you give it up, Constance? All you've done is mope since we got here. You haven't even given Arizona a chance.'

'I miss the gallery.'

'There's plenty of galleries here, just go visit some, ask for a job,' he says.

'I don't have a work visa.'

'Oh for God's sake, apply for one then,' Daniel explodes, flinging his napkin down on his plate. 'You're so negative.' He sighs, getting up. 'I've got to get to work.'

'It's a Sunday, Dad.'

'Yeah, well I still need to work on a Sunday, someone's got to pay for all this.'

Daniel flings some dollars on the table.

'I'll be in the car when you're ready.'

'Why do you ruin everything?' Cathy attacks her as soon as Daniel has left the diner. 'He was in such a good mood!'

'I'm sorry'—she sniffs—'I just don't like it here.'

'You barely leave the house, how would you know?' her daughter accuses her.

'I'm afraid,' she admits.

'What of?'

'It's legal to have guns here; your dad told me lots of people keep them in the glove compartments of their cars. There are shootings all the time. What if I come across some maniac?'

Cathy looks at her as if she is a fool.

'Honestly, Mom.' She tosses her red hair, straighter and finer in the Arizona dryness. 'You're more likely to get knocked down by a car. You can't live in fear.'

Constance is in awe of Cathy's confidence. The past week her new friend Lisa, and another girlfriend with dreadlocks, have been picking Cathy up for school. Constance sneaks a look at them from her bedroom window. Watches their comradery in the dreadlocked girl's beat-up Ford as they take off down the street. Those three in their dark clothes, not a spot of pink on them, don't care what anyone thinks of them. They don't need any boy's approval the way Constance craved it when she was their age.

Cathy belongs. It doesn't matter where they live because she is at home in her own skin. This is how it looks to Constance. Part of her is proud of her daughter, but another part of her is so ashamed of her own insecurities. What must Cathy think of her?

Back in their big house in Flagstaff, after Daniel has dashed off to show a property, and Cathy disappears to meet up with her new friends, Constance walks through their soulless rooms. They have been here a month and it still feels like a showhouse. All the things she brought with her diminish in the large white spaces of their Arizona home. The pieces of ceramics painted the purple and green of the bog, which fitted so well in their stone cottage, look lost on the vast mantlepiece. She clutches her hands as she sinks onto the huge dove gray couch. Her family are right. She hasn't made enough of an effort. Empowered by her daughter's words, she gets up again and forces herself to leave the house on her own. She gets into her new family SUV and starts to drive for the first time, her heart beating against her chest. She isn't sure where she is going to drive to. Her hand keeps grabbing space, reaching for the invisible gearshift, but eventually she begins to trust the automatic. Driving in America is easier than Ireland for sure. No sudden gear changing around twisty bends, no potholed country lanes slippery with mud and rain.

She follows the road to Sedona. Crawling down the main street, she sees the front of an art gallery and pulls in. That is what she needs. Some art to take her away from her worries.

Inside the gallery, Constance relaxes at last. This is her cathedral. A sacred space where no one will talk to her, and she can loiter as long as she wants to. All in the name of art.

The exhibition is called *Plain Rains*. Picking up the catalogue, Constance reads that the artist was inspired by a residency in one of the state parks of Texas. While there, she witnessed the torrential sub-tropical rainstorms of the region. For the first time in Constance's life, she is drawn to another landscape apart from Ireland. Images of flat river flood plains, moss-colored and vine-draped woodlands, skies dripping with rain. Most of all she loves all the artist's shades of green. The aqueous quality they give the landscape. This is not the blank pelt of city rain, but electric storms. The unleashing of the primitive that is found in the purest places. One painting stands out. It is a landscape like the others, but it shows the view of the rain falling through a window frame. There is a creek, with a sparse corridor of trees all down its length, dripping green willows merging into the green river. It is steeped in longing. It makes her feel as if she is standing in the window looking out at the lonesome landscape. The weeping willows are a reflection of the grief inside herself.

Constance wishes she could bring all these watercolors back to their new house, fill it with them. Instead, she takes a catalogue, and marks the painting of the green gallery forests, the driving rain, all protected or exposed behind a window frame.

The artist has entitled it 'Abandonment'. Constance flicks through the catalogue from cover to cover but there is no explanation behind the painting's title. Is the artist referring to literal abandonment? A landscape unkempt, forlorn, and lost in a rundown part of Texas? Or is she talking about abandoning herself the artist, or herself the viewer? Passing through the view from behind the window frame into the lush wilderness of this nature?

When she returns home to their empty house, Constance leafs through the catalogue again and she is soothed. Just by looking at the paintings. The purity of spirit expressed in them. The richness of their colors. It is as if moisture is leaking from

the pages onto her hands. She can almost smell the damp freshness of those wet woodlands. It helps her to ignore the scorching
sun outside.

When Daniel gets home, she shows the catalogue to him.

'I want one of those paintings,' she says.

CHAPTER ELEVEN

THREE DAYS AFTER, FRIDAY 5 APRIL 2019

Every time Constance encounters the startling landscape of Sedona with its misshapen mountains and red earth, she feels as if she is landing on another planet. In a way she is. It is alien territory for her. So far from all that feels safe. Her husband has become a stranger. Daniel is not the same laughing Galway boy she fell in love with over twenty years ago. He is so serious now. Full of secrets and not just the mistress. What has happened to him?

Just four days ago she had driven the same route. Everything was booked and she was ready to leave her husband and bring Cathy with her, though she'd still not told her daughter. But there had also been a little voice inside her head asking her if she was wrong. She needed evidence to confirm her suspicions and vindicate what she was about to do to her husband. So she'd followed Daniel as he drove through the shaded woods of Oak Creek Canyon, the red boulders of Sedona flashing in and out of view. He suddenly took a right off the highway. Constance had driven on and pulled in, waited. So he wasn't going all the way to Sedona. This explained why she'd lost him all the times before when she'd followed him.

The air con was up full, but her hands were sweating, her heart tight in her chest. Daniel could be working, she had reasoned. He was a realtor after all. He could be showing one of his brother's properties to potential buyers. Even so, she could not drive home without checking. She had to know for sure.

Constance turned her car around and drove back along the highway, taking the same turn as her husband.

Although those huge red boulders still loomed over her, they were hidden slightly by the forest. She consciously slowed her heart rate because she had to stay calm, whatever she discovered. She took a turn down a narrow bumpy lane and drove alongside a stream, passing small cabins along the way.

She did not have to go far before she saw the shine of her husband's silver Prius parked outside a wooden cabin, next to a canvas-topped jeep. There was no *For Sale* sign outside the cabin.

Panic swept through her. She knew with absolute certainty, her husband was inside that house with his mistress. She spotted the femininity of the building with wind chimes spinning, delicate muslin curtains on the window upstairs, and a profusion of spring flowers blooming in pots on the porch.

Constance drove past the cabin, pulling in around the next corner. She turned off the engine. Her hands clamped to the steering wheel, and her head filled with a loud buzzing noise.

She got out of the car. It was cooler than in Flagstaff. The air breathed a freshness she'd been missing since they left Ireland. Winter was fading towards spring, though the trees were still bare, and the sun blessed her with fragile light. If her task had not been so unpleasant, she might have enjoyed her surroundings, but their tranquil beauty mocked her. She walked back around the corner towards the cabin.

She approached cautiously, read the mailbox. No name, just *Luna House*. Of course, the other woman's house was called something romantic. Constance hated her.

The cabin was small, but on two different stories, with a stone patio hanging over the creek. It was sheathed in the foliage that surrounded it, like a hideaway in the heart of the woods.

Constance took another step towards the cabin. There was a light dusting of spring blossoms on the soft canvas top of the jeep. A two-seater. This woman had no need for the boring family SUV that Constance drove.

She imagined herself charging inside the cabin and catching them at it just like in the movies. But to really hurt Daniel he had to still think she knew nothing so that her and Cathy's departure would come as a complete shock. What she needed was evidence. She crept around the side of the cabin, crouching behind a low wall. As she peeked over its top, she faced onto the back of the cabin, by a bubbling creek. The porch doors were glass and she could see movement behind them. She held her breath, calming her heart, and then she turned on the video on her phone, raised it to her face. She zoomed in, gasping, as she made out what the movement was. Two people making love. Not even in bed, no, they were so hungry for each other they were fucking on the floor. She gritted her teeth, controlling her rage, as icy cold hatred poured into her whole body. She couldn't make out the woman's face clearly at all, but her husband filled the frame. His startling red hair, and his naked body as he fucked the other woman. She pressed stop and lowered her phone with shaking hands. It was too much. She'd had enough. It would be a last resort if Daniel made any trouble. She would threaten to show it to Cathy, though she wouldn't dream of doing such a thing to her daughter. But Daniel didn't know that.

She crept back along the side of the wall, her whole body trembling with shock. It wasn't as if she didn't know he was cheating on her, and yet still it was shattering to actually witness his infidelity in front of her eyes. She felt a blaze of frustrated fury. She understood now how people could commit murder because if she'd a gun, she wasn't sure she wouldn't have run back and shot the two of them.

She took a deep breath. She had to remain calm and exact her revenge with cold composure. She wanted Daniel to hurt as much as she had been hurt. Taking Cathy away was the best revenge.

Even so, she couldn't resist kicking over the other woman's flower pots on the way to her car so that all her plants upended on the ground, and one of them even shattered. It looked precious and the plant was mature, but not as old as her marriage.

'*Bitch*,' she hissed under her breath.

'*Bitch*,' she says again as she pulls up outside Luna House, the memories from Monday still raw. But as she gets out her car, she realizes the jeep is missing. She feels deflated. Now she wants a confrontation with Daniel and his mistress, and to be able to see the look on his face when she tells him that she and Cathy are flying back to Ireland in a few days. And they are never coming back.

Constance notices the broken plant pot has been cleaned up and the other plants repotted. She kicks one of them over again and climbs the porch steps, walking around the side onto the stone patio. The sound of the creek rushes by below her. There is a small table with two pottery mugs on it, and two chairs, with brightly patterned Navajo blankets draped over each one. She touches the blanket on one chair. Which one is Daniel's? She picks it up and smells it. Sandalwood, and pot, there's that aroma again which has been hanging around her husband for months.

She approaches the glass porch doors and peers inside the cabin. She sees wooden floors, covered in Navajo rugs the rusty colors of Sedona stones, and rough walls, hung with a mixture of modern art, and old Native American crafts. On the ledge above the fireplace, she spies a row of kachina dolls, staring at her with calm hostility. She glowers back. Has her consumerist husband really left her for the woman who lives in this bohemian cabin?

Constance puts her hand on the door, turning the handle. To her surprise, it isn't locked.

It is foolish to go inside. What if the other woman comes back? She might even have a gun. This is Arizona after all, and Constance is the intruder. But her need overwhelms her. She needs evidence. Do her husband and this woman love each other?

The sitting room smells sweet from a jug filled with an array of orange blossom spilling over its sides in abandon. The shelves are jammed with books. Constance can see that most of them are art books. In the middle of the room is a steep wooden staircase, almost like a ladder. Constance wonders how Daniel manages that staircase. He is so scared of heights that he had refused to clean the gutters out at the house in Galway.

There is so much beautiful stuff in this home. It makes her house in Flagstaff seem clinical and cold.

She climbs up the staircase. The floor above is open plan. Immediately she is confronted with the bed. It is unmade, tossed sheets, another Native American trade blanket draped on the floor, and clothes everywhere. Constance is astonished. Her Daniel is a neatness freak. Complaining if she so much as drops one T-shirt on her side of the bedroom floor. This girl can live like a slut and he loves her. Constance closes her eyes, pushes away the memory of what she'd seen on Monday, and climbs back down into the living room. It is then she notices another door in the corner of the space.

She enters an artist's studio filled with light. One side of it is glass, opening up a breathtaking view of Oak Creek Canyon, its lush greenery, and the mountains in the distance. But it is not the view that floors her. It is the art.

Along the walls are a series of watercolors. Some of them are finished, others unfinished. She's seen that hand before. Those brushstrokes. The texture and tone of paint that adorns nearly all of the canvases leaning against the wall as well. She walks over to the paintings. It feels as if she is wading in thick mud. She crouches down and reads the signature on one of them.

Maya D'Costa

Her heart freezes. Maya D'Costa is the name of the artist whose paintings she admires so much. Her favorite watercolor is by Maya D'Costa. She gasps. Now it makes sense. Why she'd been so surprised when Daniel presented her with one of Maya D'Costa's paintings for her birthday a few weeks after she'd asked for one. The view was similar to the one she had loved called 'Abandonment', yet slightly different. The trees more closed in, the tones of green slightly richer, as if still dripping from the last downpour. D'Costa named it 'Hideaway' and that painting had spoken straight to her heart. In it, Constance could hide away for hours. Away from the drab reality of her life as a housewife in suburban America. This watercolor of a rain-filled world expressed her heart-held dreams. She had wished she could paint like this artist. She had wanted this painting to come from her own hand.

Most of all she had been so touched by Daniel's gift. Things had been so bad between them. She could barely find the words to thank her husband.

'I'm glad you like it,' he said, yet he'd not looked in her eyes to seek approval.

'I can't believe you went to all that trouble,' she said to him.

He shrugged.

'You asked for it, remember?'

'Yes, but I didn't really believe you would buy it...'

'I didn't know what else to get you.'

He'd been odd with her. Yet for the first time since they arrived in Arizona, she felt something like hope. If Daniel could buy her this painting, knew exactly what it was that she wanted, then she had thought he surely still cared about her?

'I adore it,' she told him.

'Good.' He nodded, picking up his sunglasses. 'But I have to get to work.'

She put her hand on his arm, stopped him from leaving.

'I really love it, Daniel.'

She kissed him on the lips but he had flinched. It was an infinitesimal movement, and yet it echoed throughout her body, amplified until it felt like a slap in the face. She had felt instantly ashamed of her kiss, while her husband hid his eyes with his glasses.

'See you later,' he said as he left, not even noticing that she had been hurt by his rejection.

The door snapped shut and she sank to the floor. Why had he gone to so much trouble to get her this painting, because for all it meant to her, it apparently meant nothing to him?

Well now she knows. Daniel bought her birthday gift from his mistress. Constance had hung it above the fireplace in the house in Flagstaff. She admired that painting every day.

Constance spins slowly in the studio, feeling sicker and sicker. Yes, it's the same artist. She recognizes her touch. The lush landscapes of dripping greenery that Constance had fallen in love with. Her attention is caught by a painting still wet, covered in broad strokes of red, as if the artist is trying to desecrate her own work. She takes a step towards it, touches the wet paint with her finger.

It feels like the biggest betrayal of all: Daniel having an affair with an artist. Maya D'Costa is no Bridget Kearney. This is her worst nightmare. Constance stumbles over to Maya D'Costa's worktable. She surveys the debris of pastels, pencils, and splatters of more red paint. She picks up a sketchbook and flicks through it and makes an involuntary gasp. There he is. Her husband. A tiny pencil sketch of Daniel's face. It is good. Too good. This woman has captured him. The slight overbite of his top lip, the roundness of his cheeks, and the shape of his eyes. Constance stares at that picture of her husband. How could a face she has known over half her life now look like a stranger to her? She traces the sketch with her finger. This woman loves her husband and he is gone, gone, gone. She will never get him back.

She hears a car pulling up outside and drops the sketchbook in fright. Panic consumes her. She has to get out of this house. Her resolve to face her husband's mistress has completely dissipated now that she knows who she is.

Constance looks frantically around the studio but of course, there is only one way in. She can hear footsteps on the dusty ground outside now. Maya D'Costa will know someone is in her house anyway because Constance's car is parked in full view right outside. What had she been thinking? She intended to arrive calm and collected. Possessed with righteous truth. Now her husband's lover is going to discover her sneaking out of her house.

She pauses at the studio door. She could hide in here, and hope the artist goes out again, but what if Maya D'Costa comes into her studio? She scans the room. There is nowhere to hide. Not even curtains on those big windows.

She has to face her. Wasn't that why Constance came here after all? She thinks of Cathy and it gives her strength. They are the injured ones. She is doing this to protect her daughter, because she will tell this woman that she will never get to meet Cathy.

Constance braces herself and opens the door of the studio.

She steps into the small living area. At the same time the glass doors leading out onto the porch open but it is not Maya D'Costa who enters the cabin. A complete stranger is looking at her, equally in surprise. A man, taller than Daniel, with messy black hair. He wears a red embroidered shirt and jeans, with cowboy boots. Despite his evident confusion at her presence, he gives her a friendly smile.

'So who are you?' he asks.

'I'm looking for Maya,' Constance says, avoiding his question.

The artist's name is like thorns in her throat.

'What for?'

The stranger looks her up and down. It has the effect of making her feel indecent somehow.

'I've come to collect a painting,' she lies, quickly crossing the room.

'Well you can see she's not here.'

She can smell liquor on his breath as he steps aside.

'What's your name and I'll tell her you called by?'

'I'll come back.'

He shrugs.

'Okay,' he says, collapsing onto the couch, his body taking up its whole length.

Constance makes her way to the patio doors. All the while, she senses this man appraising her. She stumbles over the rug and bumps into the table, sending the jug of flowers wobbling.

'You want a smoke?' he asks, pulling papers and a pouch of tobacco out of his jeans pocket. 'You look like you could use one.'

The man begins to roll a joint.

'No, thank you.'

This guy looks as if he is right at home here in the Luna House of Maya D'Costa. She turns to look at him. Watching as he sprinkles grass on top of the tobacco.

'So who *are* you?'

The words are out of her mouth before she can take them back.

'Joe.' He frowns at her. 'Did Maya not tell you about me?'

He balances the joint between his fingers as if to ponder its creation.

'She's my girl,' Joe tells her. 'Maya's mine.'

LISTEN TO ME

Let me tell you that their arguments were like thunderstorms. I could sense the pressure of them building up during the days before. It made my eyes itch, my body shaky. I would take Rosie for walks in the forest. It was not a safe place, but I believed that my dog could protect me. They were so intent upon their own animosity that they did not notice when I was gone.

He was the thunder and she was the lightning. That was how it worked. Locked in a violent reaction, neither of them knew how to stop. When their storm broke, Rosie and I would hide in my bedroom. I would bury my face in her fur, and hug her shaking body as we listened to my parents tear into each other. Rosie understood. She took my pain, fear, and hurt and she lived it every day. In her soulful eyes, and her trembling limbs. My dog was the embodiment of a small child's grief.

When the storm was over, there might be temporary break. Once or twice, I had even heard my parents laughing. I hated it even more when my parents pretended everything was alright. Sometimes they would take me out for a family outing. I would be made to eat ice cream or go to McDonald's with them. They tried to make me smile and act as if I should be happy.

With all my heart, I wanted to run from them, take Rosie, and hide in the trees.

Yet like all little children, no matter how selfish my parents were, I wanted them to love me. It was only after Rosie died that I stopped wanting that too. They could have saved her, but they chose not to. I never forgave them for it.

It was not long after my ninth birthday that I noticed Rosie was limping. After pestering my parents for two whole days, my father and I took her to the vet. We were told that she had a genetic condition. Her hip was constantly dislocating, and she needed surgery to fix it. It was going to cost big money. When we got home, my father told me he couldn't afford it.

I had been desperate.

'Take my bike, sell it,' I begged.

'Honey, that's not nearly enough,' my mother told me, trying to look sympathetic.

'Even if we go ahead with the operation, it's not certain it will work,' my father tried to explain. 'It's cruel to make the dog live in pain.'

'No!' I had screamed, clinging to Rosie, who was quaking in my arms.

'I'm sorry.' My mother was crying. Even my father looked upset. But they still wouldn't save Rosie.

Three days later they took her away and they never brought her back.

When Rosie was gone, I had nothing left. Apart from the woods.

Now do you understand?

I was so angry with my parents. Deep down I suppose I have never stopped being angry. You never guessed it, did you? Never detected how deep my rage ran? Looking at me, no one would.

CHAPTER TWELVE

SEVEN MONTHS BEFORE, 17 SEPTEMBER 2018

Daniel and Maya belong to the heat. The intense soaring temperatures of Arizona in summer. During their first hot month together, their bodies are pulsing, damp, and entwined like the twisted limbs of the mesquite tree. They turn off the air conditioning and bathe in their sweat. Soundless, apart from the whirr of the fan stirring up the hot air filled with his sandalwood scent and her beating heart. Maya lies before him on her bed, her skin gleaming, and he looks at her with awe. She senses him pulled towards her, as if she possesses some kind of magic. All she wants is to encase Daniel in the soft walls of her honey gold.

The Arizonan heat brings her back to rare days of her childhood spent on holidays with her parents in California. Before they sent her to a Catholic boarding school in England, before her father left them for his mistress. Maya should be the last girl on earth who would choose to steal a husband from a wife. She has seen her mother fall apart, becoming bitter and resentful.

But Maya doesn't believe in marriage. This is how she justifies what is happening.

She and Daniel are sitting outside the cabin in the dark, cooling from the heat, with a beer and a joint.

'It's impossible to expect anyone to be monogamous for the whole of their lives,' she preaches to him.

'Some people manage it. My parents did.' Daniel looks amused as she waves the joint around in the air.

'But at what price?' she says. 'Did you have a happy childhood, or were you witness to the growing dissatisfaction of your parents?'

'To be honest, I didn't really notice,' he tells her. 'My dad was off in London working on the building sites most of the time and my mam was too busy to have the luxury of deciding whether she was happy or not. But when they were together, I thought they were happy.'

'Well, my parents were miserable.' She takes a slug of her beer. 'And then they broke up and it was brutal. My mother had impossible expectations.'

Maya always felt she possessed more maturity than her mother. 'Brainwashed since she was a little girl by her own mother that all she should want in life is the Prince Charming who will provide for her.'

'And did she try to instill that dream in you?' Daniel teases.

'What do *you* think?' She laughs. 'My mother gave up on me long ago.'

The joint has gone out. Maya flips open her Zippo, lights it and takes a big toke. All the while Daniel is looking at her.

'So you don't ever want to get married?' he asks.

'No thank you,' she says, passing him the joint. 'I have no desire to belong to another, or try to own another person.'

'But that's not what marriage is,' Daniel says in a soft voice. 'Don't you want to share your life?'

'Not all of it with the same person,' Maya says emphatically. 'There is no such thing as The One, Daniel. You can fall in love with many different people and share many precious moments.'

Maya gets up, swaying, a little dizzy. Perhaps she has gone a little overboard on the grass. She wants to stop talking. She wants to show him what she means.

She holds out her hand to him.

'Have you ever done tantric?'

Daniel raises his eyebrows, looks a little uncertain.

'Is that some kind of strange religion?'

'Oh no, darling.' She bends down to kiss his lips. 'It's all about rapture.'

He follows her into Luna House. He doesn't want to climb the stairs to her room, so they make love on the rug. It is pitch dark outside apart from an array of stars, and they don't turn on the lights. So the night seeps into the cabin, envelops them in its sensuous arms, pulling away all their inhibitions. Finally Maya persuades Daniel to venture upstairs to her bed and they make love for hours, until dawn breaks.

'I have never experienced anything like this in my life,' Daniel says to her as they watch the sun rising through her bare window. Maya lays her head upon his shoulder, her body still resonating with their love making. She feels the same way. No lover has ever touched her as deep but she doesn't tell him this. It frightens her a little.

'Let's go for a hike,' she suggests. 'Before the heat of the day.'

'I love that you're not afraid to go hiking on your own,' Daniel says, gently stroking her hair. 'Constance won't go with me. She's afraid of snakes.'

Maya tenses for a moment. She had forgotten about the wife.

'Where to today?' he asks her, not noticing her reaction. 'Boynton Canyon? Red Rock Crossing or how about Bell Rock Vortex. I loved it there.'

'Today I am taking you to the Grand Canyon,' she tells him. 'You have to see it!'

'I don't know, Maya, I can't take heights,' he says.

'But you got up the ladder to my bedroom last night!'

'That's hardly a great height,' he says. 'Besides you motivated me.'

'Well I am motivating you now,' she says. 'There will be great rewards if you face your fear and come see the Grand Canyon with me.'

'What kind of rewards?' He grins.

She snakes down his body. 'I will give you a little taster now.' She wants to obliterate thoughts of his wife through sensation and touch.

They are just setting off for the Grand Canyon in her jeep when Daniel gets a call. She deduces that it's Daniel's brother, Liam, and notes how the tone of Daniel's voice changes when he is talking to him.

'Sorry, honey, I have to view two properties on the way,' he says once he finishes the call.

'It'll be too hot to hike if we delay any later,' she protests.

'I have to do it,' he says. 'I mean that's the excuse I used for not going home last night. It's good, it means I won't have to lie so much to Constance.'

Her hands grip the steering wheel as she speeds up. She is trying to literally put distance between Daniel and his wife. Her mouth is dry, and she feels a little panicked. She should turn the jeep around and take him back to his own car at Luna House. Tell him they should stop things now before anyone gets hurt. But she doesn't because she's already fallen for Daniel Garvey despite all her preaching against monogamy. She bites her lip, furious at herself. Someone will get hurt, either herself or the wife. She's in too deep.

It takes the whole day for Daniel to view the properties and Maya is left waiting in her jeep, air con on and listening to music. By the time they get to the Grand Canyon the sun is already beginning to set and she brings him to Toroweap Point to see the view. Daniel grips her hand tightly and lets her lead him to a sun-bleached rock.

'Do we have to sit so close to the edge?' he asks nervously.

'We're perfectly fine,' she assures him. 'The precipice is way over there, and you have to get a little close to see the view. It's worth it right?'

'Yeah,' he breathes in awe.

They sit in silence for a few moments, taking in the shadows of the clouds upon the blazing red rocks, creating deep craters of darkness, and pools of brilliant color.

'Wow, it is spectacular,' Daniel says, interlacing his fingers in hers. 'So different from home.'

'Tell me about Ireland.'

'I'm from the west. Stretches of empty beaches, dramatic cliffs, with the Atlantic Ocean so wild. Waves constantly crashing onto rocks. There are places where the sea is the most amazing color, a sort of aqua green.'

'It sounds stunning.'

'It is,' he says, 'there's this road in Connemara called the Sky Road. I would love you to see it. The views are out of this world, though not equal to this.' He spreads his hands. 'Different.'

'Do you miss Ireland?'

Daniel doesn't reply for a minute.

'Not too much,' he says eventually. 'I love the west. The Irish are my tribe, and yet being in Ireland saps my confidence.' He pauses, holding her hand again.

'I got depressed a lot, maybe it was the rain.' He gives a sad laugh. 'I felt held back. Trapped. Judged by other people.'

She squeezes his hand tight, as if she understands, but she doesn't, not really. Maya has lived her whole life without caring what other people think of her.

'It's so different here in America,' he says. 'I feel I can really go for it.'

'I came here for the anonymity,' Maya tells him. 'I need a big world.'

She could add that she also settled here in Arizona so that she would be far away from her mother.

Daniel tells her more about growing up with his brother, Liam. He clearly looks up to his big brother and he makes her laugh with stories about Liam's ditsy wife, Stacey, and their hyperactive boys at their weekly barbecues. Though she must be there too, Constance isn't mentioned again, but she is the cloud hanging over them in the unblemished Arizonan blue sky. Maya tries to banish her from her mind. Daniel always takes his wedding ring off when he is with her. Maya doesn't want to know about his wife, or his life with her in Flagstaff. Every time Constance's name emerges from Daniel's lips, Maya hushes him with a kiss, and distracts him with lovemaking. She wants to keep Mrs. Constance Garvey a figment. The forgotten woman she painted that picture for a month ago.

'And where did you grow up in England?' Daniel asks her now.

'London, born a city girl,' she says. 'My mother still lives in the flat in Islington where I grew up.'

'When did your parents break up?' Daniel looks into her eyes, and she can see his sympathy. She is surprised by how much emotion rises in her chest.

'A long time ago; I would have been a kid still,' she says. 'My father and stepmother live in Miami. I haven't seen them in years.'

'I'm sorry,' Daniel says.

'Don't be,' she says, pushing down the unwelcome memories. 'I don't need him, and my mother, well, she's a handful I guess.' She sighs. 'That's why I don't want to live near either of them. My friends are my family.'

'Do you hate your father for cheating on your mother?' Daniel asks, his voice low.

'No, I don't think so.'

Maya watches three black ravens as they hop on and off the rocks around them. 'My mother is a very difficult woman. My father fell out of love with her. He fell in love with someone else. Even though it was hard for me at the time, he did the right thing.'

'I don't want to mess Cathy around,' Daniel says.

Though the evening is still warm, a shiver runs through her. 'Who is Cathy?'

He turns to look at her, frowning in puzzlement.

'You know who Cathy is. She's my daughter.'

Maya feels as if a hand is squeezing her throat, slowly, tortuously.

'I didn't know you had a daughter.' She forces the words out. She can barely breathe let alone speak.

Daniel's famous blush springs to his cheeks.

'I told you about her when we first met,' he says, not meeting her eyes. 'She's fifteen.'

His daughter is the same age she was when her father left her mother for his other woman. Maya feels winded, as if Daniel has kicked her in the stomach.

'I told you the first time we met,' Daniel repeats. 'I never lied to you.'

'Oh no, I never knew.' Maya squeezes her eyes shut, as she tries to banish the image of his daughter, Cathy. Does she have red hair like him? The same blue eyes? Is she taller or shorter than her? Does she wear braces, or glasses? Does she *know*? Because *she* had. Maya discovered her father's infidelity a long time before he came clean.

'Darling Maya, that's why I can't leave Constance yet.' Daniel puts a hand on her shoulder. 'It's because I don't want her to take Cathy back to Ireland and turn her against me.'

Maya pushes his hand away.

'Don't touch me.'

She stands up all of a sudden, swaying slightly, the Grand Canyon looming below her. Daniel grips onto his rock with both hands, her movement unbalancing him.

'I want you,' he implores. 'But I can't walk out on my daughter just yet. She's in a new country and she's trying to find her feet...'

'I'm not asking you to.' Maya suddenly finds her voice. 'I never ever want you to break up with your wife, no not for me,' she shouts at him.

Daniel stands up. His blush is gone and he is pale now. He looks sick. She can see his hands shaking.

'I love you,' he whispers, reaching out for her.

Maya feels the truth in his words. The way they cling to her, bury themselves deep inside her heart. But she pushes him away. He wobbles, looking terrified to be so close to the edge of the rim.

'Maya, please, I have vertigo,' he says, clutching his chest as if he is about to have a heart attack.

She's so angry that for a moment she wants to see him suffer in panic, but she pushes the red mist of her fury away.

'Sorry.' She takes his hot hand, pulling him away from the edge as if he is a small child. She can feel him shaking all over but is unable to look at him.

'I can't do this anymore,' she says, hearing her voice small and flat.

He remains rooted to the spot. His shock is absolute for he knows what they are, and how impossible it is to break them up in that moment. They are in the middle of it. Their great love. Yet Maya's shame is raging through her. She grabs her backpack and storms off. She has to get away from him and the crushing reality of their doomed affair. She doesn't want him to leave his daughter.

Daniel doesn't follow her. Maya sprints back along the rim and to the car park, her whole body slick with sweat, aching with sorrow. What has happened to her? It seems as if overnight, she is no longer the free-spirited artist that she had sworn she would always be. Not only is she someone's mistress, but she has fallen in love with him. He has a daughter. She has turned into the enemy. She has become the other woman—the thief—just like her father's second wife, Celeste.

Maya leaves Daniel at the Grand Canyon and tells herself he deserves it. She turns off the main route home, and drives through the Coconino National Forest, along empty roads across parched flatlands. Winding through tight forests of ponderosa pine. Snow-capped Humphreys Peak rises up alongside her, and she wants to turn back. Share this landscape with Daniel. But it is too late.

Deep down she knows she has driven this way because it passes by the part of Flagstaff where Daniel's family lives. Not just Daniel and his wife anymore, but Daniel, his wife, *and* their daughter. Playing happy families in one of those four-bedroom, three-bathroom houses, with a huge garage to the front, and a landscaped backyard. The image of respectability.

By the time Maya has returned to her little cabin in Oak Creek Canyon, the sun has long set. She feels abandoned, although it was she who walked away from Daniel. She sits on the edge of her bed with the lights off, the shadows swallowing her. She has to end it. Yet her whole being screams to be with Daniel. When he is in his house in Flagstaff, she is able to cope because she knows she will see him again in a few days. She thought she only had to compete with an unwanted wife. Knowing that she might never see him again is unbearable.

Break up.

Her mother's voice is inside her head.

End it now.

But she is unable even to pick up her phone to call him. Daniel is her oxygen.

Maya waits in the dark, wondering if he has given up on her

instead. She listens to the sounds from the wood. The rustling of small animals, the running water from the creek, and the low-pitched but loud *hoo-hoo hoo-hoo* of an owl.

At last she hears the door opening downstairs, and she knows it is Daniel. She senses his pause at the bottom of the steps that lead to her bedroom. How he takes a deep breath, so that he can make it up them to her loft. That is how much he wants her.

The shadows beneath his eyes are dark, and his red hair looks like a halo of fire.

'How did you get back?' Maya asks him.

'I got a ride.' He takes her hand. 'I'm so sorry, Maya.'

She is unable to say another word. So ashamed, so full of her need for him. She buries her face in his chest, and cries. It is the only time she will cry in front of Daniel. All the while he kisses her. The crown of her head, her neck, her collarbone, and then up to her chin, her nose, her wet eyes. That night they make love a different way. The urgent passion of their early days, the tantric explorations of the late summer have evolved into a new kind of lovemaking. Measured, ponderous, appreciative of all they risk to share their rapture together. Do they not deserve each other?

CHAPTER THIRTEEN

FIVE MONTHS BEFORE, 15 NOVEMBER 2018

Constance puts the chocolate cake in the oven hoping it doesn't sink. She doesn't know why she cares so much, but she can't bear to be looked down upon any more than she is by Daniel's brother, Liam, and his wife, Stacey. Resentment twists in her gut. She should let the cake burn. She doesn't want to host Liam's birthday party but Daniel insisted. Said it was the least they could do after everything his big brother has done for him. Yet Daniel has been out all day, calling a couple of hours ago to say that he's been delayed showing another house. Cathy's out at Lisa's, and it's all been up to her. Cleaning the whole house which takes hours because it's so big with pale marble floors, and then doing all the food. She's made an Irish stew because apparently Liam misses homecooked food but she's pretty sure her effort will taste nothing like their mother's.

Constance opens the fridge, pulls out a bottle of white wine and fills a glass. She shouldn't drink during the day but she needs something to help her face the evening to come. She flops on the couch, glass in hand, and takes a sip of the chilled wine, doing her best to smooth down the edges of her brewing anger with her husband. She is determined not to show any more cracks in their marriage to Liam and Stacey.

She's tried, she really has, to fit in, and warm to Arizona, but she feels left behind. Her family has transformed. Her husband and her daughter have become Irish American. Cathy's accent has developed a twang, and the soft lilt of home has faded away. She says 'cool' a lot, sometimes calls her 'Mom', and boys at school she doesn't like 'douchebags'. Her Cathy, the country sprite, has been spirited away. Gone is the little girl who loved to roam in their wild garden back home. The child who collected raspberries in the woods with her, or seashells along the beach. Gone their revelling in the sounds of nature. The coo of the wood pigeon, the clap of the Atlantic Ocean, and the rustle of the wind in the trees.

In America, her daughter has withdrawn into the black tomb of her clothes. She is silent yet more sure of herself than Constance has ever been. She can see it as Cathy strides down their street in her Dr. Martens, and her black fedora, not a bother on her that she is dressed like a crone in the bright Arizona sunshine. Macabre, and morose. But Cathy doesn't care what anyone thinks of her, including her own mother.

'What are you going to do with Lisa today?' Constance asked Cathy as her daughter headed off out the door that morning, her bulging book bag hooked over her shoulder.

'Just stuff,' Cathy said.

She had felt slapped by her daughter's indifference.

As for Daniel, he is completely taken in by the easy American life. He laps it all up. The big shiny car, the games of golf in the sunshine with Liam and his pals, those wretched get-togethers over beers and barbecues all summer long. How Constance detested those Saturday afternoons in Liam's house in Scottsdale. At least Cathy seemed to hate them just as much. Daniel had to force her to go. Week after week there would be a big row. Daniel yelling at Cathy to get in the car and eventually

Cathy would give in. The tension on the long drive over was so bad that Constance actually found herself feeling sorry for Daniel. Once they got there, Cathy would sit hunched on a lawn chair, her big hat shielding her face from the sun, headphones in, a look of stony indifference on her face as her cousins ran in circles around her. Constance knows that Liam and Stacey think her daughter is a freak. All in black, with her big DM boots. It embarrasses her, but also makes her feel protective of Cathy. She was relieved when at last Daniel said he had to work on Saturdays and no longer suggested they go.

She takes a gulp of wine, trying to quell the anger she feels all the time. Rather than dissipating, it has got worse the longer they are in Arizona. Daniel has taken away her life in Ireland and brought her to this land where she feels like an outcast. It was only two nights ago that she let fly at the dinner table again. Daniel had complained that she had presented them with takeout for dinner.

'What do you do all day?' he said, flicking the Chinese takeout box with his hand.

'But you like Chinese,' she protested.

'That's not the point, I thought you might have cooked something for us, seeing as you have all this time on your hands,' he said, making another dig at her.

Constance was aware of Cathy sitting opposite, putting her chopsticks down, staring at her, and she knew she should say nothing, keep the peace for her sake but she just couldn't. Her fury at Daniel was so close to the surface it spilled out.

'And whose fault is that?' She turned on her husband. 'I had a job in Ireland, I had dreams but you made me give them up. You're not even grateful.'

'Come on, Constance, it was only a little part-time job in a gallery—'

'It was more than that!'

'Well, we're here now, and there's no point whining on

about it,' he said. 'Why can't you make an effort? Make some friends. Do something with yourself, even if it's going to the gym. I mean Stacey has offered enough times to bring you, and Liam's said he'll pay for a day out for the two of you to go shopping to your heart's content!'

She flinched, hurt by the barb of his comment, and the memory of Liam's exact words. 'Let Stacey fix you up, it's all on me.'

'I don't want to go to the gym with Stacey and I can't think of anything worse than going shopping with her. I want to go home. I hate it here. You're a selfish bastard.'

'I am fucking sick of your moaning.' He slammed down the salt shaker. 'Do something with yourself. I pay for everything and look at the state of you. It's you who's ungrateful.'

Before Constance could reply, Cathy had pulled her chair back and stormed out the room and upstairs. She gasped because she had forgotten her daughter was still sitting at the table with them.

Constance had run upstairs after Cathy. Banged on the door, begged her forgiveness but her daughter had told her to go away. The damage had been done.

Constance drags herself off the couch and is shocked to see the time on her phone. She dashes into the kitchen to rescue the cake. She should have put the timer on. It's a little burnt and the inside is probably dried out, but she smothers it in chocolate icing. Besides, by the time they are eating dessert it's likely everyone will have drunk so much wine they won't notice.

An hour later, Daniel still isn't back, though Liam and Stacey, plus several of their friends, are due to turn up in less than an hour. She tries his phone yet again but it rings out. Is he punishing her? There has been no resolution from their fight the other night. Daniel has been perfectly pleasant to her, unlike the old days when he would ignore her for days. Then they would have had another row, followed by passionate makeup sex. She knows deep down they are far from reconciliation, but it's as if Daniel doesn't care anymore. It fills her with panic.

Why is he so late home on a Saturday? Surely there are no viewings going on at six o'clock in the evening? Why won't he answer his phone? She pushes her suspicions down. In Ireland he had promised her he would never cheat on her again. The States is a fresh start for their relationship. Constance stares at herself in the mirror. At her messy hair, and unmade-up face. Is it her fault?

Daniel arrives home moments after Liam and Stacey walk through the door.

'Sorry, guys,' he says, carrying four bottles of champagne in his arms. 'I was trying to get the fancy stuff and had to drive around for hours to find a liquor store that sells it.'

Her husband looks flustered, his red hair tousled, the blue of his shirt bringing out his eyes. It occurs to her that he probably looks younger than her though they're the same age.

'Wow you look great!' he exclaims, catching sight of her.

'I was just telling her, doesn't she?' Stacey enthuses. 'You should wear makeup more often, Connie.'

Their compliments should make Constance feel good, but all she can see is the flush on Daniel's cheeks. He's hiding something. She can tell.

Two other couples arrive, and a single woman, friends of Liam and Stacey. Constance is relieved that at least they have a sitter for their boys and they won't be tearing around the house causing chaos.

'Where's Cathy?' Stacey asks her.

'She's at her friend Lisa's for a stayover,' she tells her.

'Is she still dressing like a witch?' Liam jokes.

'Don't be so narrow-minded, I think she looks very stylish,' Stacey says kindly.

'She'll grow out of it,' Daniel says confidently, filling up champagne flutes with his expensive bubbly. 'Do you not remember how we used to wear those ripped jeans which fell off our arses. Grunge, we called it.'

'Jesus, don't remind me!' Liam laughs.

Constance finds herself surrounded by Stacey and her friends as they share experiences of diets and workouts. So many different ones, she loses track. She realizes none of these women will eat her chocolate cake.

'Hey, Connie, let me know when you want to get some Botox done. I've got the name of a great guy who'll give you a discount,' Stacey offers.

'I'm not too keen on someone sticking needles in my face,' she responds.

'You say that now, but believe me a few months in dry ol' Arizona and you'll be screaming for it,' Stacey's friend Jackie says, giving her a friendly push. 'You don't want Daniel looking elsewhere now do you?' Jackie gives her a big wink as she flicks the long layers of her highlighted hair.

'I better check on the stew,' Constance says getting up, mortified by the woman's comment. Unlike Daniel, she never blushes and she imagines her expression is an unreadable mask.

'Gee, she's a bit standoffish, Stacey,' she hears another woman, Crystal, say as she walks away.

'Yeah, she's real stuck up,' Jackie joins in. 'I was only trying to do her a favor. She could do with Botox. Urgently.'

Constance doesn't hear Stacey's response but what does she care? She has nothing in common with the woman apart from the fact she is married to her husband's brother.

. . .

As they sit around the table eating dinner, the conversation turns to teenage antics, dominated by Liam as usual.

'Jaysus, we were so wild, all those early morning lock-ins, and driving our cars as if we were rally drivers,' he reminisces. 'But Connie calmed you down alright, Danny.'

His words sound like an accusation.

'Well you fecked off to America,' Daniel counters. 'Leading the life of Reilly, no doubt.'

'Were you a bad boy before you met Stacey, Liam?' Jackie laughs.

'I'm not telling any secrets, now, Jackie.' Liam winks at her, while Constance notices Stacey's smile is rigid on her face. 'I was a late bloomer, didn't meet Stacey until ten years ago, but Daniel, well you got your hooks into him young didn't you, Connie?'

'Were you pregnant? Is that why you married so young?' Crystal asks. 'Ireland is real Catholic, right?'

'Crystal!' Stacey intervenes before Constance has a chance to reply. 'That's so rude. Of course she wasn't pregnant. Why, you were married for a good few years before you had Cathy?'

'Yes, five years,' Constance says tightly, hating all the scrutiny, and furious with Daniel for not speaking up and telling Liam or the stupid Crystal to shut up.

'They were high school sweethearts,' Stacey continues. 'And I think that is so romantic. Daniel, tell everyone about how you proposed. It's just the cutest story.'

'Ah no, you've heard it so many times before,' Daniel protests, knocking back his glass of wine.

'Do please,' Jackie insists, glancing at Constance. 'Us divorcées could do with a happy ever after story.'

'Okay, well at the time I thought I wanted to be in a band, and I used to write songs for Constance on my twangy old guitar.'

'Jaysus, you were brutal, it's a mercy you didn't pursue that career,' Liam intervenes.

Constance wants to slap Liam. She remembers Daniel's songs to her. She had loved each one, no matter how halting or derivative they were. What mattered was she had inspired Daniel to write music. She had been his muse.

'I will have you know I played a couple of gigs in my time,' Daniel says.

'I'm impressed,' Crystal's husband, Jeff, says. 'Shame your golf handicap isn't as talented.'

'Aw don't be mean, honey,' Crystal says to her husband. 'Go on, Daniel, finish the story.'

'Well we'd been in the pub, and were out on Spiddal Beach in the rain, God knows why because the howling wind was competing with the strains of my ancient guitar. I was playing and singing "Galway Girl", and then when I finished, I just strummed a new chord. And I sang the words, "Will you marry me, Constance?"'

'Isn't it divine?' Stacey gushes.

Constance's heart constricts at the memory. She remembers screaming *Yes* out to sea, and the two of them ecstatic on the beach. Their love as vital as the crashing ocean. But Constance can't remember the last time she has heard Daniel sing. He stopped years ago, long before Cathy was born even. She gets up suddenly, clumsy at the table, and begins to grab plates to bring into the kitchen even though some of the guests haven't finished eating. Tears are stinging her eyes as she rushes out the room. She glances at Daniel but he isn't even looking at her, merely checking his phone yet again.

In the kitchen she drops the dirty plates into the sink, not caring if some of them break. She squeezes her eyes shut trying to force the tears back down.

'Are you okay?'

It's Stacey. Her sister-in-law is behind her and places her hand on her shoulder. She nods, unable to speak.

'I'm so sorry,' Stacey says. 'I didn't mean to upset you.'

Constance turns and wipes her face with her sleeve.

'Here.' Stacey hands her a tissue, and Constance wipes her eyes.

'Thanks,' she says. 'I'm fine.'

'Are you sure?' Stacey asks, frowning.

'It's just it's been so long since we've been happy,' she whispers. 'We used to be happy, we were so in love, but it feels like that's all gone now.'

'Of course it's not gone,' Stacey says. 'It's just marriage is hard, and there will always be bad patches. Having kids changes things too.'

Constance thinks back to when she had Cathy, and how she'd struggled to cope at the beginning. Her mother had died a few months after Cathy's birth, and Constance had struggled with depression. There were days when she just couldn't get out of bed and Daniel had to do everything. He'd had to wean their daughter onto bottles because she found breastfeeding too hard. Was that when he had stopped loving her? Had he only been in this marriage for Cathy for all these years? Her throat dries with the humiliation of it.

'Come on back in,' Stacey encourages her. 'Have another drink. You two will get through this. It's hard settling into a new country but Daniel is a good man.'

Constance is touched by Stacey's kindness. She has misjudged her, and while she can't stand Liam, she shouldn't tarnish his wife with the same brush. But Stacey has no idea how deep the rift between her and Daniel is. Her husband isn't present, not even on the night of his brother's birthday dinner. She feels his absence so keenly. His physical form might be here, but she suspects his heart is elsewhere.

. . .

Finally the long night is over, and Liam and Stacey, the last of the guests, have been sent to their hotel in a cab, drunk as lords. Her cake sits uneaten on the kitchen counter. No one wanted dessert, opting for tequila shots instead. Her head is spinning as she attempts to load up the dishwasher.

'Just do that in the morning,' Daniel says, carrying in some of the dirty champagne flutes. 'It's way too late. Come on, you did a great job, thank you.'

He is smiling at her, buoyed by the success of the night. He fits right in with Liam and his pals, and all the wives love his Irish wit. Her throat tightens. What if he is having an affair with one of those women? The one, Jackie, who had told her to have Botox had been sitting next to him at dinner, flicking her hair and fluttering her eyes at him. She was sure of it.

'Are you sleeping with Stacey's friend Jackie?'

She turns on him, hands on her hips.

'What the fuck?' He laughs at her as if she is crazy.

'Well are you?'

'Of course not,' he says, still smiling. 'Give me some credit, will you?'

'This isn't funny, Daniel,' she says. 'Are you having an affair?'

'What's brought this on?' he says, looking more serious.

'You work every weekend, evenings—'

'I have to, we need the commission,' he says.

'I just feel like you're hiding something from me,' she says. 'You promised me, Daniel. You said what happened in Ireland was a one-off but if I find out that you're sleeping with someone else I will leave you and I'll take Cathy with me.'

'Nothing is going on with Jackie,' he says, spreading his arms. 'I mean she's so loud, a bit of joke. How could you think I would go for someone like her?'

'Because of Bridget Kearney,' she says in a low voice.

'Oh for fuck's sake, will you ever just let it go,' he says, plonking the champagne flutes down so hard on the counter that one of them cracks. 'If you want to give our marriage a chance you have to forgive me. You said you had.'

His voice is shaking, and he has his back to her.

'I think we should go to counselling,' she says.

Daniel turns around, eyes wide open.

'I don't need therapy,' he says to her.

'But I think our marriage does,' she tries to explain. If there was a third party, maybe they might help her get over her paranoia, or confirm her suspicions.

'No way,' Daniel protests, 'I don't want to tell a stranger about my private life. It would be about blaming me.'

'But it was you who broke our wedding vows,' she says in a quiet voice.

Daniel ignores her comment. 'We don't need marriage guidance.' He flings the dirty casserole pot in the dishwasher.

'Mind, you'll break it,' she warns him.

He glares at her and says nothing.

'I disagree, I think we need to see someone—things are bad between us, and then what happened with Bridget Kearney...' she says. 'You haven't touched me in months.'

Daniel pushes his hands through his tawny red hair. He looks exasperated.

'You'll never let me forget it will you?'

She bends over the dishwasher. He hasn't answered her question. Is she disgusting to him now? She stares at the grubby contents of the dishwasher because she doesn't want him to see her distress. How many dishwashers has she loaded and unloaded during the length of their whole marriage? Hundreds. Hundreds upon thousands. She feels so very sad. She cannot bear to look at him.

'I'm worried about Cathy,' she mutters.

'Cathy is fine. She loves it here. Has good friends and is

doing well in school. You're the problem, Constance. Not Cathy.'

She can feel her throat closing in, emotion threatening to spill. She slams the door of the dishwasher and turns it on.

'Why can't you just be happy, Constance? We've a great life here in Arizona. So much better than Ireland.'

'I want to go home,' she says, straightening up, still unable to look her husband in the face, her words half drowned by the sound of swishing water.

'But there's nothing for us back home,' Daniel says, his voice softening. 'Our parents are dead, our families scattered all over the world. This is our life now. Here. Why can't you enjoy it?'

She looks at him. He is smiling at her. Trying to reassure her, but when she looks into his eyes it is as if he is looking through her. How is it that her husband no longer knows who she is?

Daniel shrugs when she doesn't respond to his question.

'Turn out the lights when you come up,' he says before leaving her alone in the kitchen. She bangs around with no set purpose, doing what she always does. Moving pots, opening and closing cabinets, looking for something she can never find. Although she's had too much to drink already, she pours herself another enormous glass of white wine, turns out the lights and stands at the kitchen window. She does what she has done every evening for the past two months in her suburban house in Flagstaff. She looks across the parched back garden into the upstairs windows of the house behind theirs. Just one window is lit. It is *her* window.

The object of her attention stands in front of his mirror, bare-chested, a towel tied around his waist. The window is frosted over at the bottom, and all she can see is to just below his belly button. He has dark hair, but a smooth, hairless chest. She only knows him in profile. A straight nose, and high cheekbones. She imagines keen eyes, dark as a blackbird's. She wonders if she would even recognize her neighbor if she saw him head on.

He is shaving the old-fashioned way and the bottom of his face is covered in white shaving foam. It is strange. Why would he be shaving at three in the morning? She watches him with the razor to his face, as if he is slicing through snow. She imagines the tender new skin on his cheeks.

Daniel is asleep by the time she goes to bed. She creeps past her snoring husband and locks herself into their ensuite bathroom. She touches herself. Imagining that hand, with the long strong fingers, caressing her breasts, trailing down the length of her body. She would open up to this stranger just because he is not her husband.

CHAPTER FOURTEEN

THREE DAYS AFTER, FRIDAY 5 APRIL 2019

It feels like Maya has been walking the Bell Rock trail for hours, but it has not taken her away from her heartache. She sought comfort in the nature around her, but she feels just as troubled as when she arrived. All her anger is replaced by fear because on Tuesday Daniel hadn't followed her home from the Grand Canyon like that time before.

As Maya pulls up at Luna House, the evening shadows are lengthening, and light is fast seeping away. Her heart takes a tiny leap as she spies a figure through the windows. The miracle she hoped for has come true. She runs across the porch, and slides open the doors. Light floods out of her cabin and she blinks suddenly awake.

It isn't Daniel. How can it be? Disappointment swells up inside her. Leaning against the fireplace is Joe, her ex.

'Well don't look so happy to see me.'

Joe's tone is rich with sarcasm. She notices his eyelids are heavy, and his pupils dilated. He is stoned.

'What are you doing here?'

'I've come to see my girl, haven't I?' he says, flopping down on the couch and picking up his cigarette papers.

My girl? Could Joe really be serious?

'Joe, I haven't seen you since last June.'

'Well, baby, you knew I was going to Europe to tour with the band.' He begins to roll a joint. 'I sent you emails. Didn't you read them?'

'Oh yeah.' Maya sits down on a chair and unlaces her hiking boots. She averts her face because the truth is that after the first couple of rambling emails about how great the gigs had gone in Barcelona, Berlin, Amsterdam and wherever else next, she had begun to skim through them. When Daniel came into her life, she lost interest altogether. The last three emails Joe sent to her are still unopened in her inbox.

'So when did you get back?'

'A week ago,' Joe says. 'I had to sort out a few things, but I came by a couple of times you were out. You're a busy lady, Mistress Maya.'

Is there an edge to his voice? Does Joe know about Daniel? Maya sneaks a look at him, but her ex is focused on lighting his joint, his expression indifferent. He inhales deeply, and then passes it over to her.

'So, baby, what do you think?' he says as smoke plumes out of his nostrils.

'Sorry, Joe, you've lost me?'

He pats the seat beside him on the couch, gives her a smile. Maya used to think his unkempt look sexy, but now he looks like a mess.

'Come on over here, and give me a proper welcome home will ya?'

She remains sitting on her chair.

'You've been gone months, Joe.'

'Sure, Maya, and I don't expect you to have been sitting at home with your legs crossed neither.' He winks at her. 'That's not what we're about, is it? We're two of a kind. Free spirits.'

Maya passes the joint back to him. As she does so, Joe takes a hold of her hand and pulls her over towards him.

'I don't expect nothing from you,' he says. His face is inches from hers. She can smell his breath, dusky with smoke.

'I know.'

She remembers how simple her life had been when she was with Joe. Painting. Fucking. Getting stoned. No wife, no daughter, and no broken heart.

'What's your answer then?' He lets go of her hand. Past the stoned glaze, Maya can see something else in his eyes. A look she has never noticed before. Intense and dark.

'About what?' she says lightly, pulling off her hiking socks.

'Jeez, make a man beg why don't you?' He passes the joint back. 'About moving in with you. We're recording an album in Phoenix so I'll be back and forth. But thought we could share some soul time together, you know what I mean, baby.'

She wishes he would stop calling her baby. When had she ever told him she liked it?

'Sorry, Joe, it's not a good idea.'

'Aw, come on, Maya, I won't get in your hair I promise. I'll be with the boys most the time in Phoenix.'

She gets up and takes two beers out the fridge, handing him one. He's always more amenable once he's had a beer. Joe pats the space on the couch beside him again.

'I can't live with you, Joe.' Maya remains standing as she flips the lid of her beer bottle off with a quarter.

'Why's that now? Don't you think it will be cool?' Joe is still smiling at her. 'I can do some work in the yard for you, chop wood for the winter and—'

'I've met someone,' Maya interrupts him.

She doesn't know why she tells him, especially since her affair with Daniel is over. But in her heart, it isn't. In her heart, Maya is still madly in love with Daniel Garvey.

Joe takes another long pull on the joint before speaking.

'Well now, are you telling me that some man has finally caught our little Mistress Maya in his net?'

'Yes.' Maya slumps down on the couch next to Joe. 'No,' she admits, taking a huge slug of her beer. 'I don't really know what's going on, Joe,' she confides. 'But I'm all screwed up over it. I can't be with anyone else.'

'Hey, baby, you know I don't believe in ownership, right?'

'I know, it's just...'

'Well then just chill,' he says, passing her back the joint. 'It's no big deal. I'll stay with Pete in Phoenix. Okay?'

'Thanks, Joe.'

'Let's just hang out right now.'

Her body begins to melt into the couch. She can feel her muscles aching from the hike, and her head is so tired from all the thinking she has been doing about Daniel. She needs to switch off. Succumb to the moment.

'Sure, Joe, let's get stoned.'

He gives her a big grin, and Maya remembers what it was that had attracted her to Joe. He would always blow in and then out again just as suddenly. She had liked his unpredictability. It meant that she didn't have to commit herself.

'So will you read my tarot cards for me tonight?' Joe asks, beginning work on a fresh joint. 'I got them read in Barcelona but I didn't understand half of it. I didn't know my Spanish stank so much!'

'Sure,' she says, hoping he'll forget once they are stoned.

'Oh yeah and some woman was here looking for her picture,' Joe says, knocking back his bottle of beer.

'What woman?'

'Didn't say her name. Thought you'd know.'

'But I've no commissions at the moment.'

'Tall, blond, big tits, kinda sexy in a hot mom way,' he says. 'I think she was Irish.'

Irish. Maya's beer bottle slips out of her hand and crashes

onto the floor. Joe jerks with surprise on the couch next to her, spilling his grass off his lap.

'Christ, Maya, watch out, will ya?'

Maya jumps up. Her whole body trembling. She hugs her sides and stares at Joe in fright. He starts laughing at her. She must look crazy, bug-eyed from the joint, and shaking in shock.

'It was her,' she gasps. The grass has loosened her tongue. Besides she needs someone to talk to. Joe is probably the worst person, but she has no one else right now.

'Who is *her*?'

'His wife.'

Joe stops laughing. He regards Maya. His face momentarily serious, before breaking into a devilish grin.

'Oh, Maya, you are so fucked,' he says.

'She was here,' Maya mutters in horror. 'Christ, she was in this cabin, she could come back... I was the mistress, Joe, the fucking *mistress!*'

'Hey, baby.' Joe stops laughing and gets off the couch. He pulls Maya into his arms. 'You're a goddess, Maya D'Costa,' he whispers into her ear, before kissing her on the forehead.

She lets herself fall into his arms. She closes her eyes and lets him touch her. Maya wants Joe to fuck her love for Daniel Garvey right out of her. Things had got too messy, especially because of the daughter.

CHAPTER FIFTEEN

FOUR MONTHS BEFORE, 20 NOVEMBER 2018

Maya and Daniel are in the Desert Botanical Garden, one of her favorite places which she has wanted to share with him for weeks. Although the fierce heat of the summer has long waned, Maya can still feel the sun's slap upon her cheeks. As she takes her straw hat out of her bag and places it on her head, she notices a group of high school girls coming out of the center's shop. They are one mass of laughter, chat, mobile phones, sparkling nails, and long silky hair. Daniel doesn't pay them the slightest bit of notice, but Maya always looks at people. It is one of her things.

In this noisy bunch of girls, one stands out. For a start, she is dressed all in black, in DMs and a black fedora hat upon her red hair. She is carried along on the wave of her friends almost as if she is motionless. The girl is staring right at her. Maya looks behind her. Surely that girl is looking at someone else with such a penetrating gaze? But there is no one behind Maya. She nearly says to Daniel, *Look at that girl staring at us*.

Yet just as she is about to, she realizes who this pale-faced staring girl with the long red hair might be. Her stomach drops in horror. At that exact moment, Daniel puts his arm around her waist, and burrows his face into her neck, kissing the tender skin. She feels hostile eyes boring into her back as they keep walking. She hates herself, and yet she cannot stop it.

She is being paranoid. It is just some nosy schoolgirl watching them. If it is Cathy Garvey, wouldn't she call to her father? Or surely Daniel would have seen her? But then all his attention was on Maya. She had seen it with her father and Celeste, when Maya had felt that nothing she did could ever get his notice. She had seen her father and Celeste all over each other in public, and never made them aware of her presence. She had been the same age as Cathy. Maya remembers how much she hated her father for cheating on her mother, and how she hated Celeste even more. The thought makes her feel sick.

But instead of pulling away from Daniel, or even telling him her suspicions that his own daughter has seen them, she points out one of the flowering cacti which have inspired her recent series of paintings. She pushes the truth down because she's not ready for a reckoning. Not yet.

LISTEN TO ME

You knew what I was capable of. You knew how the anger inside me made me act. And yet you still did it. You pushed me, as much as I pushed you.

There is no such thing as unconditional love. Not between father and daughter, nor between husband and wife. Not in my world.

I grew up twisted by the conflict between my parents. I could only respond to betrayal with revenge. So, what happened was inevitable.

The first time I orchestrated death was wicked, because I lost control.

I took the rage I felt at my parents for having Rosie put down out on an innocent. I didn't mean to do it. It just happened.

A week after Rosie was taken away from me my father came home with a big cardboard box.

'I have a surprise for you,' he said, looking pleased with himself.

Inside was a squealing puppy. It even looked like Rosie. The same breed, chocolate brown, with soft floppy ears. A girl dog too. But it wasn't Rosie. The puppy was nothing like my beloved hound.

'I don't want it,' I said, and my father had looked shocked.

'Come on, now,' my mother said. 'Look how cute she is.'

She took the puppy out of the box and forced her squirming body into my arms.

'Go on, hold her,' she tried to persuade me. 'What are you going to call her?'

I had dropped the puppy onto the floor.

'She doesn't want it,' my mother said to my father.

'Of course she'll want it.'

'I told you it was too soon.' She turned on him.

'You always have to be right, don't you?'

They started into each other. I felt myself become invisible. Their raised voices agitated the puppy and it began to whine.

'Get used to it,' I whispered to the stupid creature. 'They don't care about you.'

I picked the puppy up again, took it upstairs and I dumped it on the floor. It immediately pissed on my carpet. I hated it. Rosie never did anything like that, even when she was a puppy. It ran around the room like a maniac. When I looked into that little dog's eyes, it wasn't normal. It was wired crazy. There was no intelligence, no understanding. Not like Rosie. It kept jumping up at me and pulling on my clothes. It ripped my best jeans, chewed up all my boots. It barked and barked all night long. My father would tell me to shut it up, but I would poke the puppy then to make it bark more. It was wild, and out of control. No one could tame that stupid puppy.

We never had to worry about Rosie running off, but as soon as that puppy got outside it would tear off into the woods for hours. My mother was terrified it would get run over if it got out the front of the house. She asked my father to put up a fence, but the puppy got bigger and bigger and soon it could jump over the fence easy.

'Control your dog,' my father would tell me. 'What's it called anyway?'

I never gave it a name. It was just It.

When I think about that poor dog now, I feel really bad. The way I treated it proves that I was not normal, right from the beginning. How could I be so cruel?

But when I pinched and poked that dog, when I pulled its tail and watched it jump around, tearing at their things, destroying the house, it gave me some kind of joy. It was a way I could get back at them.

It was always going to end badly for that dog.

I take the blame for its death because I knew exactly what I was doing when I left the back door open. It went bounding out into the garden. I calmly unlatched the gate and left it wide open. It ran straight out into the road, and smack into the oncoming traffic.

I regretted it immediately. Ran out onto the road screaming.

It was lying on its side, panting its last breaths, red streaking its chocolate brown coat. I knelt by its side, and I looked into its eyes. And, for the first time, it looked at me with knowing.

'I'm sorry,' I whispered to the poor dog.

That dog always knew I would destroy it. It had been frightened of me, a mere child, from day one. What happened to the dog taught me that fear can push anyone over the edge. No matter how solid they might seem.

I wanted my parents to be as afraid as that dog. As I was.

I wanted you to feel the same fear.

And I guess you did. At the end.

CHAPTER SIXTEEN

THREE DAYS AFTER, FRIDAY 5 APRIL 2019

As she drives back towards Flagstaff through Oak Creek Canyon, Constance feels as if the woods are pressing in on either side of her. These are not like the woods back home in Ireland, with their moss carpet, and fairy rings. These woods are spiky, dry, and brittle. There is something sinister about them. She glances at her door to check she is locked inside the car. Ever since she has come to live in America, she has not felt safe.

Light is fading fast. She reads the clock on the dashboard. She has been much longer than she planned. She connects to her Bluetooth and rings Cathy's number. The first time her daughter's phone rings out. Nothing unusual. Cathy is very lax about answering her phone. The second time she picks up.

'What is it, Mom?'

'I just called to let you know I'll be back in twenty minutes, love.'

'Whatever.' Constance can hear the sulk in her daughter's voice. 'I'm not home anyway.'

'But what about dinner? Are you still at the library?'

'Nope, I'm at Lisa's. I told you we're working on our math project together. Her mom will give us something to eat.'

'What time should I pick you up?'

'No need.'

'I don't want you walking home in the dark...'

Her daughter interrupts with a frustrated sigh as if her mother is an imbecile.

'Lisa's mom will drop me when we're done, or I might stay over.'

The hostility in Cathy's voice hurts her.

'So I planned a trip to Scottsdale Fashion Square for your birthday tomorrow...' Constance tries to sound upbeat, as if she hasn't noticed Cathy's rudeness.

'Listen, Mom, I don't really care if we go out.' Cathy pauses for a moment, her voice a little softer. 'What with things the way they are with you and Dad, I'd rather we didn't okay?'

'Just us two, no Dad,' Constance pleads. 'A girls' day out. It'll be fun.'

'Thanks, but no thanks.'

Constance grits her teeth. 'But it's your birthday,' she protests.

'Exactly, it's my sixteenth birthday so I'd rather not go out with my mother. I want to hang out with Lisa.'

'But Cathy—'

'Have to go,' she interrupts.

Before Constance can try to persuade her otherwise, Cathy has hung up on her.

She feels a mixture of hurt and confusion. Since Cathy was about twelve years old, her moods have swung between silent and sullen to flashes of indignation and frustration. Constance remembers one time, not long after Daniel had been made redundant, when Cathy lashed into her about how pathetic she was not to have a proper career.

'How could you live off Dad all these years?' her daughter had criticized her.

'I was looking after you.'

'Oh don't give me that,' Cathy said dismissively. 'Plenty of women, *single* women even, manage full time jobs and children. You've only got me... and I'm not even a baby.'

'But I work at the gallery.'

'Part time and for peanuts.' She looked at Constance in disdain. 'I am never going to let myself be dependent on a man.'

'Well good for you,' Constance said, her heart burning with humiliation.

The sun is glaring in her eyes as Constance drives into the outskirts of Flagstaff. Her head is throbbing. It all feels too much. Cathy despising her, and Daniel gone. Her daughter has always been a daddy's girl. Once she announces they are returning to Ireland, Cathy will hate her even more.

Constance drives past their turn-off from the highway. She can't bear going home to that big empty house yet again. She keeps going all the way into the historic downtown of Flagstaff. Across the railroad tracks and onto the iconic Route 66. Daniel loved this part of Flagstaff, said it reminded him of the whole beatnik culture. Constance remembers that when they first met Daniel had carried around a battered old copy of Jack Kerouac's *On the Road* in the back pocket of his jeans for months on end. He had spoken of his dream to hit the road and be free from all of his family and Ireland. He had presumed that she would want that dream too.

But Constance has always been a homebody. Over the years, Daniel transformed from that lanky lad with wanderlust into the silent serious watcher of their failing marriage. He had not spoken of his dreams to travel in years. The furthest they had gone before they had moved to America was a disastrous holiday to Majorca when Cathy had been eleven. Constance had got food poisoning from tiramisu (her husband and daughter had turned down dessert of course) and had spent the holiday stuck in the apartment sick as a dog while Daniel and Cathy had gone exploring over the whole island. She had hated every minute of it. Felt left out and abandoned by them. She had missed Ireland and just wanted to be home again.

Maya D'Costa is bound to be a great traveler. Just her name is enough to make Constance think of foreign lands. She is an artist too, probably exhibited all over the world. She imagines Daniel confiding in Maya D'Costa. The two of them making plans to travel together to lost islands, and beautiful beaches.

And yet there had been another man inside Maya D'Costa's Luna House today. What had this Joe meant when he called Maya D'Costa his girl? Is she sleeping with Daniel *and* that wild-haired druggie? What kind of woman is she? Constance wants to be disgusted, but she isn't at all. She clenches her jaw, bites her lip, and tastes blood. She is jealous of Maya D'Costa.

Without even realizing it, Constance is driving back over the railroad tracks, and in a loop around Flagstaff. Round and round in a circle like the headless chicken she feels she is. She drives past the library, one of Cathy's favorite haunts, and finally pulls into the small parking lot behind the red-brick Monte Vista hotel. She turns off the engine and opens the window of her car. Now the light has gone, cool air floods into the car. She picks up her phone and opens Google. She can bear it no longer; she has to see a picture of this woman. She types in *Maya D'Costa*. No Twitter nor Facebook nor Instagram. Not even a website. What kind of artist is she? Surely all artists nowadays have websites? There are several reviews of her paintings. All of them glowing. Then something pops up that makes her tremble. Coverage of the exhibition in Sedona called *Plain Rains*. With shaking hands, Constance chooses one of the articles and clicks on it, waiting as her phone slowly downloads.

Maya D'Costa is smiling up at her. She is *so* young. Beautiful *and* talented. Tears well in her eyes. How could she ever have competed with this radiant creature? The photograph is a shot of the artist at the opening of the exhibition. She is holding a glass of champagne in her hand and beaming at the camera, her eyes molten brown, outlined deftly in black. Dressed in a full-length sleeveless silver dress that clings to her body like luminous fish scales, Maya D'Costa possesses a tiny yet feminine figure. Her beauty is not of the ordinary kind. Constance can detect the rebel in her. The artist has a tattoo on her shoulder. Constance zooms in on it. A tiny blue hummingbird bright against her dark skin. How cool is that. She is wearing dozens of silver bangles, her fingers are littered with rings with an assortment of different stones, and her nose is pierced. If Constance had decorated herself in such a way, she would have looked like an eccentric, but Maya D'Costa looks enticing. Her hair is a long sheath of silken black, with streaks of red in it. Constance instinctively touches her own hair. It is cut short in what she had hoped was a gamine style, but she fears ends up making her look masculine.

When Constance first had her hair cut, back home in Ireland, Daniel had complained about the loss of her long blond locks. Constance was surprised that he cared at all.

'But, Dad, haven't you noticed that nearly all middle-aged Irish women get their hair chopped off, especially if they live in the country,' Cathy piped up. 'They call it the Culchie Crop.'

Her husband and daughter had sniggered. Constance tried not to show her hurt.

'The ends were all split,' she said in defense. 'I needed a change.'

'I'm sorry, Constance, it *is* nice,' Daniel said to her, but she could tell he was lying.

She had meant to grow her hair when she got to Arizona. Just as she had meant to join a gym and lose some weight. She also meant to mix with the mothers of Cathy's new school friends. Make her own friends. Constance has not done any of these things. Unable to cope with the irritation of the in-between stage of growing her hair, especially as the climate in Arizona makes her hair so flat and flyaway, she got it cut again. She can't face the energy involved just getting to the gym, let alone working out. As for making friends... this is an ordeal for Constance. It always has been. She has no understanding of how Americans interact. It all seems so falsely cheerful. What are people *really* thinking of her?

Constance looks back down at the charming Maya D'Costa. She looks like she would have friends. Many of them. And still, she steals another woman's husband.

Constance's phone begins ringing in her hand. It gives her fright. Liam's name comes up on the screen. She silently curses. The last person she feels like talking to is her brother-in-law.

Constance waits until the phone rings out but then it just begins to ring again. Reluctantly she answers it.

'Hi, Connie, how's it going?' Liam's voice is a strange mix of American and Irish accents. It adds to the overall sense of fake whenever she speaks to him.

'I'm grand thanks.'

'Is Daniel there?'

'Nope.'

Constance presses the phone to her ear as she watches a woman get out of her car in the hotel parking lot.

'It's important. I can't get hold of him.'

The woman walks past her car, swinging a blue leather bag onto her shoulder. She is around the same age as Constance. Her hair is as short as hers, and *she* looks good. Constance watches the woman cross the street and walk off, swinging her hips with inner confidence. She could be that woman if she wanted to be. Strong and self-possessed.

'I'm sorry, Liam, I don't know where he is,' Constance says. She is tired of lying, pretending that everything is alright.

'He didn't turn up today at the viewing,' Liam continues,

sounding cross. 'He was supposed to be back in. He can't just not turn up, not even ring the client. He's cost me thousands; you don't piss off these people.'

'It's nothing to do with me,' Constance says. 'He's gone.'

'What do you mean he's gone?' Liam rants. 'He rang in on Tuesday and told me he had food poisoning. Said he'd be back today. That's why I set up the viewing.'

Constance's cheeks sting as if slapped by her husband's deceit.

'Well he was lying, Liam, because he's gone for good.'

Constance hangs up before Liam can say anything else. The phone begins ringing again but she throws it onto the passenger seat and starts up her car. She just wants to get home now and bury her sorrows in a big glass of wine. She wants to forget what has happened for one evening at least. Tomorrow she will have to wake up and face her new reality. Life without Daniel. She will have to tell Cathy they are moving back to Ireland. And Constance is dreading her daughter's reaction.

CHAPTER SEVENTEEN

THREE DAYS AFTER, FRIDAY

'I've missed Mistress Maya's flowers,' Joe says, as he pushes his hand into the waist of her combats. He unzips them to reveal the tattoo of faded roses. Their stems entwined, spread across Maya's pelvis.

'I want you so bad, baby,' Joe says, brushing his lips against hers. He smells of grass, and tastes of beer and bourbon.

He pushes his tongue into her mouth. Her head is spinning. She is stoned. Wiped out. Everything feels wrong. She has slept with Joe hundreds of times before, but he feels like a stranger now. A wave of repulsion sweeps through her and she pulls his hand out of her panties. He tries to go again, but she pushes him away.

'No, Joe,' Maya tells him, pulling up her combats and fastening them. 'I'm sorry but I can't cheat on Daniel.'

He looks at her incredulously.

'You're not serious?' he says. 'The guy's married. He was cheating on you *all* the time with his wife. '

'No he wasn't. They stopped having sex.'

'Oh right.' His voice is sarcastic. 'That woman is hot. I *saw* her. Course he was still banging her.'

Maya knows in her heart that Joe is wrong.

'No, Daniel told me they hadn't had sex for over a year.'

'Oh come on, Maya, I'm a guy right? I know guys. He wants to have the best of both worlds, believe me.'

'Not all men are like that, Joe.' She is surprised at how defensive she is of Daniel.

'I never took you for dumb,' Joe says, giving her a hard look.

He shrugs. She can tell he is trying to look as if he doesn't care about her rejection. 'I don't give a crap either way,' he says, pulling two more beers out of the fridge and handing her one. 'Just thought we could hang out. You know, share some loving. No big deal.'

'Sorry,' she says, relief surging through her.

'Hey, it's you I feel sorry for missing out on my big dick.' He grins but his smile doesn't quite reach his eyes. 'You got anything to eat?'

Maya makes them a huge mound of nachos. Joe likes it hot, so she puts extra green jalapenos on it, the kind Daniel can't handle. She can't think of two more different men than Joe and Daniel. She remembers hikes with Joe, and how he'd leap with confidence from rock to rock. She pleaded with him to be careful. Daniel gripped her hand so tight on Tuesday when they were at the Grand Canyon. But she had let go of him. Shaken him off. She remembers that.

She had been so angry with Daniel for breaking up with her after all his promises. She wanted to hurt him as much as he was hurting her. She can't remember what she actually screamed at him. It is a hot blank in her head. Like yesterday when she vandalized her own painting with red paint. She hates this side of herself. Irrational. Messy emotions. How she felt as a powerless little girl. It is all wrong. Negative, and base. She is heartbroken, that's what it is, and she has so little to show for their affair. Daniel only gave her one precious gift—everything else was experiences, and roses. Maya puts her hand on her wrist, but the watch Daniel gave her for Christmas is missing. She needs to wear it, right now. Her head is foggy from all the joints that she and Joe smoked. She can't remember when she last had it on. She always takes it off when she is painting in case she gets it splattered. She staggers into the kitchen and begins to pull open drawers, bursting with all the small things she likes to collect. Stones, leaves, dried flowers, and bags of herbs. Candles come tumbling out, sticks of incense, an array of stash boxes, and little bells tinkling onto the floor.

'Are you okay, Maya?' Joe asks her from the couch.

'I can't find my watch,' she says, sounding panicked.

'Who cares what the time is? It's dark, that's all I know.'

Maya ignores him. His presence is an irritation to her now. She climbs up the stairs to her bedroom, throws clothes around the room.

'You sound like an angry bear up there,' Joe calls up. 'Hey get your tarot, will you?'

She opens the drawer of her bedside cabinet and pushes her hand right to the back of it. To her relief, her fingers clutch the hardness of the watch's face. She pulls it out. Holds it up to the moonlight. It is twenty-three minutes past eight. She straps it onto her wrist, and immediately she feels held by Daniel's love. This watch reminds her she is still lost inside Daniel's heart. How will she ever find her way out again?

When she comes back downstairs, Joe is rolling another joint. She wishes he would go, but then he's too stoned to drive. She shouldn't smoke any more tonight, and nor should he. After a certain point, Joe transforms from chilled-out dude to paranoid basket case when it comes to dope.

'So did you find your watch?' Joe asks, as he scoops up a handful of nachos and shovels them into his mouth.

'Yes.'

Joe pulls at her hand with his greasy fingers so that he can examine the watch. 'So he gave you the watch, I guess.'

Maya nods, still gazing down at the ivory watch face, and the golden hands.

'Not cheap,' Joe says as he drops her wrist.

Maya circles the watch face with her fingertip, avoiding Joe's scrutiny. She can sense his mood changing.

'He's dumped you,' he says. She can hear something like glee in his tone. 'You know that right?'

'I don't want to talk about it.'

'I promise you, baby, you will never see that man again.'

Joe's eyes are half closed, but she senses that he's not drowsy. He's watching her.

The energy in the cabin has changed. She is strangely unsettled. There is something different about Joe. She picks up a bunch of sage out of the bowl on top of the fireplace, and lights the end of it, waving it around the room to clear the bad energy. Joe is fumbling with his papers and grass. She prays that he will fall asleep soon. The last time he smoked too much grass, he had a huge rant about the other members of his band. He had been sure they were trying to get rid of him and asked her again and again if he wasn't the best mandolin player she had ever heard.

Maya can't shake from her head what he just said.

I promise you, baby, you will never see that man again.

How could Joe be so certain? He has never met Daniel.

'Come on, Maya, get out the tarot,' Joe demands from behind her on the couch.

She doesn't want to read Joe's tarot cards and predict his true intentions. Let alone discover what he might have already done.

CHAPTER EIGHTEEN

THREE DAYS AFTER, FRIDAY

As Constance drives down the street for a moment she thinks she sees Daniel's car. It's the same type of car, in the drive of the house behind theirs. The man in the mirror's car. It's the first time her secret obsession has crossed her mind all day. She shakes the image of those hands gripping the razor's handle from her head. She is pathetic fantasizing over a complete stranger when her own husband has strayed.

She turns into their street, pausing before opening the automatic doors of their garage. She looks at her US home. It's a new building, twice the size of their Irish cottage with a large porch and a pool out the back. Inside the lounge is vast, the walls cream, the floors marble. Her mother would have thought it the height of luxury.

Constance hates it. The brightness and the light. She wants to be back in her little stone cottage, sitting in the shadows by the window. Watching the rain pelt down, sweeping across the beach. The Atlantic Ocean wild and roaring. Constance misses her Irish rain so much. In Arizona occasionally it rains, but it's violent, sudden, and short. What she misses are those soft rainy days in the west of Ireland, when she is wreathed in a gentle mist of rain, clinging to her sweater like tiny pearls. Her skin soft as flower petals in all that moisture, but in Arizona she is dry and itchy. She keeps getting heat rashes on her thighs. She is forever covering herself in body creams and lotions, but this desert air seems to suck them out of her almost immediately.

Constance sits down at the breakfast counter, sweeps her hands across its unblemished marble top. The house hums around her, as desolate as a vast desert. She takes out her phone, scrolls down to Cathy's number. She wants to call her daughter and beg her to come home. But she can't because Cathy would despise her even more.

A shopping trip in Phoenix was a terrible idea. Cathy has no interest in fashion. Driving lessons? Money? She's a useless mother because she has no idea what to give her daughter for her birthday.

Constance picks up her phone and searches for Frances' number. She will know what she should do.

But Frances sent her a voice note last week asking when to expect her and Constance still hasn't replied. If she calls her, she'll only ask her if she's spoken to Cathy yet. She's ashamed of her relationship with Cathy. Frances is so close to her two girls, especially Sophie. She puts the phone back down on the counter. She has to talk to Cathy before she calls Frances.

The doorbell rings. It's so loud that it makes Constance jump. She walks down the hall, realizing she has been sitting in the dark. She turns on the light.

It's the cop car she sees first. Her throat constricts in terror. Cathy. Is she in an accident, hurt, worse than that? Suddenly her obsession over Daniel and his mistress seems trivial compared to this possibility.

There are two cops on her doorstep. A man and a woman.

'Mrs. Constance Garvey?' the woman asks.

'What's happened? Is it my daughter?'

The man steps forward. 'No, Ma'am, this is nothing to do with your daughter.'

There is a buzzing in her ears growing louder and louder. Constance finds herself staring at the female cop's hands. They are big for a woman's. The skin weathered, too old looking for her face.

She begins to shake. Something is seriously wrong; she can see from the stern expressions on their faces. They are here because of Daniel.

Constance sits on the big dove gray couch staring up at Maya D'Costa's painting above the fireplace. She remembers that sometimes she had caught Daniel looking at it, and she had thought he might be appreciating what she liked. How stupid she had been. It had been nothing to do with her. Daniel had been looking at the painting because he was thinking about his lover, right in front of her eyes. But none of that matters now because Daniel is gone.

The fake Tiffany lamp bathes the painting in golden light, drawing out those emerald tones, the twists of verdigris upon the river.

Constance glares at it. She wants to take it down and smash it. The anger wells up inside of her, and she clutches her shaking hands. The cops still haven't told her why they're here, only that it's to do with Daniel. They insisted she sit down which means it's serious. Her thoughts stray to Liam. She always thought he was shifty. What have the two brothers got themselves caught up in? She remembers Liam's anger earlier, his accusation that Daniel had cost them thousands of dollars.

'My name is Deputy Peters from the Coconino Sheriff's Office,' says the woman. 'And this is Special Agent Lopez of the National Parks Investigative Services Branch.'

Constance notices that the man isn't in police uniform but wearing belted fawn trousers, a green check shirt, and holding a Stetson hat with the National Parks insignia in his hands. He looks familiar, but his name, Lopez, means nothing to her.

'Ma'am, a body was found this morning in the Grand Canyon, alongside your husband's I.D.,' Deputy Peters says bluntly.

'What?' she gasps in shock. 'Whose body?'

'We believe it is your husband,' Lopez says more gently. 'He was found by a park ranger.'

'No!' She brings her hands to her face. What are they telling her?

'Mrs. Garvey, this is a big shock, let me make you some tea,' Deputy Peters offers, looking uncomfortable.

Without waiting for a response, or any direction, she disappears into Constance's spotless kitchen. She supposes that the cop has done this before. Delivered bad news, and then made tea, or coffee for the victim's next of kin. Constance's throat is so dry she begins to cough.

'Peters, can you get Mrs. Garvey a glass of water,' Lopez calls out. 'Just breathe,' he says to her, his brown eyes rich with concern. 'You've had a terrible shock.'

Peters returns with water, and a steaming cup of tea. Constance grabs the water and knocks it back. She takes a breath, but she still can't speak. Questions tumult in her mind. What had happened to Daniel? How had he died? But he can't be dead. He can't. She realizes the last time she saw him alive, he was fucking Maya D'Costa in her Luna House. The thought makes her feel sick and she gets up, running to the downstairs toilet where she throws up. The cops wait patiently, in silence. She wills them away, for time to go back, for this not to have happened, but when she returns to the lounge, toilet paper bunched in her hands to wipe away the tears, they are still there.

'I'm sorry for your loss, Ma'am,' Deputy Peters says, handing her the tea. 'Drink this, it'll help.'

Constance takes a sip, her hand trembling as she raises the cup to her lips. It is possibly the worst cup of tea she has ever drunk, sickly sweet, but she keeps on sipping. The deputy must have put half a bag of sugar in it but the sweetness, though revolting, gives her strength.

'It looks like an accident,' Special Agent Lopez says. 'It happens I'm afraid, more than you might think. Especially outsiders hiking in the Grand Canyon. They go too close to the edge...'

'He fell?'

'Yes, from the rim,' Lopez confirms.

Daniel falling. Falling. Her heart pounding in horror at the thought of it.

'Did someone see him fall?'

Constance's heart is accelerating even faster. She just can't imagine it. This is all a bad dream. Any minute now, Daniel will come marching into the house. Ask what these strangers are doing in his lounge, drinking tea with his distraught wife.

'There are no witnesses that we know of,' Lopez tells her. 'As I said, he was found by a park ranger on patrol this morning.' He coughs, avoids her eye. 'We're not sure exactly when he died. We'll know more when we have the autopsy report.'

'He must have gone too close to the edge and slipped. We've had a few similar incidents in the Grand Canyon the past couple of years,' Deputy Peters adds.

They are wrong. Constance thinks of the time she and Daniel went to the Cliffs of Moher back home. He'd been so nervous to be that high up he refused to walk the cliff path with her.

'But that can't be,' she protests. 'Daniel would never have gone too close to the edge. He's terrified of heights.'

The deputy says nothing, but Lopez leans forward in his

chair. His eyes are keen, shimmering almost black. She cannot help thinking how different he looks from pale, red-haired Daniel.

'Your husband suffered from vertigo?'

'Yes, he didn't even like to climb ladders. There is no way he would have gone close enough to the edge to fall.'

'Do you know why he was at the Grand Canyon?' he asks Constance. She feels him scrutinizing her.

'No,' she says in a small voice, not daring to look at either of them.

'I'm sorry to ask you this, Mrs. Garvey, but was your husband suffering from depression?' Deputy Peters asks. 'Was he under pressure at work, or had money troubles? How were things at home?'

Constance looks up in surprise. The deputy's cheeks are flushed, but the expression in her eyes is steady. What is she really asking her? Constance sees Lopez giving Peters a stern look.

It's clear what Deputy Peters is implying but Constance knows it is even less likely that Daniel killed himself than fell by accident.

'He didn't kill himself,' she says. 'Daniel wouldn't. But I can't believe he would fall off the Grand Canyon. He is so careful... are you sure it's Daniel?' she blurts out.

'His I.D. was found near the body.' Lopez's expression is apologetic.

'But someone could have stolen it,' she says in a weak voice.

'That's why I need to ask you to come to the Medical Examiner's Office to confirm his identity.'

Constance shrinks in her chair. Her cup of tea wobbles on her lap, spilling onto her pale pink linen skirt.

Lopez takes the tea from her, placing it with care upon the table.

'Do you have any family living with you?' he asks her.

'My daughter. She's at a friend's.'

'Do you want to call her?' the deputy asks. 'We can go pick her up for you.'

Constance looks in horror at the police officer.

'No!' She takes a breath. 'No, I want to wait until I'm sure.'

'Is there another adult relative or a friend you can ask to come with you?'

Constance shakes her head. The only person she could ask is Liam and he is the last person she wants to see right now. She has to do this on her own and be absolutely sure before she tells anyone.

'He has a brother, but I don't want to call him, not yet.'

'You shouldn't be on your own.' the deputy says.

'Deputy Peters is right. Can we not call someone for you?' Lopez pushes.

Constance stares at them unblinking. All she wants is to be on her own.

'When was the last time you saw or heard from your husband?' Deputy Peters continues to question her.

The room is spinning. Constance feels sick again to the pit of her stomach.

'Monday morning.'

'Four days ago?' Deputy Peters clarifies.

She nods.

Lopez frowns, pulling a small red notebook out of his back pocket and writing something down.

'So, you hadn't seen or heard from him since then? You didn't report him missing?' the deputy continues.

She shakes her head. She knows what they are both thinking. What kind of wife doesn't worry when her husband goes missing for four days?

CHAPTER NINETEEN

THREE MONTHS BEFORE, CHRISTMAS
DAY 2018

Maya stares at the blank canvas, trying to summon some inspiration, but she feels empty. She never used to mind spending Christmases alone. But today she cannot help feeling lonely, and her thoughts continually stray to Daniel and how different his Christmas Day, surrounded by family, is to hers.

It has taken years for Maya to banish the depression she used to feel at Christmas time. Her father left her and her mother to be with Celeste and set up a new home in Miami. Every year they invited Maya for Christmas, but she refused. She hated Celeste and besides, she couldn't leave her mother alone in London.

The festive season for Maya became dragging days and cheerless evenings in her mother's flat in London. Every night they would watch the round of Christmas movies. Her mom drunk as usual. Though years have passed, Maya's mother never seems to adjust to the fact that she is divorced. She still refers to Maya's father as her husband and wears her wedding ring. It frustrates Maya. Her mother had been just over forty when her parents broke up. Young enough still. She had plenty of admirers but as soon as a new boyfriend was forced to listen to her mother's bitter monologues on how her husband cheated on her for years and ran off with the bitch mistress, he would fade away. No one likes a scornful woman.

They were lonely Christmases with her mother. Maya had no siblings. They had no contact with her mother's family back in the States. Her grandparents were uptight Baptists that her mother had turned her back on when she went to London and met Maya's father. Maya's grandparents had never got over the fact their daughter had married an Indian, *and* a Catholic. That he went on to become one of the most celebrated artists in America was a fact that her mother's family had always ignored. Maya has never been tempted to build bridges and visit either her mom's family in Minnesota, or her father and his second wife in Miami.

Maya thought that nothing could be as bad as those dreary drunk Christmases with her mother in her damp flat in Islington, but today is worse. She can't help comparing who she has become with herself last year. A content and self-contained woman. Daniel has dismantled her and left her yearning. She understands a little about her mother's pain now. She had judged her so harshly, but her mother was nursing a broken heart, for years.

Maya puts down her palette and paintbrush, wiping her hands, and picks up her phone. She looks up her mother's number and presses the call button. It's three in the afternoon in England, and her mother has already had a few.

'Hello, honey,' her mother slurs. 'Merry Christmas!'

'I'm sorry I wasn't kinder to you. I'm sorry what Daddy did to you,' Maya suddenly blurts out.

'What's all this?' her mother says, startled.

'I'm sorry he left you for Celeste...'

'But it's not your fault. It's that bloody bitch. I can't believe they're still together. Knowing Antonio, he's probably cheating on her anyhow.' She is off and Maya immediately regrets stirring it all up again. She listens to her mother berating the other woman for half an hour before she manages to get a word in.

'Mom, please, you need to let it go, it's ruining your life,' she says.

She hears her mother take a sip from her drink, the clink of ice in her glass.

'You don't know what you're talking about, Maya. How could you? You've never married anyone, let alone been in a committed relationship.'

Maya feels patronized, and though she shouldn't react, her mother is drunk and lashing out; she can't help herself.

'I'm in love,' she says.

'Oh, well, that's fantastic.' Her mother's tone changes, all warmth and excitement. 'Tell me all about him. Or is it a she? I have never been quite sure.' She giggles.

'His name is Daniel. He's Irish,' she confides.

'Good for you, a lovely Irishman, it's about time you settled down,' her mother says. 'Well, I am delighted for you, darling. At last, your prince has come. Is he there, can I say hello?'

'No, he's not here.' Maya bites her lip. Her mother's attitude is irritating her. She doesn't care about her life as an artist. It's clear she measures her daughter's success on her marital status.

'Why not, darling? Where is he? Oh, Maya, are you pushing him away, trying to be independent? Don't lose another good man because of your pride—'

'He's married!' Maya interrupts before she can stop herself.

There is a stony silence on the other end of the line.

'Mom, are you still there? Mom?'

'Maya, how *could* you?' her mother says before hanging up.

She thinks about ringing back but what can she say to make her mother understand? Her daughter is the other woman, and her mother will never see things from that perspective.

Maya slides open the glass doors and sits out on her porch, wrapped in blankets, smoking a joint. She watches the sunlight and the shadows chasing each other across the Sedona skyline. She has done it now. Admitted her love for Daniel to another person, even if it is her mother all the way over in England, drunk and furious with her.

She thinks of Daniel on his family holiday in Colorado. She imagines him walking the snowy streets of Aspen with his family. It is like an image in one of those Christmas movies. He is weighed down by boxes in multi-colored, sparkling foil wrapping, and with trails of long lengths of ribbon. His daughter is by his side, holding her daddy's hand, excitement shining in her eyes. And his wife is there too, beside him. Constant Constance, who owns Maya's beloved. The three of them walk together in the falling snow with Christmas lights sparkling all about them.

What does she expect? That Daniel abandon his family at Christmas time? He told her weeks ago that Liam had paid for the whole holiday, renting a chalet in Aspen where the two families were going skiing.

Daniel tried to make it up to her. They celebrated their own Christmas two weeks ago. He managed to get away for one night and they had such fun decorating Luna House together. Maya never bothered with Christmas trees before, but he insisted. They drove out to the Old Time Christmas Tree Farm, where they gave them a measuring stick and a saw and they trudged through acres of cypress Christmas trees to find the perfect fit for her cabin. Afterwards they drank hot apple cider while Daniel got her to pick a Christmas garland. That evening they decorated the tree together. Hanging baubles off each other's ears, trailing tinsel through their hair, kissing and teasing. She'd made a beautiful star out of card and golden paint, sticking it on top of the tree instead of an angel.

Daniel made Maya excited about Christmas for the first time since she was a little girl. He even cooked her a traditional Irish Christmas dinner with turkey, potatoes, gravy, even Brussels sprouts. He forgot that she didn't eat meat, but she didn't remind him. She had been so touched by his effort.

After Daniel cleaned up, they sat together on her couch in front of the fire. It had turned cold outside, and the clear night sky was clustered with stars. They stared into the pulsing fire, watching the wood as it crackled and crumbled like fallen cities.

'It's not Christmas without a fire in the hearth,' he said, tucking the hair behind her ears and kissing her neck.

She squeezed her eyes shut, willed it to really be Christmas Day, not their pretend Christmas. Imagined herself in Ireland with Daniel at Christmas time. Dark, cozy nights by the fire, snow falling outside. Midnight mass in the flickering candle light. Accepted by his family. Part of his tribe.

'Don't leave me,' Daniel whispered. 'I can't bear to be without you.'

She twisted around on his lap, her cheek brushing his.

'Daniel, you can't walk out on your daughter.'

His gaze warmed her, and he pulled her to him.

'I love you,' he said. 'I love that you are so selfless. I wish we could be together all the time.'

She put her hand to his mouth. 'Shush,' she chided him. 'It's enough that we're with each other right now.'

He spoke to her with his body. They made love in front of their fire. And while they did so it began to snow, lightly, a soft smattering that left a fine glaze of unblemished white all around them, far, far away from their guilt.

The next morning Daniel left early, while Maya was still asleep. When she got up, she found a small box wrapped in gold foil and tied with long spiraling sprays of silver ribbon on her work bench.

She peeled the wrapping off slowly, her heart pounding. In front of her was a small black case. She opened it. Inside was a watch. Not a dainty sparkly thing, but a watch with a large face, and a wide leather strap. Daniel knew exactly what she would like without even asking her.

Maya looks at the watch now. Its face so huge upon her narrow wrist, but she loves it. She is surprised to see it is late into the afternoon. How long has she been sitting outside getting stoned? She gets up and wanders back into her cabin. She needs to cook something to eat. She picks up her phone but there are no missed calls. Her mother hasn't called back. But there is no message from Daniel either. He will ring her, of course he will as soon as he has the chance.

Maya makes herself a stir fry, and gets a beer from the fridge. She settles on her couch, waiting for Daniel to call. He promised he would. When she's finished eating, she makes another joint to fill the space between waiting. She smokes slowly, meditatively. Maybe she should call her mother back. Tell her she's not like Celeste. But it's now the middle of the night in England, and she has a feeling her mother will have a go at her, no matter how Maya justifies what is happening to her.

For a moment, she sees herself through her mother's eyes, through Daniel's wife's eyes if she knew about their affair, through his daughter's eyes. It makes her feel sick. She's not a bad person, and yet she is doing this terrible thing which will hurt other women. She glances down at her phone. It's midnight now and still Daniel hasn't called. Christmas is over. She gets up, taking the watch off, and leaving it on the book-shelf. She crosses her arms, swaying from the joint. He doesn't love her because if he did, he would have called her today. He knew she was on her own and how hard Christmas is for her. She has to end this. Before all these women—herself included—get hurt.

CHAPTER TWENTY

THREE MONTHS BEFORE, 7 JANUARY 2019

'No one walks in Houston, Mom, it's dangerous,' Cathy moans. 'Everyone drives.'

'It's broad daylight, don't be ridiculous.'

But the walk is longer and more unpleasant than Constance expects. Concrete sidewalks alongside a road heavy with traffic. No shade. The Texan sun so bright even though it's January. By the time they arrive at the Rothko Chapel, Constance is damp with sweat. She can sense the anger radiating from her daughter.

However, once they walk inside the chapel, Cathy calms down. She seems very taken with it. No surprise really since the paintings are all black, her daughter's daily uniform. They sit within its shaded, spiritual confines for a long time, Cathy getting up every now and again, circling the chapel and examining each of the paintings one by one.

'They're not just black, are they?' she says as she sits back down next to her.

'Yes, you're right, that's what Frances said too,' Constance murmurs as she gazes at the huge canvases. 'There is so much depth and layering within them.'

She can't wait to talk to Frances about the Rothko Chapel. Her best, her only friend, who she is about to see in a few hours. She's eager to see her, and yet there is also a small part of her which is dreading it because she's not sure she can lie to Frances. Originally, Daniel was supposed to be with them in Houston. It was going to be a two-day stopover on their way back from Christmas in Colorado. But on New Year's Day, he told her he had to get back to Arizona for work. It was clearly a lie because Liam had said nothing about it, and he was spending another week in Colorado with Stacey and their boys.

'But you're supposed to hang out with Cathy while I see Frances,' she protested. 'It's been planned for ages. She's on a quick trip to visit a potential client who wants her to buy art for him.'

'I'm sorry, Constance,' Daniel said, tight-lipped. 'It's work.'

'But Liam isn't going back—'

'That's because he's the boss; he might be my brother, but I still have to prove myself, there's a lot of competition with the other realtors.' He pushed his hand through his red hair, his eyes not meeting hers. Liam would never fire Daniel. Not necessarily out of loyalty but because he loved lording it over his little brother. Taking every opportunity he could to remind Daniel that he was the big success and had saved the day for his failure of a brother. Everything they had—their big house in Flagstaff, the SUV—was thanks to Liam. Constance had never liked him. Not since the night before their wedding when she had overhead him telling Daniel not to marry her. That she wasn't good enough for him. She had been so pleased when Liam had left for the States and they hardly saw him anymore, but now she was constantly in his company, him interfering in their lives.

She should have been grateful because Liam had clearly gone to a lot of expense and trouble to organize their family Christmas in Aspen but as much as she tried, she hadn't enjoyed it. Right from day one Liam insisted they get out in the snow and ski. Liam, Stacey, and their boys were all good skiers while Daniel and even Cathy seemed to pick it up quickly. Constance was a disaster. Stacey had spent a whole morning trying to teach her, but she just kept falling over. She couldn't keep her balance at all.

'It's okay, just keep at it,' Stacey had said patiently. 'It'll stick.'

But Constance had given up. Said she had a headache and went inside their chalet. It was a relief to sit on the big couch with a steaming cup of tea, and look out the window at the others skiing down the slopes outside. For a few moments, she had appreciated the magical sparkle of the snowy mountains, beneath the clear blue winter sky. But before long, she began to feel lonely. She wished she hadn't given up on the skiing because it looked like they were having fun. Even Cathy and her younger cousins seemed to be getting on at last. But she'd been left out, and ended up cooking the dinners every day because the others were out skiing. In the evening, everyone was so exhausted they all went to bed early. Constance would lie next to Daniel listening to the rhythm of his breath and feel like such a loser. It was a relief when it was time to leave, despite her annoyance that Daniel was flying straight through to Arizona.

But now, in the Rothko Chapel, she feels she is in a place where she belongs again.

'Black is a color associated with depression. And yet Rothko's paintings make me feel quite the opposite,' she remarks to Cathy.

'Black is not depressing,' her daughter responds. 'It's safe.'

Once they are back outside again, Cathy continues to discuss the chapel with her. 'I love that it's a place for everyone of all religions and philosophies,' Cathy says to her. 'A place for human rights.'

'Yes, it's special.' Constance is pleased that for once, Cathy is opening up to her. 'I believe the founder set it up specially in mind for civil rights activists to gather together.'

'I want to be a human rights journalist,' Cathy announces, gazing at Barnett Newman's Broken Obelisk sculpture as it rises from a reflecting pool. Constance looks at her daughter in surprise. This is the first she has heard about Cathy's career plans. She bites back the temptation to tell her daughter that she might be unrealistic in her aspirations. She has never once known her to write anything.

'That's great, Cathy,' she says.

As they walk across the street to the Menil Collection, Cathy talks with passion about shocking human rights abuses, especially in America.

'It's not getting better,' she says, sounding angry. 'It's getting worse.'

Constance has not seen her daughter so animated in months. She feels a swell of pride.

————

Frances jumps up and waves as soon as Constance and Cathy enter the hotel restaurant. Emotion sweeps through Constance as she sees Frances' big smile, and she pushes back the tears. She has missed her so much. As the two women talk breathlessly to each other and Frances fills her in on all the news from the art world, Cathy retreats into her old monosyllabic self, taking out her phone and tapping away on it.

'You look great!' Frances says to Constance. 'It must be all the skiing on your fancy trip in Colorado!'

'Mom didn't ski,' Cathy says, looking up from her phone. 'She was scared.'

'I wasn't scared,' Constance says, embarrassed. 'I just didn't like it.'

'Oh I am with you there,' Frances says. 'Tried it once myself. Hated it. All that fuss with boots, skis, gloves, hats. You spend all this time going up the mountain to whizz down it in one minute.'

After dinner, Cathy declares she is tired, and goes up to their hotel room to bed. Constance and Frances stay on to have a nightcap at the bar.

As soon as she has taken a big slurp of her gin and tonic, Constance confides in Frances. 'I think Daniel might be having an affair.'

'Oh no, not again.'

Constance feels a twinge of guilt that she broke Daniel's confidence and told Frances about Bridget Kearney. But she needed someone to talk to at the time, and besides, he was the one who cheated on her so why should she feel bad that Frances knew?

'Are you sure?' Frances leans forward on her bar stool and places her hand on Constance's knee.

'Yes, pretty sure.' Constance nods. 'He's always telling me he has to stay over when he's showing properties, but Liam never does that. When I try to call him, his phone is off. And there's just something about him...'

She takes a big slug of her gin.

'He barely touches me anymore. He's sort of switched off.'

'But who do you think he's having an affair with?'

'I've no idea. I followed him one time but lost him just outside of Sedona. I felt like such a cliché afterwards—the suspicious wife tailing the cheating husband.'

'I'm so sorry,' Frances says, compassion filling her eyes.

'I don't know what to do.'

'You haven't confronted him?' Frances looks at her in alarm.

'No, I don't have any proof. Sometimes it feels like it's all in my head, but then my instincts tell me I'm right.'

'Ask him. Surely, that's a good place to start?'

'It's not that easy. What about Cathy?'

'It's precisely for Cathy's sake that you need to know. I mean that's why I left my husband. I couldn't bear to bring the girls up surrounded by such tension.'

'You're right, I know. But we've been married over twenty years.'

'And he's making a fool of you.' Frances signals to the bartender to bring them another drink. 'I don't understand why you aren't angry.'

'I am angry,' she retorts. But the words sound flat, without emotion.

'Come on, Constance,' Frances says, her voice softening. 'You can do it. When you get back to Arizona, just pack up your things and come back to Ireland with Cathy. You can stay with me.'

'I couldn't land on you like that!'

'Look, my business is expanding. I now have international clients—I mean this guy in L.A. is spending big money and I need someone I can trust to scout new artists. I could offer you a higher salary now.'

Constance stares at Frances in shock.

'I couldn't pull Cathy out of the middle of the school year, it would be so disruptive,' she says.

Frances taps her fingers on the bar counter.

'The longer you leave it the harder it will get to leave.'

'I know,' she says. 'But Cathy loves it in Arizona. She has really good friends. I don't think she will want to go back to Ireland. You don't happen to want someone in America to scout art for you?' she asks, thinking of the Maya D'Costa paintings she adores.

'Sorry, not right now but opportunity awaits you in Ireland.' Frances smiles slowly, as the bartender arrives with two more drinks.

. . .

As Constance flicks through the inflight magazine on the plane back to Arizona she thinks about Frances' offer of her old job in Ireland. Could she return to Galway? Their house has been sold and she and Cathy would have to stay with Frances until they got everything sorted. The idea of being free from the suffocating atmosphere of her marriage already makes her feel lighter. It depends on Cathy. She's what's most important.

Encouraged by their conversation outside the Rothko Chapel, Constance turns to Cathy now. She has headphones in and is looking at her phone, but Constance indicates for her to take them off.

'What?' Cathy scowls at her.

'So is your school very different from Our Lady's back home?' she asks. 'Do you like it? Are you settled?'

'Yeah, sure it is, better than home,' Cathy says, beginning to put her headphones back on.

'I'm not finished,' Constance says.

Cathy pauses, glaring at her.

'So is it strange being in school with boys now?' Constance asks, trying to warm the conversation up a little.

Cathy gives her a haughty look.

'I've friends who were boys back home. Don't you remember Darren O'Reilly?'

'Oh yes, of course, but you know it must be different to be in school with them...'

'God, Mom, it's not the seventies anymore!' Cathy interrupts, shaking her head as she makes to put her headphones on yet again.

Constance is irritating her daughter, and yet she can't stop herself from probing.

'So are there any cute boys in your class?' she asks, giving her daughter what she thinks might be a cheeky smile.

Cathy rolls her eyes but says nothing in reply. Constance has never known Cathy to date anyone back in Ireland or in

America. At one time she thought maybe Darren O'Reilly was keen on Cathy, but when Constance once asked her if they were dating, her daughter had burst out laughing. 'Give me some credit, Mam!' Constance had been relieved. She hadn't liked the boy much. Felt he was always laughing at her behind her back.

In Constance's mind Cathy is still a child, but Frances' two girls both have boyfriends. Sophie lost her virginity at just thirteen years old. Constance had been shocked on her friend's behalf. But Cathy doesn't seem that interested in boyfriends. Maybe her daughter is queer? She wonders if she could ask her. It doesn't bother Constance either way, as long as Cathy is happy. She thinks of all the time her daughter spends with Lisa. Even now, Constance can see pages of text as Cathy reads her phone.

'So what's that you're reading?' she asks, trying to lean over Cathy to see.

'None of your business,' is the smart reply. A hand covering the text.

'Come on, Cathy.' She finds her voice rising in irritation. 'Will you not even tell me that?'

She sees a faint blush on her daughter's cheeks.

'Okay, don't make a scene,' she says gruffly. 'It's just a textbook for school. I downloaded it.' But she still doesn't show her.

They sit in silence for the rest of the short flight to Phoenix. Cathy reading her iPhone with headphones on, while Constance continues to flick listlessly through the inflight magazine.

To her surprise, after not hearing from Daniel during the whole time they were in Houston, he's at the airport to meet them. He also has presents. A necklace for Cathy and flowers for her. He kisses her on the cheek and gives her a hug.

'It's good to see you,' he says.

Are her instincts wrong? Is she merely paranoid? She immediately feels bad for telling Frances that Daniel is cheating again. What if she's wrong?

She smells the bunch of roses he has given her, but they have no scent, and are a plastic shade of pink. It feels like an empty gesture.

Father and daughter link arms on the way to the car park in the airport. It is a long time since she has seen such closeness between Daniel and Cathy. How could she take Cathy so far away from her father? If she went back to Ireland, Cathy would lose Daniel.

On the way home, Daniel takes them out for dinner in Scottsdale in a fancy steak restaurant.

'I missed my girls,' he says, smiling at Constance, and ruffling Cathy's hair. 'I've spoken to Liam and I am going to cut back on the weekend viewings so we can all spend more time together.'

That night Daniel makes love to her for the first time in months. She lies beneath him, searching his face for the truth, but his eyes are closed as he comes inside her. Within a few seconds, he is asleep beside her, snoring softly. She lies on her back, her body humming with frustration. Daniel wants to be with her again. So, the affair must be over, even if it ever did exist in the first place.

She slips out of bed, and pads downstairs to the kitchen to get a glass of water. She stands in the dark at the kitchen window staring across the patch of land to the house of the mystery man. Daniel has come back to her but it's not enough. The light flicks on in the bathroom window opposite, as if its occupant knows she's waiting for him. He is shirtless, and is shaving, again in the middle of the night. She slips her hand inside her silk pajama bottoms and begins to stroke herself. She is already on edge and it doesn't take long to come. She gasps as she bends over the sink, her glass clattering on its side as water drips off the counter and onto the floor. She is shocked at herself. What if Cathy had come in? Or Daniel? But she feels a flint of retaliation in her heart, and when she thinks back on the whole day, she knows Daniel well enough to see the guilt in his eyes, his words, and his actions. He has been lying to her for weeks, and she's not going to let him get away with it this time.

CHAPTER TWENTY-ONE

THREE DAYS AFTER, FRIDAY 5 APRIL 2019

Her husband is dead. Not only that. He has died a dramatic death. Fallen hundreds of feet in the Grand Canyon. He will be a news story. She imagines people from back home in Ireland reading about it on the internet. Will it become one of those newsfeed stories on Facebook?

Irishman falls to his death in Grand Canyon.

It makes Daniel sound stupid. As if it is his own fault. How on earth is she going to tell Cathy?

Lopez is holding her elbow and guiding her out of the morgue. The smell of the place has permeated every pore in her skin. She is sick to her core. Toxic, as if she needs to scrub the place off every inch of her body. Yet she didn't cry. Nor did she touch Daniel, or sob, or kiss goodbye the man she has spent half her life with.

Daniel was messed up. He was lain before her, but he was in bits, ravaged from the fall, and from the exposure. Although she confirmed his identity, in her heart he was not *her* man. He was long gone.

They walk down a long corridor and up some stairs, following the medical examiner into his office. She can still smell the clinical morgue, taste it in her mouth. Constance slumps into the chair Lopez pulls out for her. As the medical examiner takes out the initial autopsy report, Constance feels herself breaking out into a sweat. The room is so hot. His voice drones on. The estimated time of death was on Tuesday afternoon. He begins to list Daniel's injuries. The broken ankle, the damaged ribs. But what do they matter now? She just needs to know what killed him.

'Excuse me, can you open the window?' she interrupts the man.

Lopez springs up from where he's sitting beside her. She's almost forgotten he is there.

The medical examiner continues to read her the report. The open window makes no difference. She is hot and dizzy. Nothing makes sense. How can Daniel have fallen off the South Rim of the Grand Canyon? He is afraid of heights. He would never have gone so close to the edge. And yet he had. Suddenly it's clear to Constance whose fault it is. It is Maya D'Costa, who persuaded Daniel to take such risks. That's what she needs to believe happened, because Daniel would never have been so reckless otherwise. He would never have done that to Cathy.

'My husband did not kill himself,' she interrupts the medical examiner. 'I promise you he would not have done that to his daughter.'

The man coughs, clearly uncomfortable with her outburst, but Lopez looks at her, his eyes steady, their brown as dark as charcoal.

'I spoke with the park ranger who found him this morning,' he says. 'She says that if someone is on their own, it is most likely a suicide.'

'But I don't think he was on his own.'

Lopez stares at her. She feels like she knows him, but it can't be possible because she knows no one in Arizona.

'If he had been walking with someone else, they would have reported his fall,' Lopez argues.

Her throat is thick with tension. She almost has to spit the words out.

'But they didn't. They left him there. Maybe they hoped he might never be found.'

Special Agent Lopez takes out his little red notebook as he looks at her with interest.

'One thing is sure,' Lopez tells her. 'When I questioned Park Ranger Nolan this morning, she told me it's not a route she usually takes on her patrol. It was quite by chance she found him.'

'So he could have been missing forever?' Constance whispers.

No one speaks. Constance can hear the traffic outside. A distant siren, and panic inside her chest. Can the two men hear it? A rattling inside her. The fear, the unease, the horror of what has really happened to her husband.

'He wasn't on his own,' Constance insists.

Lopez pulls a pencil from the spine of his notebook.

She takes a breath. She is past embarrassment. Her husband is dead. It is time to protect herself.

'Daniel had another woman. He left me for her. That's why I didn't report him missing.'

She looks straight into Lopez's eyes. She can see sympathy in his gaze. It gives her courage.

'You need to ask *her* what happened to Daniel.'

CHAPTER TWENTY-TWO

TWO MONTHS BEFORE, VALENTINE'S DAY 2019

Maya has held out for six weeks, ignoring Daniel's texts, phone calls, and once hiding in her studio while he banged on the front door of Luna House. She thought he would give up, but he hasn't and her will is weakening.

And then, on her birthday, which also lands on Valentine's Day, there is a card pushed under her door when she comes down in the morning. She sighs, picking it up, knowing it's most likely a Valentine card from Daniel, but to her surprise it's a birthday card. She's never told him when her birthday is. Inside are written the words *Talk to me*, geographical co-ordinates and a time, *1800 hrs*. She opens her front door, but he is nowhere to be seen. In front of her is a carpet of red roses strewn outside her cabin. Their sweet luxurious scent wafts over her as her heart aches for Daniel. He has broken through. She can't keep ghosting him. It's only fair she explains to him why they can't see each other anymore. Besides, when she punches in the map co-ordinates on her satnav it brings up the luxurious Enchantment Resort. He's clearly gone all out, the least she can do is put him out of his misery.

· · ·

They meet in the bar at the Enchantment Resort surrounded by Valentine balloons and pink hearts. As soon as Maya sees Daniel, she realizes this has been a mistake. All she wants is to touch him, kiss him, make love to him. Chemistry fizzes between them as she sits down, and she can see Daniel is restraining himself from touching her too. How can she break up with him now? *But you must.* She hears her mother's voice inside her head. *He's a cheater.*

'How'd you know it's my birthday?' she asks him.

'I read your birth date in the catalogue for your show,' he says, looking pleased with himself.

'You got one of the catalogues?'

'Constance bought it.'

The mention of his wife's name is a sharp reminder of their situation.

'I don't believe in birthdays,' she says.

'Don't be such a killjoy.' Daniel gives her a flirtatious smile. But it only annoys her, because how can he mention his wife in one breath and flirt with her the next?

'Daniel, I need to tell you the reason I've been ignoring your calls,' she says, stirring the olive in her martini.

'What's going on?' he cuts across her. 'I've been going crazy.'

She looks up at him as she pops the gin-soaked olive into her mouth. His blue eyes are blazing, and her heart tightens. This is going to be so hard, but she has to do it.

'I can't keep doing this,' she says. 'I thought I could keep things light, but it seems I've fallen for you. Sooner or later your wife will find out, and you've a daughter too. I don't want to hurt these women.'

Daniel doesn't say anything for a moment, just regards her with his hypnotizing blue eyes.

'I'm sorry,' she says. 'I don't want to be the other woman, the shameful secret knowing you're constantly looking over your shoulder in case someone you know sees us. I hate the lies.' She takes a breath. 'So after this drink, I'm going to leave, okay?'

'Do you love me?' Daniel says, staring at her intently. 'Because I love you.'

'Please don't say that.' Her voice breaks as she struggles not to cry.

'But do you?'

'Of course I do,' she admits. 'I love you too.'

Daniel leans forward and takes her hands.

'I'm so sorry, Maya, that I've made you feel like this, especially after what you experienced as a child.' He pauses, licks his lips. 'I am going to ask Constance for a divorce. Cathy's nearly sixteen, and she's old enough to understand. In fact, once she gets used to the idea, I think she'll be happier. Things are so toxic between me and Constance. It's bad for everyone.'

'But I don't want them to be hurt,' Maya begins to say.

'Honey, they're hurting right now. My wife is miserable. I want her to be happy, I do, and if we break up, she has more of a chance of that. We don't love each other anymore.'

'And Cathy?'

'She's never home because the atmosphere is so bad. She will get over it, in fact I think she'll learn to love you too. I mean you're going to be such a cool step-mam.'

'What are you saying?' she whispers, tears spilling down her cheeks.

'Marry me,' he says. 'I want us to be a family.'

'I don't believe in marriage, remember?' she says, a smile hovering around her lips.

Daniel cocks his head on one side.

'But I do,' he says. 'I want you to know how much I love you, and how committed I am to you.'

She considers his proposal. She feels a little blindsided, and struggles to remain composed.

'I am not giving up Luna House,' she says.

'Of course not, I was hoping I could move in with you,' he says. 'Constance will have to have the house.' He raises her hand to his face and kisses it.

'I am madly in love with you, Maya D'Costa,' he continues. 'I can't live without you.'

'Don't say that,' she says, but she can resist no longer as she leans forward and kisses him on the lips.

'So?' he asks, peering into her eyes.

She gives him a little nod, and a smile breaks across his face.

'You've made me so happy,' he says. 'I promise we'll be together soon, and everyone will know.'

CHAPTER TWENTY-THREE

TWO WEEKS BEFORE, 22 MARCH 2019

Everything is in place. Has been for weeks. Constance isn't sure why she's stalling because she's certain Daniel has resumed his affair. It happened on Valentine's Day, if not before. She knows not only because he forgot to give her anything, but he didn't come home either. She'd cooked his favorite, beef bourguignon, and bought an expensive bottle of red wine. The beef had gone in the bin, while she had drunk the whole bottle of wine on her own. As usual Cathy was out, and Constance was left sitting waiting for Daniel, her phone calls not answered. Staring across her yard, at the darkened windows of the house opposite. Even her mystery man was out.

When Daniel turned up the next day with excuses that he had to show a property in Prescott late in the day, and ended up staying over, Constance could smell the other woman on him. She realizes that she had always smelled her because that's what had been different when Daniel had come back to her. He had smelled like he was hers again. Now his clothes stink of woodsmoke, and outdoors, his hair of tobacco, and something else feminine and sensual seems to seep from his skin. It makes her want to throw up.

For the past month, Constance has been squirrelling away money for her and Cathy's new life, moving money from the joint account into her old personal account in Ireland. Frances has lent her the money for the plane tickets home, and promises she will pick her and Cathy up at the airport and bring her back to her place until they find their own. The job is ready and waiting for her in Frances' gallery, and yet Constance has held on. Every time she sees a moment of tenderness between Daniel and Cathy it cuts through her heart. Is she doing the right thing for Cathy if she takes her away from her father? Frances assures her she is, though Constance is conflicted. But then something happens which makes up her mind.

Wednesday night and Constance is in the kitchen cooking when she hears Daniel's raised voice.

'You should show me some respect, Cathy!'

She steps out into the hallway and is shocked to see father and daughter glowering at each other. Both are white-faced, and thin-lipped with rage. Cathy usually reserves her moodiness for Constance, not her dad.

'Remember it's me who's paying for the food on the table,' Daniel is lecturing. 'I deserve a bit of civility at least.'

Cathy gives a sarcastic snort.

'You're so full of shit, Dad.'

Constance is shocked by the tone of Cathy's voice. Surely Daniel will explode, but to her surprise he storms past his daughter, and out the house while Cathy runs upstairs. Constance hears the bedroom door slamming. She knows better than to follow her.

She goes back into the kitchen, slides onto a chair, and stares at her simmering pot of Bolognese sauce. She gets up and turns it off. It seems likely it is going to be left uneaten anyway.

She imagines Daniel tearing off down Highway 89A towards Sedona, to the secret location of his hidden love. She is certain he has gone to be with his mistress. Maybe he won't come back at all? It would make things easier.

She pours another glass of wine, turns off the kitchen lights and sits in the dark, staring out across the back yard to the darkened house of her man in the mirror. She wills a light to turn on. To take her away from her broken family, but the house remains still and closed up for the night.

A short while later she hears Cathy opening her door and coming downstairs. The light switches on in the kitchen. Her daughter starts to see her there.

'Why are you sitting in the dark?'

'I like it.'

'You're weird!'

Cathy opens the fridge, and takes out some juice. Her face is blotchy, as if she has been crying. Constance wants to ask her if she is okay, but she doesn't want Cathy to get angry again.

'Are you hungry? I've made spaghetti Bolognese,' she says instead. It is the only way she can show her love, by feeding Cathy.

'No thanks, I told you I don't eat meat anymore,' Cathy says, pouring juice into the glass. 'Where did Dad go?' she asks, not looking at Constance.

'I don't know, probably over to Liam for a beer.' Constance sighs. Now is not the right time to tell Cathy about her father's infidelity, especially when all she has are suspicions. No evidence. 'What was that all about, Cathy?'

Her daughter takes a sip of her juice, framing her top lip with orange. She says nothing for a moment. As if she is sizing Constance up. Cathy takes another sip of her juice. She looks as if she is about to say something but Constance can bear the silence no longer, and cuts across whatever she is about to say.

'Why's your father mad with you? What have you done?'

Cathy raises her eyebrows. Says nothing but again Constance has the feeling her daughter is looking down on her.

'You need to tell me what set him off,' she pushes.

'It's none of your fucking business, Mom!' Cathy slams down her glass on the counter. The remainder of the juice splashing all over to spatter the worktop. 'You know what, you both deserve each other. You really do.' She heads back upstairs again before Constance can say anything else.

It occurs to her that maybe Cathy knows about Daniel's mistress too. But how? He has kept it so well hidden from Constance. All she is going on is instinct. How would Cathy know? A few seconds later, she hears music pounding overhead.

That night Daniel doesn't come home again. She tries calling but after the fifth missed call she gives up. As she lies in bed awake, she realizes that he is forcing her to do something. Making it so obvious to her he is cheating that she has to break up with him. 'Coward,' she whispers, as tears trail down her cheeks. Her curtains are open, and she gazes at the waning gibbous Moon, the pristine stars in the dark Arizona sky, as its tone changes while the hours pass. As the sun begins to rise, her hurt turns to anger. She is sick of being the victim, the wronged wife. Daniel is going to pay for what he has done to her. She is going to take his daughter away, and Cathy will know every-thing. She will know that it's Daniel who destroyed their family, and she will never forgive her father.

LISTEN TO ME

I could not understand why my mother didn't leave my father. He cheated on her, humiliated her, and still she stayed. I lost all respect for that woman.

He would let her down again and again, but sometimes it seemed to me that she wanted him to. It gave her the opportunity to take on her favorite role. The victim. All the bad things that happened to my mother were never her fault of course. She was the wronged wife. The martyr who sacrificed her own happiness for the sake of her family.

'I've never betrayed you,' I would hear her sob at him.

I began to despise her.

What had happened to the truth?

He didn't want to be with her, so why did it take him so long to leave?

'Your father doesn't want to walk out on

you,' my mother once said. 'He loves you so much.'

So now, it was *my* fault?

I was so angry with her I could not speak. I banged out of the back of our house and took off. I marched like a soldier off to war, until I got to the woods. Only in the secret shade of the trees did I let my whole body sag. How dare she make me feel guilty?

It was hopeless.

I had seen my father with his mistress.

It had been winter and I had been walking home from school. The temperatures had dropped suddenly, and I had wanted to test the ice on the frozen lake, prolong returning to our miserable house. I knew what I would walk into when I got home. My mother sitting by the window in the kitchen, everything polished to perfection, her eyes red from tears, and a large glass of wine in front of her. Her whining voice. I could not bear it.

Trudging through the thick snow in my boots, I did not feel the cold, although my teeth were chattering. I went through the trees, and out the other side where the lake spread before me. Silent and becalmed by stretches of ice. I could see it was not sturdy enough to step upon although I was craving to test it out. I could see bubbles of water trapped within the ice, and scatterings of pebbles on its surface where some of the boys had tried to shatter it.

As I thrust my frozen hands deeper into my pockets and turned to head back home, I noticed a car parked by the side of the lake. I hadn't seen it on my way over. I took a step forwards. Stared in surprise. It looked like my father's car. Without thinking, I approached the vehicle. As I got closer, I could see that the windows were all steamed up. I felt a prickle up my spine. Whispers, sighs. I stared intently at that steamed-up glass. Walked around my father's car until I could see through the front windscreen.

I knew exactly what I was looking at. She was pushed up onto the back seat, and my father had his back facing me. He was pushing into her.

He did not turn, he did not see me, but I knew for sure it was my father.

The woman had her head tilted on the back seat, but it was as if she sensed my eyes upon her. She dropped her head and looked right at me. Cool as they come.

I turned away in disgust. Ran.

CHAPTER TWENTY-FOUR

THREE DAYS AFTER, FRIDAY 5 APRIL 2019

Detective Lopez drives Constance home from the Medical Examiner's Office. He doesn't mention Maya D'Costa in the car. All Constance assumes is that he and Deputy Peters plan to question her. Constance wonders how the other woman will react to the news her lover is dead. But she doesn't care what Maya D'Costa feels. It is her husband who is dead. *Hers.*

Her eyes are dry and tight, but she has not cried, not since she threw up in the toilet earlier. Lopez must think she is cold and unfeeling. As each wave of pain hits her, she withdraws further. The world is a dull haze around her, and she wants to shut it all out. But she can't. She has to face Cathy. Tomorrow is her daughter's sixteenth birthday. She will be back from Lisa's by now. Constance rang her from the medical examiner's to see if she was on the way home but her daughter hadn't answered. She'd been forced to leave a voicemail that she was out but back soon. Constance is frantic to get home to her, and yet at the same time dreading it. She has no idea how Cathy will react. She's not sure even what to tell her. Accident? Suicide? How can she tell her daughter that her father is dead the night before her sixteenth birthday? It is beyond cruel.

'I have to tell you something, Mrs. Garvey.' Lopez begins to speak again as they pull up outside her house. Constance can see the light on in Cathy's room, and her throat constricts in panic. Her daughter is home.

'Call me Constance, please,' she insists, irritated that now he is talking to her. He had the whole car journey to speak, but she has to go. Her daughter needs her.

'Okay, Constance,' he says in his low drawl as she opens the door. 'I feel I should tell you that we're kind of neighbors.'

'We are?' Constance starts, completely taken by surprise.

'Yeah, I live in the street behind you.'

She is halfway out the car door. She looks at him over her shoulder. He is giving her a significant look.

'My yard faces onto the back of your house.'

Constance is speechless. She just keeps staring at him.

'I believe your kitchen window looks out over the back of my house,' he continues.

She is a small creature caught in his headlights. Now she knows why he looked faintly familiar. He is the man in the mirror. He turns away from her, gazing out his windscreen at the road. My God, it is him, the profile, the high cheekbones, and the straight nose. She is horrified. Does he know? Nothing he said suggested that he had seen her staring at him across their back yards, but then how does he know her kitchen window looks out on his house? He is an investigator after all. He will have detected her nightly observations. Constance slams the car door closed, unable to respond.

He looks at her again, and she can see it in his eyes. The knowledge of her spying on him, but rather than continue talking about it he reaches across and offers her his card out the open window. Constance takes it automatically.

'So, call me, if you think of anything.' He hesitates. 'I only live a minute away.'

He drives off, clearly sensing her discomfort and not waiting for her to reply. Constance tucks the card into her pocket. Now her nightly fantasies of the man in the mirror seem pathetic compared to the vast enormity of what has happened to her family. Daniel is dead. She is a widow. Unbidden, a guilty thought surfaces. She and Cathy can return to Ireland without the trauma of facing Daniel. She'll have to change the tickets because they are booked for a few days' time, but at least Daniel isn't in the way anymore. It's a terrible thought but she can't help it after weeks of anxiety over how to tell Daniel that she's taking Cathy back to Ireland.

Before she goes upstairs to Cathy, Constance calls Liam.

'So has Daniel turned up, he still hasn't answered his phone,' Liam snaps. 'He's really landed me in it.'

'That's why I'm calling, Liam.' She takes a breath. The next words she speaks are so hard to believe they're true. 'He's dead,' she says bluntly, not knowing how else to say it.

'What the fuck!' Liam cries out. 'What do you mean he's dead? What happened, Connie? What happened?'

'He fell off the rim at the Grand Canyon.'

'But he was scared of heights, why would he go there?'

'I know.' She licks her lips. 'The cops think it might be suicide.'

There is a long pause. She notes that Liam isn't shocked at the idea of it. Nor does he ask why his brother was at the Grand Canyon when he should have been at work or in bed with food poisoning. Of course, Liam must have known about the affair. How else could Daniel have kept it a secret from her?

'We'll come straight over,' Liam is saying to her. 'We'll get a sitter for the boys and we'll be there in an hour.'

'No,' Constance says in a panic. 'I haven't had a chance to tell Cathy yet.'

'Ah God, the poor kid, it's her birthday tomorrow, isn't it?'

'Yes, I'm sorry, Liam, I'm really done in and I have to call your sisters in Australia, and deal with Cathy...'

'It's okay, I'll ring them, don't worry about that. If that's what you want, we won't get in your way tonight.'

But he insists they will be over first thing the next day.

Cathy's door is locked. Since when has her daughter started locking her bedroom door? Loud music pounds inside the room. Constance knocks on the door, but either Cathy is ignoring her, or she can't hear her.

'Cathy!' She bangs on the door with the flat of her hand. 'Cathy!'

The key turns. Now is not the time to lecture her daughter on it, but she makes a mental note to take away the key at the first opportunity. The door swings open and there stands her scowling daughter. She is wearing a huge black T-shirt, her bare legs long like a colt's. Her skin is as pale and fragile as a baby's, yet there are dark shadows under her eyes, and though wan as the Moon, her cheeks are damp with sweat.

'What?' she asks.

Constance's stomach cramps as the music blares out of the room. It sounds to her like a mesh of missed beats and disharmony. It sounds like the violence of her husband's big fall in the Grand Canyon.

'Can you turn down the music?' Constance asks, her voice shaking involuntarily.

Cathy stomps over to her bedside locker and turns off her iPhone. Instantly the speaker is silent.

Constance surveys the pile of books on her daughter's bed, the mess of clothes on her floor. Her eyes roam the room, for she can't look at her face.

'So tomorrow is your birthday,' she says weakly.

'Yeah, thanks.' Cathy shrugs. 'Is that it?'

'No, but, I know it's your birthday tomorrow, and this

shouldn't be happening but it's... it's your father,' she says slowly, feeling like throwing up.

'So he's not home for my birthday.' She shrugs. 'Whatever. I'm going over to Lisa's house in the morning, anyways.'

'Anyway,' Constance finds herself correcting her.

'Whatever.' Cathy narrows her eyes at her.

Desperation sweeps through Constance.

My daughter can't stand to be in the same room as me. What have I done to deserve her contempt?

Cathy is already shutting the door.

'No, it's not that,' Constance says, pushing her foot in the door. 'I need to come in.'

'I don't want you to come in, this is my space, you promised when we moved in...'

'Cathy, listen to me!' Constance jumps at the urgency of her own voice.

The expression on Cathy's face changes instantly. She looks at her mother through guarded eyes, as she steps back and sits down on her bed.

Constance walks into the room. Stands over her daughter. She looks tiny, curled up on her bed.

'This afternoon the police called to the house,' she says at last. 'And I was out just now because I was with them.' Although she is clutching her hands to stop them from shaking, she sounds quite calm.

Cathy sinks back against the headboard of her bed. Her face has completely shut down, and Constance has no idea what her daughter is thinking.

'And, I just had to, well, your father—'

'I don't care,' Cathy interrupts.

She looks at Constance with such loathing that her mother steps back in shock.

'Cathy, you don't understand.' Constance plows on. Squeezing her eyes shut and spitting it out. 'Daddy is dead.'

Her daughter gasps like a stranded fish. Constance opens her eyes again. She wants to go to her, take her in her arms. She wants the two of them to cry and wail together, but the tears won't come, and Constance finds she can't move. The horror of what she has just said has turned her to stone.

'What happened?' Cathy struggles to get the words out, yet she isn't crying. She is whiter than ever, and shaking, but tearless, nonetheless.

'He was at the Grand Canyon, and there seems to have been an accident,' Constance's voice cracks. 'He fell.'

'No, no,' Cathy says, shaking her head. 'He couldn't have! He never went to the Grand Canyon. He wouldn't have gone. He was scared of heights!'

'I know.' Constance nods like a robot. 'I know.'

She manages to move towards the bed, and sits down on the covers. She takes her daughter's cold shaking hand in hers, squeezes it.

'But, love, he did go to the Grand Canyon.' She takes a large gulp of air. 'I just had to identify him.'

Cathy's head snaps up and she stares at her. Her daughter's eyes are the same as Daniel's. Constance is pinned by their blue intensity. A sob rises involuntarily. She suppresses it. She has to be strong for Cathy.

'Was *she* there with him?' her daughter asks her.

Her words punch Constance as she looks at her daughter in astonishment.

'You knew about *her*?'

'Of course I knew, Mom,' Cathy says.

Constance can hear the pity in her voice, see it in her eyes.

'I've known for months.'

CHAPTER TWENTY-FIVE

FOUR DAYS AFTER, SATURDAY

All Maya wants to do is paint. It's what she does when she's upset: bury herself in her art. Usually it works. Before long she becomes immersed in the creative process, and her spirits begin to lift. But today, she can't concentrate. Maya can still see Daniel's face the last time she saw him on Tuesday. His shock at her fury and her jealous rage.

'Maya, calm down,' he tried to placate her. 'This isn't you.'

Maya had pushed him away.

'I hate you!' she screamed at him. Daniel had become her father leaving all over again.

He appeared stunned. Confused by her sudden madness. He looked as if he might say something, but instead he shook his head and walked away. He had put her in an impossible position, and Maya had been furious because there was nothing she could do to change it.

It had been their second breakup in their time seeing each other. And it was clearly their last, because since Tuesday she hasn't heard one word from Daniel, unlike last time.

Maya takes up her palette and attempts to mix the colors of the canyon rocks.

'I love you,' Daniel had said to her, but it hadn't been enough.

They are from different worlds, and different generations. He is twelve years older than her. Maya thought it didn't matter, but it does. Daniel believes in responsibilities, and she believes it's more important to be true to yourself. It frustrates her that in the end, he didn't take the risk to live his life how he wanted to.

Maya puts down her palette. It's no good. She's too wired to paint. She shouldn't have smoked so much weed with Joe last night. She can hear him still sleeping on the couch. His soft snores rippling through the silent house. That man could stay up for days, but when he crashed, boy it was monumental.

She gets up from her workbench, stretches to the ceiling of her studio. She tries not to think of her and Daniel making love on the paint-splattered floor just last week. How he had massaged her with warm vanilla and ginger oil as she came again, and again. She squeezes her hands and orders the image out of her head. She has to accept that she will never see him again.

Yet she feels an unusual anxiousness, so much so that her whole body is aching. A sensation of needles in her arms and fingers, and a stabbing dull ache in the side of her head. Opening the door of her studio, she creeps past the sleeping Joe. She wants to be on her own hiking on one of her beloved trails. She needs to get her head together. She wanders into the kitchen to make some green tea. As she does so, she hears a car pull up outside. Hope surges through her. At last, a miracle. He is back. At last.

Maya runs out the back of the kitchen, her little red kettle still in her hand. Why is she running? Of course it can't be Daniel. He left her.

She rounds the side of the house, and indeed it's not Daniel's car but a cop car that has pulled in next to her jeep.

The car comes to such a sudden halt that the tires whip up loads of dust. It fills her mouth. She watches two cops get out of the car. She watches them walk towards her. She can feel herself fading away, as if her whole body has turned to dust.

The force of her grief shocks her. Maya is flattened by it.

Tears stream down her face. Her darling Daniel is gone forever. It is all her fault. She abandoned him.

She knows of one other person who died in the Grand Canyon. A friend, a beautiful Polish girl, only twenty-five, who had been aiming to be the youngest woman to hike the whole length of the Grand Canyon. It had been a freak accident. She had stepped on a ledge that looked perfectly safe, that any of the group might have stepped on, but it had given way beneath her and she had fallen three hundred feet to her death. That's how it is in the Grand Canyon. It's a harsh, unforgiving landscape. It doesn't wish to be conquered. It should never be taken for granted. And you never leave someone behind in the Grand Canyon, no matter how mad you are at them. She has done that to Daniel twice.

But Special Agent Lopez tells her that he has fallen from the rim. He hadn't gone down into the canyon on a trek and got lost. He hadn't tried to negotiate any difficult terrain as her Polish friend had. He had fallen from a spot that they had gone to dozens of times. Shoshone Point. He knew the way back. And he would never stand too close to the edge. She tells Lopez that.

'Daniel's scared of heights,' she says to him, wiping the back of her hand across her eyes, trying to contain her tears. 'I don't see how he could have fallen,' she says, trying to control the wobble in her voice. 'He wouldn't have gone right to the edge of the rim. Definitely not on his own.'

'That's what his wife told us,' Deputy Peters from Coconino Sheriff's Office says to her.

She winces at the mention of the wife. She can feel the female cop's censuring glare. She knows she is judging her. The way Maya is dressed in her cut-off shorts, and billowing chiffon top, slightly see-through. She isn't wearing a bra either. The deputy is looking at her hummingbird tattoo on her shoulder. Maya notes her wedding ring. The woman clearly thinks Maya is as good as a prostitute.

'He wouldn't have gone off the path. Not on his own,' she insists.

'So what do you think happened that made him go right to the edge?' Lopez asks her, his expression stern. 'Do you think he was on his own?'

She shakes her head, squeezes her hands sticky with sweat. She knows that Lopez is insinuating that Daniel has killed himself, but she can't believe it.

'No,' she whispers. 'I don't know.'

Even as she says it, she remembers how upset Daniel had been. Should she tell the officers about what had happened between them on Tuesday?

One of the last things Daniel promised her was that they would be together in another lifetime. But it hadn't been enough for Maya. His promise had felt like an excuse. It had made her furious.

Now he is gone from this world, and the only chance their love will ever have is in another lifetime. It seems a pathetic concept. All her esoteric beliefs of ancient past lives in Egypt and connections during the Renaissance feel like rubbish.

'If you believe he wasn't on his own, who was he with?' Deputy Peters' tone is sharp, almost accusatory.

Maya steps back, her hands shaking violently, her stomach heaving.

She is never going to kiss Daniel again. She is never going to stroke the golden hairs on his arm, or feel his cheek against hers. She is never going to make love to him, ever again.

'Let's go inside,' Lopez says. 'You need to sit down.'

She's forgotten about Joe. He is awake when she comes in with Lopez and Peters, sitting on the couch with an innocent look on his face, all signs of last night's joints cleared away.

'Who's this?' Lopez immediately asks.

'What's going on, Officers?' Joe asks at the same time, giving Lopez a cold look. He is no fan of the law.

There's something comforting about the sight of Joe, and his shaggy hair. Maya is glad he is there. She wants to hide in one of his bear hugs.

'Joe,' she says in a trembling voice. 'Something terrible has happened.'

'Who is this person?' Peters asks her.

'He's my friend. Joe Burns.'

'What's going on?' Joe asks the deputy.

'He's dead,' Maya says, her voice rising. 'Joe, he's dead!'

In one quick movement, Joe is off the couch. Maya falls into his arms. She buries her head in his chest and lets out a loud sob. She can't say another word. The pain sweeps through her. She wants to die too.

'Is it her father?' she hears Joe ask the officers.

'No,' Lopez says. 'Not her father.'

She pulls back from Joe's chest. A voice inside her head is telling her to step away from him. How does this look? To be in the arms of another man.

She wipes her wet face with the back of her arm.

'Daniel fell off the rim in the Grand Canyon,' she tells Joe. 'He's dead.'

'Holy fuck!' Joe exclaims.

A wave of desperate longing sweeps through her. She can't

bear to speak to Special Agent Lopez or Deputy Peters anymore. She just wants to be left alone, but it is clear the two officers want to ask her more questions. Lopez has taken out a little red notebook from his back pocket.

'If you could take a seat, Miss D'Costa,' he says, producing a pencil from the spine of the notebook. 'We need to ask you a few questions.'

No, go away, leave me be, Maya screams inside her head, but she nods her head in assent and sits down on the couch. Joe sits down next to her. He takes her hand in his. It is inappropriate but she is too devastated to pull away from him.

'Mr. Garvey's wife has told us that her husband was with you the day he disappeared?' Lopez asks her. 'Is this true?'

She can't speak. She stares up at the two officers blankly.

'How long had you been seeing Mr. Garvey, Miss D'Costa?' Deputy Peters asks her. The female cop's eyes are icy as she stares right at her.

'Well hey, Maya's my girl, officer,' Joe speaks up in a valiant attempt to protect her.

'Miss D'Costa, we really need you to answer us,' Lopez insists.

'Can't you see she's upset, man,' Joe says.

Maya can hear a hostile tone in his voice. The last thing she needs is Joe acting out.

'It's okay,' she says, gently extricating her hand from his.

'So, for how long were you having an affair with Mr. Garvey?' Lopez asks.

'There is no point denying it. The wife told us about you,' Peters adds, a threatening edge to her voice.

'About nine months,' she says in a small voice. She looks down at her bare feet. She remembers she had painted her nails silver for him. He said he loved the way silver shimmered against her skin. She gulps as tears begin to rise again.

'And you used to go hiking in the Grand Canyon together?'

'Yes.'

'So were you with Daniel Garvey at the Grand Canyon on Tuesday?'

The two cops are scrutinizing her.

She doesn't know how much to tell them. They will find out soon enough, anyway. All she wants is for them to go now, let her be so she can wail and rant and cry out to the mountains. She will deal with the consequences the next day.

'No,' she lies.

They are gone now. The sun is sinking behind the Sedona red rocks, and the trees' shadows are dark diagonal lines reaching out towards her. She wants to run away from all this pain. Through the trees and up the walls of the canyon, and disappear like a puff in the melting sky. It is a beautiful sunset, the kind that makes you glad to feel alive. But she isn't glad, because Daniel will never see a sunset ever again. He will never see the love in her eyes. Or hear her tell him how he is the center of her world. She is spinning around, with no center now.

'Maya, honey, come inside.'

Joe is still here. A part of her wants him to take off and leave her be so that she can lie down in the red earth. Pray for a rattlesnake to come bite her. So that she can fall asleep and wake up in Daniel's new world. But a part of her wants Joe to stay. She lets him lead her back into Luna House and sit her down on the couch. He has made soup. She's not sure out of what, but it is salty and hot with spices, and it gives her a little strength. He rolls up a huge joint, and he makes her smoke most of it. She falls into a kind of daze.

Joe helps her up to her bedroom, and onto the bed. She is like a ragdoll, unable to even undress herself, so Joe takes her shorts off, and unbuttons her blouse, his hands accidentally brushing against her nipples.

He lies on the bed next to her, and he holds her in his arms as she weeps again.

'I loved him, Joe,' she cries. 'I really loved him.'

The room is spinning, and she feels sick and ugly. She doesn't deserve happiness. She has spent her whole life trying to find that balance, but she will never have it. She and Joe are facing each other on her tiny bed, and his face is coming in and out of focus. It must have been a strong joint. His eyes are changing color from brown to green. A flash of Daniel's blue. Back to brown. She is losing hold of her body. Her soul flying up out of her. She is terrified.

'Fuck me,' she hears herself mutter.

Joe says nothing, but somehow, he is naked and somehow he is on top of her.

'Fuck me hard,' she begs Joe, fury sweeping through her. How dare Daniel leave her. How dare he!

For a brief moment, as they are making love, within a tiny chasm her grief is gone. Afterwards, it descends upon her again heavy and fast. She is sick with herself.

Joe cradles her, kissing her cheeks wet with tears, trying to console her.

'Forget him, baby,' he whispers. 'He was no good for you. Forget him now.'

CHAPTER TWENTY-SIX

FOUR DAYS AFTER, SATURDAY 6 APRIL 2019

Katarina opens her notebook and pulls out a picture of Our Lady of Guadalupe. It has been folded, and unfolded so many times that the image is fading. When her mother had first given it to her, the Virgin's cloak had been a rich brilliant blue, dotted with golden stars, her tilma a glorious yellow cocoon encasing her, and edged in orange. She doesn't know why it is she still carries it around with her wherever she goes. She has long stopped believing in God. And yet it is hard to shake her mother's old traditions.

She stares at the familiar face of Our Lady of Guadalupe. She asks for her strength to help her through this time of separation from her husband. She prays for the soul of the dead man she found yesterday morning in the Grand Canyon, and she even asks for Our Lady's help with his family. Katarina doesn't want to have to meet them.

The body had been taken to the Medical Examiner's Office in Flagstaff for official identification and an autopsy. After she and Special Agent Lopez bagged the body, loaded the basket stretcher and signaled for the chopper to take off, they had taken pictures of the impact site. The special agent had taken out a small red notebook and taken copious notes.

'Looks like our man fell from Shoshone Point,' Lopez said, craning his neck and looking up at the jagged walls of the canyon.

'Reckon it was suicide?' Katarina ventured.

Lopez didn't reply. Continued to make notes in his book although he didn't share them with her.

She had never worked closely with the special agent before. He had been on duty assignment in the Grand Canyon for just three months. Shane had spoken about him. Had said he was solid. He was clearly the silent type too.

What had Lopez been looking at exactly?

The puddle of dried blood. The view of the deadly rim above. The vast chasm that Daniel Garvey had fallen down.

Thinking his name makes her feel a little sick. She tries not to think of the moment when he fell.

For the past week, Katarina has been having these recurring nightmares of falling. She wonders if any of the other park rangers suffer from bad dreams like these. They are constantly clambering up and down ravines, and rocks, negotiating narrow cliff edge trails. Called on for search and rescue in the most precarious of situations. You have to be on your guard the whole time. In her night-time subconscious she slips, and falls off one of those rocky precipices. The falling takes so long. It never ends. Fear coursing through her body. Buffeted by the cross-winds. Battered by the sun's harsh hand. Flung into the land. All of her breaking up into tiny little pieces. She wakes up screaming. Missing Shane more than ever.

With shaking hands, she hunts for her phone and calls him, but he never answers. Even his voicemail is enough to soothe her. Just to hear his slow drawl. Nothing ruffles Shane. She lies back down and closes her eyes. She remembers the first months they were together in the trailer in the Grand Canyon. It had been the happiest time of her life.

Her phone rings. She doesn't make a move until she has the urge to suddenly lunge for it before it rings out.

'Hello, this is Katarina Nolan.'

'Good morning, Park Ranger Nolan.' A male voice. She recognizes it. 'It's Matt Lopez here.'

'Right.' Katarina stands to attention, wide awake now, on alert.

'I'd like to ask you a few more questions about the body you discovered in the South Rim district yesterday.'

'Sure.'

'Standard procedure for the paperwork.'

She licks her lips. 'So I guess it was suicide?'

'And why do you say that?' Lopez asks her.

'Well, I told you yesterday that there seemed to be no ledge fall at Shoshone Point.'

'But still more likely to be accidental though. Statistically.'

'Yeah but he was on his own. Most people don't hike on their own in the Grand Canyon.'

'Possibly, Park Ranger,' Special Agent Lopez says. 'Well we can discuss what you think happened to Daniel Garvey this afternoon at two.'

Daniel Garvey. She wishes he hadn't said his name. It makes her feel sick again. To think he is a real person, rather than the tangle of limbs she sat with yesterday morning.

She gets up from her bed, swaying a little, and goes into her little kitchen. She turns on the tap and splashes cold water on her face. Picking up the bottle of hand cream, she squirts some onto the palms of her hands. Rubbing them together while thinking. This meeting with Special Agent Lopez is crucial. She has to provide the right evidence and put this case to rest. Show him her skills and potential as a park ranger. It has always been her dream to become a special agent of the Investigative Services Branch, just like Lopez.

Katarina will convince him that Daniel Garvey is one more suicide in the Grand Canyon. A dramatic gesture with no thought of the consequences for his loved ones.

As she waits for Special Agent Lopez, Katarina watches a family of four sitting outside the café. The kids are eating ice creams and making a mess of it. Two boys between the ages of six and eight she reckons. One of the kids drops his ice cream and starts wailing. The father does nothing, just stares at his kid almost coldly as he drinks his coffee while Katarina watches the wrecked-looking mother trying to mop the kid up. In the end she brings him back into the shop to buy another ice cream. It all looks so exhausting.

Katarina had started out in her life as a park ranger working on many different kids' camps. Indeed, she had done her stint as an interpretative ranger and taken kids on guided tours. Yet the truth is she has no desire to have her own children. She likes kids when it's all fun and adventure, but not that nitty-gritty stuff of discipline and boundaries. She'd be no good at that. She really doesn't want to be a mother. Does that make her unnatural? It annoys her that so many of their friends had expected her and Shane to have children. They were happy just the two of them. Why mess that up?

What she wants more than anything is success and respect in her profession. To help protect the National Parks—and root out any behavior that threatens the institution both physically, and morally. She wants to become a special agent. If this investigation goes well, maybe Lopez could help her?

'Morning, Ranger.'

The first time Katarina met Special Agent Lopez, with a name like his, she expected him to look a little like her too. Maybe even more Mexican. But though he is dark-haired, it's clear that his heritage is Native American. This afternoon he is an arresting figure in his uniform, with his dark glasses, and gleaming jet hair, mostly hidden beneath a green baseball cap.

Lopez requests that she accompany him to the point on the South Rim where Daniel Garvey had fallen. They walk to where Lopez's jeep is parked and drive along Desert View Drive.

'I want to get your perspective on the site,' Lopez tells her as he turns into the car park at Shoshone Point.

They walk in silence along the slight uphill incline of the trail. Through the sparse pine forest, scattered with oak, Katarina keeps a look out for deer or elk, but today they are keeping their distance. All she can hear are birds rustling in the branches of the trees.

Eventually the land opens out to a small viewing area with picnic tables and a barbecue pit. The place is deserted though. It's still early enough in the season for Shoshone Point to be empty.

Katarina points at the promontory, with its lone standing stone, like a ragged tombstone of solid sand.

'So that's where he must have fallen,' she says. 'Several hundred feet.'

Lopez walks out onto the narrow promontory, glancing up at the tombstone before taking another step forwards and peering over the edge.

'So you were off trail when you found him?'

'Yeah, I was taking a detour.'

Katarina joins Lopez at the edge of Shoshone Point and looks at the view. It never fails to fill her with a sense of awe, no matter how many times she has seen it.

'It's a long way down alright.' Lopez's voice sounds distant beside her. She listens intently. The silence billows around them. In the distance, very faintly, she can hear the raging waters of the Hance Rapids. That is the thing about the Grand Canyon. Its peace is an illusion.

'So do you think Daniel Garvey jumped or fell?' the special agent asks her.

'I think suicide is most likely. Did he leave a note?' she asks him.

'Well according to his wife, he was afraid of heights,' Lopez says.

She feels the intensity of his gaze upon her.

'It would seem a strange way to kill yourself if you had vertigo, don't you think?'

'Maybe that's precisely why he did it this way?' Katarina suggests, taking a step back from the edge. 'It takes courage to kill yourself. He finally overcame his fear.'

'Pretty sick irony though, Ranger?'

She kicks the dusty ground.

'Yeah, it's sad.' She watches Lopez as he circles the small area. He turns his back to her and crouches down by one of the prickly grape-holly bushes. He seems to be checking the ground all around it.

'They already took photographs yesterday,' she tells Lopez. 'Did you see the report?'

But Lopez doesn't reply.

She wants to leave now. Why does she have to show Lopez this place anyhow? Surely he was out here yesterday, with the other investigators?

Lopez is still crouching by the shrubs. He has taken a small red notebook out and is writing in it.

'Did you find something?' she asks him.

'Nope,' he says, not elaborating.

She steps back from the edge and sits down on a ledge of rock. Takes her hat off and wipes her forehead with the back of her hand. There is no shade on this point, and it's a warm day for April. Not long since the snows had closed half the roads in the park. Spring is so short in the Grand Canyon. She can smell the intensity of the summer approaching. The long days of rescuing idiot tourists who get themselves lost and dehydrated. The season of wildfires will be upon them. She and Shane liked that work. The exhilaration outweighed the dangers. She finds herself hoping he will be back soon. So that they can work as a team yet again.

'Okay, well thank you, Ranger, we can go now.' Lopez is straightening up, putting his notebook back in his pocket.

'What do you think?' she asks him.

He raises his eyebrows at her, clearly unimpressed by her inquisition.

'Too soon to conclude.'

'Suicide then?'

'Maybe, maybe not,' he says, his expression unreadable.

Although she is still hot, his words send a chilling shiver down her back. Why is Special Agent Lopez being so obtuse?

CHAPTER TWENTY-SEVEN

FOUR DAYS AFTER, SATURDAY

Constance dreams that she and Daniel are in an airport racing to catch a plane, but he keeps running in a different direction to her.

Daniel! she calls out. *Daniel, this way!*

She is on a downward escalator as she sees him going on the up escalator. She calls to him again, but he doesn't hear or see her. His eyes are fixed on where he is going. Up and up. Away from her. Toward the other woman.

Constance wakes with a start. She reaches out for Daniel. Of course, he is not in the bed with her.

She lies on her back. Lets the tears slide out of her eyes, down the side of her face, and onto her pillow. She has lost him forever. She will never be able to fix their marriage now.

She tries to remember their last proper conversation without tension or hostility. She clutches onto the few moments of truce between them. He had put his hand on her shoulder. Squeezed it. She remembers now. It had been Monday morning. The day before he lost his life. He had said, *See you later*.

He had smiled. His eyes had been sad. The faded blue of washed denim.

She picks up her phone on the bedside locker and looks at the time. It is four minutes past two in the morning. Fragments of the dream are stuck inside her head. She wants to talk to Daniel so badly. She needs to ask him.

Would you have chosen me in the end? Like the time before?

If she had actually told him she and Cathy were leaving, would he have given up Maya D'Costa to get her back? Had her husband's affair been a cry for her attention? That was why Daniel had been unfaithful before. But this time it was different. Maya D'Costa is different. Her husband had fallen in love with her. Love had not come into his first infidelity.

Maya D'Costa is a very different kind of woman from Bridget Kearney. It had not been a one-night stand. Her husband had pursued the artist. It had been the death of him.

Constance sits up, pulls the covers off her hot body. She falls out of the bed. Her whole body humming with restlessness. She glides by her daughter's bedroom door, pausing to listen, but she can hear nothing. Is her daughter sleeping? Could it be possible after the weight of what she learned last night?

She carries on down the stairs, and into the lounge. There it is. Maya D'Costa's sublime watercolor hanging over her fireplace. 'Hideaway'. Constance stands in front of it, staring. The painting's beauty makes her angry. How can such a wicked person produce a painting so iridescent, so divine? Why has God blessed this bitch with such talent? It's not fair.

Constance reaches up and takes the painting down. She considers smashing the frame, ripping up the watercolor and burning it in the fireplace but she can't bring herself to do it. It is art after all. And to Constance no matter who made it, that means it is sacred. In the end, she opens the sideboard, and pushes the watercolor into its dark recesses.

Her heart racing, she stumbles into the kitchen and opens

the fridge. Pours herself an enormous glass of sparkling water. Her head is pounding, and her throat so dry she thinks she might choke. She takes a big gulp of fizzy water as she stands at the window staring out at Special Agent Lopez's windows. His house is in darkness. The man in his window had been her fantasy. She had not wanted him to be a real man. She had wasted all these weeks thinking about a stranger, when she should have been trying to get her husband back. If she had succeeded, Daniel would never have gone to the Grand Canyon. She would never have met Special Agent Lopez.

Constance is heavy with sorrow. She knocks back the rest of her water, but it does nothing to ease her headache. She drags herself back upstairs, turning at the doorway of her bedroom. She can't bear to get back into the vast emptiness of her bed.

Constance opens Cathy's door, thankful her daughter has not locked it. Light from the hall illuminates the sleeping form of her child. The curtains are open, and she sees the bright yet tiny slip of silver crescent against the dark Moon. She slips into the bed beside Cathy, and her daughter stirs. She puts her arms around her, and inhales. Her daughter smells different. Not how she remembers her scent in Ireland. She pulls her daughter closer to her, and feels the rhythm of her breath against her chest. Her daughter doesn't push her away.

'I want Daddy,' her daughter whimpers. 'I want my daddy.'

'I know, sweetheart,' Constance says, her voice shaking with emotion. 'So do I.'

Cathy begins to cry. Constance feels her daughter's torment in each racking sob. Her pain turns to fury. Maya D'Costa is going to pay for what she has done to her family.

LISTEN TO ME

I have told you before how hard I found it to make friends.

'Why don't you ever have anyone over?' my mother would pester me.

She would get herself another drink while becoming tearful over the fact that she had lost contact with all her girlfriends since she had got married. I knew it was all a lie. My mother had been as friendless as I.

In some of his better moments, my father would ask me if I wanted him to take me and a friend to the town pool, or out for pizza, but I always refused.

'Haven't you got a best friend? Don't you want to have fun?' he'd ask me, clearly mystified.

But it was their fault that I never had any friends because I never wanted to bring anyone home. Especially after the disaster of my tenth birthday party.

Even at that young age I had known it was
a bad idea, but my mother had persuaded me.
Told me she had booked a clown, and a magician. She had bought bright yellow invites
that she made me fill in and give to everyone
in my class at school. I hated the color
yellow, but of course my mother didn't want
to take that on board. She dressed me up in
canary yellow to match the invites and patent
black shoes with white socks. I felt like a
freak when all the other children were in
jeans.

To be honest, I was surprised that anyone
turned up in the first place. I really did
have no friends. I guess it was pure curiosity
to find out more about me.

You know all about my early school days.
There really is no need to pity me. As I have
already said, I didn't have any friends, but
that was my choice. I was never bullied or
picked on. Sometimes even one of my classmates
might try to befriend me. Offer me some snacks
at break, or ask me over to play, but I always
said no. I was a loner right from day one.
Just like you. That's why we always understood
each other.

Back to that dreadful party. My mother had
tried. I have to give her that. The house was
filled with balloons and streamers, and she
had been baking all day. There were little
cupcakes with lemon icing, and a big chocolate
cake with birthday candles, as well as stacks
of snacks and big bottles of Coke. I was never
normally allowed to drink Coca-Cola at home. I

began to tuck into it before anyone had even turned up.

There was something not quite right though. My mother was rushing around, her face all red, and her voice raised a pitch. She ordered the clown to smile more, the magician to entertain us with better tricks, and screeched at the children to play this game and that. She was kind of demented.

By the time the clown and the magician had packed up and left, my mother was in the middle of organizing a game of musical chairs. At that precise moment my father came home. As soon as I saw his face, I knew there was trouble.

He stormed into the front room, and it was as if he didn't even see me or anyone else at the party. All he had eyes for was my mother.

'In the kitchen. Now,' he hissed at her.

Some of the kids tittered in embarrassment. My mother didn't even look upset. In fact, she looked far from it. Her cheeks were flushed, and her hands were shaking as she put down a chair. There was a triumphant look in her eyes.

'Not in front of the children,' she said, following him into the kitchen and behind the closed door.

'You do know I've lost my job because of you,' I heard my father accuse my mother.

'I don't know what you're talking about,' she said. 'We can't discuss this now. I have to get back to the children.'

'No, you've got to phone my boss up. Tell him it's not true.'

'What's not true?'

'Don't pretend you don't know what I'm talking about.'

My parents continued to bicker. I could feel the eyes of all my guests on me. Twelve ten-year-olds, all holding their breath as they heard my parents' voices beginning to rise.

'Shouldn't you go in there?' Frankie, a weedy boy with black hair, said to me.

I shook my head, too mortified to speak.

'You've destroyed our lives.' My father's voice was rough with anger. 'Well done. How do you think we're going to manage now?'

'Don't blame me!' my mother screeched. 'This is your fault.'

'Wow,' a girl called Carla giggled. 'Your parents are mental!'

All the kids laughed in response to her remark.

'I think you should all go now,' I said, suddenly finding my voice.

'But we haven't had tea yet,' Carla protested.

I opened the hall cupboard, pulled out coats and jackets.

'Really just go, all of you.' I could feel myself close to tears. 'Now!' I yelled, opening the front door. 'Go away! Fuck off!'

I had never said such a bad word before, but I had heard my parents saying it once or twice to each other.

All my classmates looked at me in stunned silence. We could hear my parents laying into each other.

'Just go away now!' I shoved Carla first out the door.

I sealed my friendless state by destroying any sympathy my classmates might have had for me by throwing them out. Most were protesting that they needed to call their parents to collect them. I didn't care. I slammed the door on the whole lot of them. I watched from the window as they all sat down on my front lawn and waited to be collected. Before too long, I saw them playing chase. I was an oddball, and no one wanted to know me.

I went up to my bedroom and I lay on my bed thumping the pillow in rage. I hated my parents for ruining the party. But I hated myself more for trusting my mother. For thinking that for one afternoon I could be like any other ten-year-old and have a happy birthday party.

My parents fought for hours. It was a bad one. I had long stopped caring about the details of their fights. It was all venomous words, but they never actually hit each other. They always stopped short at that. They were locked in a game together. Their arguments were part of their relationship. I do believe there was a part of them that actually enjoyed being joined in such conflict all the time.

Later my father went out—I heard the door banging—and then a while later I heard my mother crying. I tiptoed down the stairs and spied on her in the kitchen. She had the bin out and was throwing all the party food away. Sobbing her heart out as if it had been her birthday that had been ruined.

The next morning at breakfast, my father said he was sorry about the party. He tried to make it up to me by offering to take me, and two of my friends camping for a weekend. But I said I didn't want to. It was not that I didn't like camping, it was that I had no friends.

You once told me that you had been the center of your parents' universe when you were a child. I had been so jealous of that because I don't think I even existed in the same universe as my parents.

It was clear they loved each other more than they loved me. The obsessive nature of their hate proved that.

It is the same with us. I love you more than anyone or anything else in the whole wide world. And that is why I hate you too.

CHAPTER TWENTY-EIGHT

FOUR DAYS AFTER, SATURDAY

Maya needs to force herself to take some steps forwards into a life without Daniel. The first part of that is owning up to the truth. That is why she is driving to the Grand Canyon to talk to Special Agent Lopez.

The sides of her jeep are open. She has always liked to feel the warm wind caressing her, and her hair flying all over the place. The jeep is shuddering with the effort of keeping up, but she no longer cares if it isn't that safe. Spring is ruined for her now. Life has turned to death.

When she woke up this morning, Joe was already gone. She is confident that true to form he won't come back for a good while. To think of what she did with him last night fills her with regret. It was a terrible betrayal to Daniel. Afterwards, she told Joe that it was well and truly over between them. There was no reason for him to ever come back to Luna House.

Everything is such a mess. Maya needs to talk to someone. She even wishes she could call her mother, but there is no way that she could tell her about what's happened to Daniel after she told her they had split up weeks ago. She thinks fleetingly of her father, but he is like a fading dream to her now. She has not seen him in so many years. Maya has a half-brother and a half-sister she has never met. They are still children. The eldest just about thirteen. She has never even seen a photograph of either of them. It is as if her father has rubbed Maya and her mother out. They are his mistakes, and now he has a new family. Well, she doesn't need him or his family. She is used to coping on her own. She has friends. They are her family.

Can she consider Joe a friend now? Maya swallows back a wave of shame. She used him to deal with her grief. But then surely Joe knew that she had been in a state. He had just been trying to make her feel better.

She feels a sudden wave of desperation. Again, a need to talk to her father but Celeste is always in the way.

Would it have been like that for Cathy Garvey if Maya and Daniel had made it? Maya had been the same age as Daniel's daughter the last time she visited her father. She guesses Cathy Garvey would have hated her just as much, if not more than she had hated her stepmother, Celeste.

Maya grips the steering wheel. No, she would have done things differently, because she knows how Cathy feels. She would have tried so hard. She cares about Cathy, whereas Celeste has never appeared to care about her. It would have been so completely different because Daniel loves his daughter. And Maya's father never loved her.

Even so, despite Maya's good intentions, Cathy hates her. That is evident. Daniel underestimated his daughter. He had handled it all wrong.

It wasn't until the incident in the Bird Cage Saloon in Prescott that Maya knew for certain that Cathy Garvey had known about them for several months. That night Maya had recognized her. Her instincts had been correct that the school-girl staring at her in the botanical gardens all those months ago had been Cathy Garvey. Why had she not confronted her father or told her mother?

Two weeks ago, Maya and Daniel had gone to see the singer Candace Devine perform in the Bird Cage Saloon. She had suggested that rather than Daniel come to her house in Oak Creek Canyon, they meet there. She had booked them a room in the St. George, and they planned to share breakfast the next day in the diner below, before he headed back to work. His excuse to his wife had been an early viewing in Prescott for a client so he needed to stay over.

The venue was packed but they found a table in the corner. Daniel had seemed excited. He looked younger to her that night. His hair a richer red and his eyes brimming with anticipation.

'This is great,' Daniel had shouted to her over the sound of the crowd. 'I haven't been to a gig in so long.'

'Do you like Candace Devine?'

'Don't know her, but I love live music,' he had declared. 'Actually, I play a little myself.'

'You'll have to play for me sometime!' She had been delighted by his enthusiasm. 'You'll love her. She has the most awesome voice.'

He had put his arms around her waist and squeezed her, gave her a whopping kiss on the lips. They had stood arm in arm looking over the heads of the crowd at the stage as the band took their positions.

A moment later Daniel's good mood evaporated. She had felt him suddenly stiffen beside her. She turned to him. Daniel had a look in his eyes that she had never seen before. Absolute fury. It had shocked her to see the sudden change in him. She had followed the direction of his gaze. The first thing she had picked up was a face she recognized. A girl's face. Pale, red hair, blue eyes lined in black kohl and red lips. She looked young, possibly just about twenty-one, but unlikely. Where had she seen that girl before?

The red-haired girl had been with a man. He had looked a

good bit older than her. He was good-looking in a clean-jawed cowboy way. A look that had never appealed to Maya. Indeed, she had never appealed to this kind of man either. They always wanted white girls.

Daniel had been completely rigid beside her. She had heard him muttering in a low voice.

'I don't fucking believe it.'

'What is it? Daniel?'

But he had let go of her. It had been as if she was no longer there. He had pushed through the crowd, shoving people out of his way. The girl saw him, and in that moment Maya had remembered. She was the schoolgirl who had stared at her at the Desert Botanical Garden. She looked so much older in her makeup and dressed in a skintight mini-skirt, tiny scarlet top, and high heels but behind the mask, Maya could see it was the same girl. The one she had imagined might be Cathy Garvey.

The girl took a step back into the chest of her companion as soon as she saw Daniel. She looked shocked, and yet Maya could also see a glimmer of challenge in her eyes. Maya followed the trail Daniel had left in the crowd, but just when she got within earshot she stopped. What was she doing? She couldn't approach Daniel's daughter. Of course not.

'Cathy, what the hell are you doing here?' she had heard Daniel say to his daughter.

'Well I could ask you the same question,' Cathy had said, pointing right at Maya.

Daniel had looked over his shoulder at her. His blue eyes had been dark with displeasure. Maya wasn't certain what she should do. Stay. Walk away. It was too late now. Their secret was out.

'Who is this?' Daniel had said, glowering at Cathy's companion.

'Hey.' The guy put up his hand protectively. 'There's no need to be hostile.'

Daniel took Cathy's elbow.

'Come on, I'm taking you home,' he had said to her. 'What's your mam going to say about this?'

Maya had felt a finger of ice trail her spine at the mention of Cathy's mother.

'I don't think you want to tell Mam anything, do you now?' Cathy had said to her father, her tone taunting. 'Because I could tell her plenty back.'

'That's enough, come on,' Daniel had said to Cathy, dragging her away from the cowboy. They were making a bit of a scene. Maya saw the bouncers looking over at them.

'Hey don't push her,' Cathy's cowboy had said to Daniel. 'Who do you think you are?'

'I'm her father.' Daniel had turned on him in an icy voice.

The guy flinched.

'Do you know that she is only fifteen,' he had hissed at him in a low voice.

'No way,' the man had protested, but his eyes were darting everywhere. Maya could see he was lying. 'She told me she was twenty-one. At college.'

'I could have you arrested right now,' Daniel had said to him. 'Don't you dare come near my daughter again, else I'll have you done on statutory rape...'

'Look, I didn't know, right,' the cowboy had protested.

'Guys, can you take this outside else we'll have to call the cops?' One of the bouncers loomed over their group.

'Hey, I'm gone,' the cowboy had said. He had plowed through the crowd, and out the door without a second glance at Cathy.

'Let's go,' Daniel had said to his daughter, as she glowered at him.

'That was rude, Dad; he was just a friend.'

'I'm not a fool, Cathy,' Daniel said as he pushed her towards the door.

'Aren't you forgetting someone, Daddy?' Cathy retorted in a voice laden with sarcasm. 'What about your *girlfriend*?'

'Shut up, Cathy.' Daniel dragged his daughter out the door of the bar.

Maya had watched them go. Daniel had said nothing to her. He hadn't even waved goodbye. She had been aware of some people looking at her. How many had listened to that little altercation?

She had walked back through the throng and leaned on the bar. Candace Devine had just taken to the stage. Maya had taken a deep breath, pushed the tears back. He would come back for her. Surely? Or at least send a text? Candace had launched into a powerful rendition of her song 'Tell Me How To Stop'. Maya had felt almost winded by the impact of the lyrics on her. As if her vulnerability was being channeled through Candace Devine. She had felt so ashamed of her co-dependence.

But Maya had waited patiently. Trying to let herself get lost in the power of the music. Yet she could not switch off from her fears. Why had Daniel not even sent her a message? With Candace Devine's set over, Maya had pushed her way to the door and stumbled out onto the street. There had been no sign of Daniel and his renegade daughter. He was probably back home in Flagstaff by now. The two of them having had a screaming match in his car all the way. At the end of the day, what could he do? He couldn't tell her mother, because if he did, Cathy would tell her about Maya. So what then? Was it over between her and Daniel?

She had needed a drink.

There was a bar next to the hotel. It was a bit of a dump, but she hadn't cared. She went straight to the counter and ordered a shot of Wild Turkey. Then another. The bourbon had burned her throat, but it had made her feel better. So what if she never heard from Daniel again? It had to end one day. Everything ends.

She had ordered another drink, and turning to look over at the pool table, she had seen two cowboys playing. As she had watched them, she realized one of them was the tall fair man she had seen with Cathy Garvey. He looked older in the brighter lights over the pool table. She had felt a flutter of disgust. Daniel's daughter should have been dating a fumbling high school boy, not this towering adult male.

Maya had ordered another bourbon. As she had knocked her drink back, she watched the blond cowboy leave. When he reached the door, she distinctly saw him take a gold wedding band out of his jeans pocket and slip it onto his finger. He was married too, just like Daniel. Another liar.

———

Maya slows down as she approaches the entrance to the South Rim of the Grand Canyon Park. Her chest is tight with dread. Only four days ago, she had been entering the park in such a different state of mind. Brimming with love, and expectation. Restless to be with Daniel.

Within a few hours, she had driven away from him forever. The red mist had descended as it had done to her before, and all her memories were lost in an inferno. Fury in her heart, as passionate as the love that resided there as well.

It is time for all the lies to stop. She has to tell the truth as much as she can. Because she needs to know what happened to Daniel. Although she's afraid, she hopes that Special Agent Lopez can tell her. Is it all her fault?

CHAPTER TWENTY-NINE

FOUR DAYS AFTER, SATURDAY

Constance can hear the sea. Waves sweeping the beach behind their stone cottage, and the seagulls calling to her. She wants to jump out of bed, pull on her wellies, and walk along the beach. Feel the spray from the ocean patter her damp cheeks, and the wind wreak havoc with her hair. She wants to find a pretty shell to decorate for Cathy, attach it to a small twist of leather to tie around her daughter's slender neck. A birthday present unequaled in meaning and tenderness.

Cathy's birthday. Constance sits up in bed, panicked. She is in Arizona, not Ireland, and she has no present. She remembers sleeping in Cathy's bed last night and for a moment Constance is confused. Why had she been in Cathy's bed? Why had she been comforting her daughter?

Daniel is dead. Her husband. She is a widow.

It is as if she is out of her body, yet her mouth is dry, and her throat feels sore. She picks up her glass of water by the bed and drinks it down. It's eight in the morning. She lies on her bed and closes her eyes. She should be feeling more. Her husband has died in a most dramatic way. And yet she is hollowed out.

Empty of emotion. She has felt so alone for so long now that the impact of Daniel's loss can't penetrate her. All she cares about now is Cathy.

Her daughter had known about the other woman, and she had never told her.

Of course she couldn't, Constance reasons. Cathy had been stuck in the middle between her and Daniel. It shouldn't have been up to her to tell her. Yet at the same time she feels betrayed, and a flash of anger at Daniel. How dare he put Cathy in that position?

'How did you meet her?' Constance asked Cathy the night before. 'What is she like?'

'Oh no,' Cathy said to her. 'It wasn't like that, Mom.' She sat forward on her bed, crossed her legs. 'I was never introduced to her.'

'But where? When?'

'I was on the school trip to the Desert Botanical Garden in Scottsdale. He was there with her. Though he never saw me.'

'That was last November!'

Cathy shrugged. 'I know.'

Constance felt devastated. Her daughter had known for so long and never said a word.

'I couldn't tell you, you know that right? I thought you didn't know.'

Constance patted her daughter's arm.

'I know, love.' She sighed. 'It doesn't matter now anyway, does it? Because of what's happened.'

It felt like the longest conversation that she and Cathy had had since they had arrived in America. It had taken Daniel's death to get them talking.

'I hated him,' Cathy whispered, her eyes huge and loaded with tears. 'And now he's dead, and I feel so bad.'

Constance took her trembling daughter in her arms and held her as she cried. Everything was such a mess.

'I wish we'd never come here,' Cathy said fiercely. 'Why didn't you leave him?'

'It was complicated.'

Cathy pulled back.

'I used to blame you. It always seemed like you were getting at Dad.' She sighed. 'I was sick of all the arguing. I just wanted it to end.'

'You wanted us to break up?' Constance asked her incredulously. 'No one wants their parents to split, surely?'

'It would have been better than living in a battleground.' Her daughter sniffed loudly, pulling away from her. 'It's been awful watching the two of you at each other all the time. I can't remember when you were happy together. Why did you stay if you hated him so much?'

Constance caught her breath.

'I didn't hate him,' she said in agony. 'I loved him, Cathy.'

'I don't think you and Dad have loved each other for a long time.' Cathy sighed.

'It doesn't matter now anyway,' Cathy spat out. 'Dad's dead. He killed himself. He didn't love us enough. Not even her.'

'That's not true, Cathy. They think it was an accident...'

But her daughter had pulled her covers over her head. She heard a muffled 'Go away.'

'Cathy darling.' Constance tried to pull the covers off her, but her daughter had them clenched tightly in her hands.

'Leave me alone.'

She had given up and gone downstairs into the kitchen. She had poured herself a big glass of red wine, turned out the lights and stared yet again across her backyard at the back of Matt Lopez's house but the special agent wasn't home. She imagined him at his desk working late into the night. Looking at photographs of her dead husband's body and waiting for a more extensive autopsy report.

Special Agent Lopez was sitting there trying to work it out.

Had Daniel Garvey been pushed off the rim of the Grand Canyon? If so, who would want him dead? It just wasn't possible. Daniel must have fallen, took a risk, and lost balance because of his vertigo. Or was it one more tragic suicide at the Grand Canyon?

Constance had never known Daniel to suffer from serious depression. He had been down when he lost his job in Ireland but that was normal. Anyone would be like that. But in all their years together he had never made her feel as if he was struggling with life. He just wouldn't do it to Cathy. She felt certain.

She had drunk nearly the whole bottle of red wine, staring at the dark shadow of Matt Lopez's house. It seemed that he lived alone. She had never seen another soul in that bathroom window apart from him. She had stood there for hours, waiting. Eventually, just after midnight, she had seen a light go on in the house. She imagined the raven-haired special agent walking up the stairs of his house, heading for his bathroom. Her body shivered involuntarily as she thought of his hands, those long fingers. Of course he could not see her in the dark, but maybe he could sense her watching.

She backed out of the kitchen so fast she knocked over the rest of the bottle of wine. She tried to mop it up as best she could. On her knees on the white tiles, the wine that looked like blood, as she placed strip after strip of kitchen roll over it, sobbing with despair.

She had staggered upstairs again, fell into her bed, her head spinning from all the wine. Her last thought as she had passed out was of the Grand Canyon, and its huge desperate chasms. She hates that place.

It is her daughter's sixteenth birthday and Constance has done nothing about it. She looks at her alarm clock again and groans inwardly. Eight-thirty. Liam is due over in about forty-five minutes.

As soon as Liam is in that door, it really will be official. Constance curls up on the bed. All she wants to do is hide. She has to get herself together, but she feels catatonic just like when her mother died.

Late last night, she'd called Frances and she is flying out to them on Sunday, getting in Monday evening. Once she's here, Frances can help her organize everything. The important thing is to make sure Daniel is brought home to Ireland. She feels sick at the thought of one of those big country funerals. Hundreds will come and she will have to shake the hands of every single soul in their small townland. All those pitying faces. And the talk. Remembering Daniel. She will be in the spotlight. Having to look like the grieving widow. Will they expect her to say a eulogy? The thought makes her feel even more sick.

She must think of something else.

Cathy's birthday. Her daughter is sixteen and because of what has happened, it might pass by with barely any acknowledgement.

Daniel was a good present buyer. Surely, he had got Cathy something? It would mean so much to Cathy to have some token from her father. It would be something that would help heal the pain of her loss in some small way.

Constance gets out of bed and pulls open the drawer by his side of the bed. It feels surreal to look at all of Daniel's bits and pieces. A foil wrapper of aspirin, only two pills left in the packet, a stick of lip balm, a scrap of paper with a list of stuff he needs for the garage (Daniel had been a great list writer). The list now takes on greater significance.

Inch nails, hammer, screwdriver, wood varnish...

So he had been planning to build something. She has no idea what. Now he never will.

Underneath the list is a folded piece of paper. She takes it out. It is a travel itinerary for Daniel Garvey, Constance

Garvey, and Cathy Garvey: a United Airlines flight from
Phoenix to New York, and then on to Shannon. It is dated for
the next day. It must be some kind of mistake. But she reads the
date again. There is no doubt about it. Daniel must have been
planning a surprise holiday by taking them home for Easter. She
looks at the ticket again. There is no return itinerary. These are
one-way tickets. Constance feels a sharp stab in her chest.
Could it be true? Had Daniel planned to bring them home to
Ireland? It appeared for good. Why hadn't he told her? Why
had he suddenly changed his mind? She doesn't understand.
What about Maya D'Costa?

With shaking hands, she shoves the tickets back into the
drawer. She can't take it in. Her fingers bang against a small
black box. Knowing instinctively that it is her husband's
birthday gift for their daughter, she takes it out and opens it.
Inside is a delicate silver chain, on the end of it a tiny blue
hummingbird. It has to be something Daniel bought for Cathy.
Her daughter had fallen in love with the Arizona hummingbirds. She had developed a fascination for them, insisting they
fill their arid backyard with hummingbird feeders.

Bearing her father's birthday gift, unsure of its effect, but
trusting her instincts that this is something beautiful in a black
day, Constance knocks on her daughter's bedroom door. There
is no answer. She turns the handle, and is glad to see it isn't
locked, but when she walks in her heart drops. The bed is
empty. Cathy isn't in the room.

She races around the house calling for her daughter but the
place is empty. In the kitchen, she finds a note from Cathy on
the counter.

Gone to Lisa's house. Sorry. It's not personal.

What kind of message is this? *It's not personal!* Of course it is personal. Her father has just died and rather than be with her mother, Cathy has run away. How did Cathy think that her new friend Lisa, who Constance barely knows, could console her? She has only met her mother twice. Is she an adequate person to take care of her? Constance picks up her mobile and immediately rings Cathy's number. She doesn't answer.

Flinging on a pair of jeans, and a dirty sweater, not even bothering to straighten her hair, Constance tears out the house. For once she doesn't care what the neighbors think of her. The drive to Lisa's only takes a few minutes. She pulls up outside with a screech, slamming on the brakes.

Lisa's mother answers the door. She looks as alternative as her daughter. Braided black hair, studded ears, and a nose ring. Before she has the chance to speak, Constance demands to see Cathy.

'I'm so sorry about your husband...' the other woman begins to say, avoiding eye contact.

'I want to talk to my daughter,' Constance says. 'Get her please.'

'Come in, please,' Lisa's mam says. 'Can I get you anything. A coffee?'

'No, just my daughter,' she snaps.

Lisa's mam disappears. Constance stands in her kitchen, clinging onto the breakfast counter. She feels like she is speeding very fast down a tunnel. All she can see is her daughter, running away from her. She has to catch up.

'Mom, what are doing here?'

She turns. Cathy is standing in the doorway of the kitchen. For once she isn't wearing black. She has on a pair of blue pajama bottoms, and a silky gray robe. She has dark smudges under her eyes. She looks tired, and cross.

'What do you mean what am *I* doing here, Cathy? What do you think you're doing? You should be home. With me.'

'I just had to get out,' her daughter says. 'I can't sleep at home.'

'But why didn't you come in to me? Wake me up?'

Cathy shrugs.

'We should be together,' Constance says.

Cathy crosses her arms. Says nothing.

'You belong with me, not here, with strangers.'

'Lisa and her mom are not strangers,' Cathy says.

'Well they are to me,' Constance protests.

'Well that's because you've never made any effort to know them.' Cathy glowers at her.

'That's not true, I'm always telling you to invite Lisa over.'

'Yeah, to our House of Hell,' Cathy spits back. 'Do you even know her mom's name?'

Why is Cathy doing this to her? Of course she doesn't know her name. But it doesn't matter. Because Daniel has died. And she needs Cathy with her. Nothing else matters apart from that.

'Come on,' she says. 'Get dressed. We're going home.'

Cathy shakes her head.

'I don't want to.'

'You can't run away. Your uncle Liam and Stacey are coming over. You need to be with your family.'

'Oh God no, they do my head in.' Cathy looks sick.

'They're your family. You belong at home,' Constance insists.

'But I feel safe here. With Lisa. And Julie,' she says pointedly.

Constance feels like screaming. She takes a deep breath.

'Cathy, you have to come with me. You've no choice.'

'But it's my birthday!' she suddenly roars at her. 'Don't you get it? It's my fucking birthday! I don't want to spend every birthday until the day I die remembering what happened.' Cathy's words seem to echo around the kitchen.

Lisa's mother Julie appears, looking a little nervous. 'Everything okay here?' she asks, looking at Cathy.

Her daughter nods. Constance can see she is biting her lip to stop from crying.

'She needs to come home with me,' Constance appeals to the other woman.

'Cathy, honey, don't you think you should go with your mom?'

'I can't, please.' Cathy speaks up. 'In that house I see Dad everywhere. I can't bear it.'

'She's welcome to stay as long as she wants.' Julie turns to Constance. Despite her tough exterior Julie's eyes are swimming with concern. 'Maybe she needs a little space?'

Constance wants to slam her hands into the woman's face. How dare she speak as if she knows Cathy better than her? But then maybe she does. Her daughter spends more time in this house than her own. Lisa appears in the kitchen now. She puts her arm around Cathy's waist, and her daughter buries her head in her friend's shoulder, beginning to shake. She is actually crying. Lisa and her mother look at Constance in appeal. She feels like a monster. It's all wrong, but she doesn't know how to make it better.

'I am so very sorry about your husband,' Julie says. 'If there is anything at all I can do...'

'Well, I suppose you could look after Cathy this morning,' Constance says with reluctance.

Cathy looks up from her friend's shoulder. She gives her mother a weak smile, through her tears.

'I'm sorry, Mom. I just can't see Uncle Liam, Aunt Stacey. It's too much.'

Constance's chest is so choked she can barely speak.

'I have a birthday present for you,' she says in a small voice.

'Come get me later, okay? And you can give it to me then.'

Despite Cathy's tears, Constance can see the determination on her daughter's face. There is no way she is going to give in.

'We'll take good care of her,' Julie says, putting her hand on Cathy's shoulder.

Maybe it was just as well, thinks Constance as she drives back home. This is going to be a horrific morning. Liam and Stacey all over her.

Why, why? they will keep asking her. And she will see it in their faces. They will blame her. What kind of wife is so unbearable that her husband throws himself off the Grand Canyon?

––––––

'So I spoke to Deputy Peters at the Coconino Sheriff's Office on the phone first thing,' Liam is saying to her.

While Stacey cooked them breakfast, Constance had taken a quick shower. They are now all seated at the dining table, and she is attempting to eat one of Stacey's golden pancakes. Daniel had loved his sister-in-law's fluffy pancakes, which he would pile with blueberries and cream.

'It looks pretty likely that Daniel took his own life.' Liam sighs, shaking his head.

Stacey begins to cry again. 'I just can't believe it,' she sobs as she reaches for the maple syrup and drenches her pancakes with it.

'But do you think Daniel was really in that state of mind?' Constance asks him.

'Well, he was very depressed wasn't he?' Liam says to her.

'He was?'

'All the money worries?'

She has no idea what he is talking about, but she doesn't

want Liam to know that she has so little a grasp on their finances.

'Daniel wouldn't kill himself over money.'

'Lots of men his age do,' Stacey says in a quivering voice, taking her husband's hand in her own. 'They feel like they've failed their family.'

'Even with the work I gave him, I don't think he was coping well with all that debt you guys built up in Ireland,' Liam adds.

Constance is cold with unease. What is Liam talking about?

'But we sold the house.'

'Yeah, but that was a drop in the ocean, wasn't it?'

She stares at her brother-in-law. He looks so different from Daniel. He has a long thin face, sandy hair, and his skin is leathery and tanned from all the years in Arizona.

'Anyway,' he sighs. 'It does no good wondering why. He's gone.' Liam's voice cracks. 'I can't believe it.'

'I keep thinking he's going to walk in the door and join us for pancakes,' Stacey says.

Constance stands up suddenly. She can't bear this talk. She wants them to leave. She needs to be alone. And she wants so much to be by the sea. To run on the beach and scream at the waves. But she lives in Arizona. Landlocked. Miles and miles away from the ocean.

'I'm sorry,' Stacey says. 'I'm so sorry, Connie.'

Her sister-in-law gets up from the table and attempts to put her arm around her. She shakes her away. Stacey is only trying to be kind, but she can't bear her to touch her. If she lets one tear drop, she will fall apart completely. She has to hold it together for Cathy.

'Did Deputy Peters say when we can get Daniel back?' she asks Liam, her voice sounding cold and almost businesslike. 'We need to organize getting him to Ireland for the funeral. '

'No,' he says. 'But I guess if it's suicide not too long.'

'You know, he could have been pushed,' Constance says, annoyed that Liam assumes Daniel would take his own life.

'What?' Liam looks at her in shock. 'But who would do that?'

'Whoever he was with.' Constance turns and stares right into Liam's eyes. He is blinking like crazy. It is clear to her that Liam knew about Daniel's affair. She feels a flare of rage.

'*She* could have done,' Constance says. 'The other woman.'

LISTEN TO ME

Why is it that so many men think it is quite okay to do things with underage girls? Remember, I told you all about what had happened to me?

I had been on holiday with my parents. The routine every year was to go to a resort. Somewhere hot and sunny where my mother could baste herself by the pool all day long, and my father would go off and play golf. I was expected to lie on a sun lounger next to my mother but I didn't like sitting in the harsh sun. So instead, I would stay in the cool shade of our room all day long. I would lie on my bed and read book after book. I devoured fictional worlds because they were my only escape. I would only swim early in the morning before the pool got busy, and the heat of the day had sprung.

During the day, their separation was a kind of peace. Evenings could go either way. Too much drink and laughter. Too much drink and harsh words. Tears. Recriminations. I felt tense the whole time. Afraid what every night would bring.

One morning I got up early as usual to swim in the pool. The only other people up at that hour were a few middle-aged men walking around the pool on their phones looking self-important. They just couldn't switch off to be with their families on holiday. They didn't seem to notice me, and I didn't mind them, as I slipped into the pool in my new yellow bikini. But this particular morning, I had been surprised by a splash at the deep end of the pool. A body moving under the water, past my pedaling legs. A head emerged, water streaming down a face, black hair slick, streaked with gray. He smiled at me and without thinking, I smiled back. He looked about the same age as my father.

'Hi,' he said, bobbing up and down.

'Hi', I said, feeling shy. I wanted to get out of the pool but somehow it seemed rude. There were only the two of us.

'I've seen you every morning,' he said to me, and as he spoke, I felt something brush against my thighs. It was his hands. Before I could do a thing, I felt his fingers slip under my bikini bottoms and touch me in a place I had never been touched before. I should have slapped him, and swum away, or shouted out. But I did nothing. I stared at the smiling face of this man, as he stroked me with his fingers. I could feel my breasts swelling in my bikini top, my nipples hardening.

'Stop,' I whispered at him, but the man smiled even wider, and continued to stroke me.

'I don't think you want me to stop *now* do you?'

'Stop,' I begged. 'Please stop.'

I closed my eyes, felt the water holding me up. This trembling deep inside me. My head was screaming at me to get away from the pervert. Yet my body was paralyzed.

'Good girl,' he whispered, as I experienced my first orgasm, my body flapping in the water like a drowning butterfly.

I was immediately repulsed, and kicked out with my legs. I felt his hands pull on my bikini bottoms but I grabbed them back, and kicked him again hard. I was seething. I kicked and I kicked. Glad to hear him cry out in pain. I swam to the other side of the pool like a demented creature and hauled myself out of the water. I ran all the way back to our apartment.

My parents were sitting on the balcony eating breakfast. They were arguing. They didn't even notice me as I ran into my bedroom, collapsed on my bed, and buried my face in my pillow, sobbing and shaking with shame. The sound of the man's curses ringing in my ears.

I refused to go back down to the pool for the rest of the holiday. My parents gave up asking me why.

I knew what that man did to me had been

wrong, but even worse was that he had made me feel dirty. I craved to be touched again. This time by someone I could love. And failing that, I touched myself. Every time I came, I remembered the guilt and shame that I had felt that first time in the swimming pool on holiday with my parents. It was only with you that I began to feel clean again. You took away my disgust at my own desires and made me see the beauty of pure passion. My love for you suffused all of me. My heart. My mind. Even my body.

And then you ruined it. Turned all that was good about us bad.

You knew all this about me, and yet you still went ahead. You did the worst thing possible.

CHAPTER THIRTY

FOUR DAYS AFTER, SATURDAY

Katarina is just about to knock on Special Agent Lopez's door when it is flung open from the inside. A young Indian woman storms out. She is beautiful in a bohemian way, long black hair with red streaks and her arms jangling with bangles. Katarina takes a step back but not quite in time. The hippy woman bangs into her as she sweeps by. She doesn't apologize, indeed she doesn't even seem to see her. Her eyes are glazed with tears.

Katarina takes a few tentative steps into Lopez's office. The agent is seated at his desk, poring over some papers. He barely looks up at her.

'I have the surveillance material that you requested, sir,' she says.

'Thank you, Ranger, it's not so urgent now,' he says, looking up at her.

Katarina waits for further explanation. She is dying to know who the beautiful hippy was who had looked so upset.

'She's admitted being at the Grand Canyon on the day Daniel Garvey disappeared. I don't know why she lied in the first place,' Lopez says, scratching his chin.

'Who is *she?*' Katarina asks.

'Maya D'Costa.' Lopez sits back in his chair, indicating for her to sit down opposite him.

'She was with Daniel Garvey just before his fall.' Lopez stares right at her. Katarina finds his scrutiny slightly uncomfortable. 'He was having an affair with her. They used to meet at the Grand Canyon and go hiking.'

Katarina feels her whole body jolt in surprise. Daniel Garvey had been a cheater. What was it Shane always said: *What goes around comes around.*

'So she saw him fall off the rim, right?' Katarina asks Lopez.

'No. She says not. Well of course she says not, because why would she not have reported it otherwise?'

Katarina feels a chill creeping down her spine.

'Can she say why he could have taken his own life?'

Lopez says nothing for a moment.

'So is that what you think, Ranger?' Lopez asks her. 'Do you really believe Daniel Garvey's fall wasn't an accident but intentional?'

'I can't say,' she says, feeling self-conscious. 'But *you* said it might not be an accident.'

'Sure.' He nods at her.

'So, I guess he could have killed himself.' Katarina pauses, licking her lips.

'I am not convinced that Daniel Garvey was a suicidal man, Ranger,' Lopez says to her. 'There was no note. His wife seems certain that he had no intention of killing himself.'

There is sudden tension in the room. Lopez pushes the sheets of paper on his desk towards her.

'This is an initial autopsy report. Take a look if you want.'

Katarina shakes her head.

'It's not in my remit, sir. I'm just a park ranger.'

'That's not true, Katarina,' he says to her.

She is surprised he uses her first name.

'You are a valuable pair of eyes and ears. You were first on the ground to find Daniel Garvey. Your opinion counts.'

Katarina picks up the report, scans the page.

'The cause of the bruising on the back of Daniel Garvey's head is inconclusive,' Lopez says. 'But you showed me Shoshone Point. Did you see anything that could have been used to hit him? Push him off the edge?'

'Pushed?' Her words echo his faintly.

'Yes, he could have been pushed off the rim.'

Katarina puts down the report and stares at Lopez. She is surprised that the special agent seems to be so interested in her opinion.

'Well there's no tree there. So no branches to hit him with,' she says. 'I guess a rock could have been used. But we didn't find anything.'

'That's true, but maybe the perpetrator threw the rock over the edge after Daniel.'

She shivers. Murder rarely happens in the Grand Canyon. Special Agent Lopez is way off track in his analysis.

'So who do you think might want to kill Daniel Garvey that day?' he persists.

'Well I guess if he was having an affair, maybe his wife?'

'But it wasn't the wife who was at the Grand Canyon with Daniel.' Lopez pauses. 'Something happened between Maya D'Costa and Daniel Garvey in the Grand Canyon on Tuesday. I don't think Maya has told me everything.'

'What did she say?'

'She said that they argued. She walked off and left him at Shoshone Point on his own.'

'Were there any witnesses?'

'She says she can't remember.' Lopez leans forward on his chair. 'Nor can she remember how their argument ended.'

'Seriously? She must be lying.'

'Yes, that's what I was thinking too, Katarina,' Lopez says, taking his little red notebook out again and flicking through the pages.

'You know I think you should go through the security footage for me,' he says. 'Keep an eye out for Maya D'Costa and Daniel Garvey. It might give us an idea of where they were when she supposedly walked out on him.'

For the rest of the afternoon Katarina can't shake the image from her head of tearful Maya D'Costa charging out of Special Agent Lopez's office. Beautiful, broken, and fragile. Women like that always got around men, but not it seemed Special Agent Lopez. He told her that Maya D'Costa had asked to see Daniel Garvey's dead body.

'Of course I couldn't agree to that. She isn't family,' Lopez said, his eyes steeped in disapproval.

It's clear to Katarina that the special agent is suspicious of Maya D'Costa. She is after all a woman who has stolen another woman's husband. She should not be pitied.

Her shift over, Katarina decides to grab something to eat at the Canyon View Information Plaza rather than head straight back to the trailer. She is just about to walk off with her burrito, when to her surprise she notices that Maya D'Costa is sitting at a picnic table outside. It has been hours since she had seen her storming out of Lopez's office. Now is her opportunity. There are no other free picnic tables, so she has the perfect excuse to go over. Maya D'Costa is bent over a mug of tea, dipping the string on the teabag up and down in the hot water.

'Is this seat taken?' she asks.

Maya looks up at her as if she has been shaken awake. Her eyes are red-rimmed still.

'No,' she says in a shaky voice. 'Go ahead.'

Katarina settles herself down, takes a bite of her burrito. She can feel Maya looking at her.

'Sorry, have we met?' Maya asks her.

'Not really, you bumped into me on the way out of Special Agent Lopez's office earlier.'

'Oh,' Maya says, her voice so faint that Katarina can hardly hear her. 'Oh yes, sorry.'

Katarina puts down her burrito. She has a chance to impress Special Agent Lopez. What if she can get Maya D'Costa to confide in her?

'I just want to say I'm very sorry for your loss,' she says.

Maya's eyes fill with tears again. 'You know about Daniel?' she whispers.

Katarina nods. 'Yes,' she says. 'It was me who found him.'

Maya gasps, clutching her hands to her breast.

Is this woman for real? There is something rather over the top about her grief. It makes Katarina a little angry. But she conceals her annoyance, tries to look sympathetic.

'They won't let me see him,' Maya says tearfully. 'But I can't go to the funeral. I need to see Daniel one last time to say goodbye.'

She wipes her tears away with shaking hands.

'I can't bear it.'

'It won't help you to see him dead,' Katarina says. 'I promise you.'

'I don't understand how he fell,' Maya says to her. 'He was afraid of heights. He wouldn't have gone to the edge without me.'

Katarina looks down at her burrito.

'He could have jumped on purpose,' she says in a low voice.

There is a tense pause.

'Daniel did not kill himself.' All of a sudden, Maya's voice is firm.

Katarina looks up and stares into Maya's eyes. They are rich, limitless brown.

'He loved his daughter too much,' Maya says to her. 'He would have done anything for Cathy. She came first.'

Katarina can hear the bitterness in Maya D'Costa's voice. So, she was jealous of the daughter, not the wife. She wonders if she had said the same to Special Agent Lopez. Maybe Katarina can get her to say more?

CHAPTER THIRTY-ONE

FOUR DAYS AFTER, SATURDAY

Maya wishes she could be free of the heavy weight of her grief.

She sits back on the bar stool in Bright Angel Lodge and lets the park ranger order them both another shot of tequila.

'That's the last one for her now, Kat,' the bartender says to the park ranger, nodding at Maya.

Maya has no memory of how the park ranger persuaded her to go drinking with her. Maya had made it a rule never to drink tequila again. Not after that time, five years ago when she woke up naked and in bed with a guy she barely knew. Tequila had been to blame. Something happens to her when she drinks the spirit. It taps into her most free self. And that isn't necessarily a good thing.

But tonight, Maya wants oblivion. She wants the pain to stop in her chest. Katarina hands her a segment of lemon, along with the salt. She cups her shaking hand and dips it into the salt, presses her lips to it before knocking back the shot, and sucking on the lemon. The hit is immediate.

Maya had told Special Agent Lopez that she had been with Daniel at Shoshone Point. She told him they had argued.

'Over what?' Lopez asked her.

'He didn't want to hike with me,' she lied. 'We had a small argument. And I left him.'

Maya chases the tequila with a slurp of beer.

'I shouldn't have left him,' she now confesses to the park ranger who found Daniel.

If Katarina Nolan hadn't taken that route on her patrol, Daniel's body might never have been found. Maya can feel waves of hysteria threatening. Daniel fell hundreds of feet off the rim of the Grand Canyon. What kind of a pointless end is that?

'What I don't get is why you both went to the Grand Canyon if he was so scared of heights?' Katarina is asking her.

Maya thinks she is being insensitive, but the tequila is working its way through her body, loosening her mind and her tongue.

'We had gone for hikes before,' she says. 'I was helping him get over his vertigo.'

'Never been bothered by heights,' Katarina comments, taking a sip of her beer. 'Don't like scorpions though. Check my boots every morning for the little critters.'

'It wasn't really working,' Maya confides in Katarina. 'He could only bear to go close to the edge if I held his hand, and then not really that close either. He was really terrified.'

'So why did you leave him on his own at Shoshone Point?'

Maya takes another sip of her beer. She can feel all the alcohol swirling around inside her head. Something is clearing. She is beginning to remember.

'We had a big argument,' she says. 'And I stormed off.'

Katarina persuades the bartender to give them one more shot of tequila. This time Maya doesn't bother with the salt and lemon and knocks it back in one. She can feel wildness creeping into her heart. She looks at the park ranger again. She has long dark hair and brown eyes, just like her, though her skin is paler than Maya's. Her Stetson is sitting on top of the bar, with its National Parks insignia: the bison and the sequoia tree with the snow-capped mountains. She is still wearing her ranger uniform. Brown trousers with a thick leather belt, and a buff shirt with a crest on it. The sleeves are short, and her arms are toned. The clothes hug the shape of her body. She looks fit.

'Is it my fault he died?' she asks Katarina.

'No, of course it's not your fault,' the other woman assures her.

'If I had gone back to him... well...' Maya gives a big sob. 'If I had followed him...' She can't continue.

She is shaking so hard it is impossible to control her voice. She gets up off the stool. She has to get out of this bar.

'Where are you going?' Katarina asks her, putting a firm hand on her arm.

'Restrooms,' she mutters through her tears.

Maya doesn't go to the restrooms. Instead, she walks right out of the back of Bright Angel Lodge, and towards the wall to the rear. She teeters up to it, almost blind with tears and grief. She could climb over it right now. Drop down into the Grand Canyon after Daniel. But before she has a chance to climb onto the wall, she feels a hand on her arm, pulling her back.

'Hey, watch it there,' Park Ranger Katarina says.

'I want to go climbing.' Maya sobs. 'I want to be with Daniel.'

'Come on,' Katarina says. 'You've got to get it together.'

Maya stares at the park ranger through her glaze of tears. She can see the power and strength of this woman.

'Thank you,' Maya whispers. 'Thank you for finding Daniel.'

The ranger looks uncomfortable. 'Just doing my job,' she mutters. 'Come on, I'll give you a lift. I only had one shot.'

Katarina helps her over to her truck. Maya clambers in unsteadily. She has no idea where her jeep is.

'You can crash out at mine,' Katarina says as she starts up the engine.

Maya looks at her companion's face. The irises of her eyes are so dark they look black. All she can see is a tiny glimmer of the white in her eyes in the night shadows.

'You know I was so angry with Daniel I can't remember what I said or did just before I walked away from him.'

'What do you mean you can't remember?' Katarina asks, an incredulous tone to her voice just like Special Agent Lopez had had.

'It happens to me sometimes,' she explains. 'Blackouts. Well, more like red mists. When I get really mad.'

There is a long pause.

'I really want to remember. It's driving me crazy,' Maya admits.

'Well let's take it step by step,' Katarina suggests.

Her voice is gentle. Maya is touched by the kindness of this woman. They are strangers after all.

'Tell me the last thing you remember, and we'll try to take it back from that point onwards. See if you can re-trace your steps that day.'

Maya squeezes her eyes tight. Takes a deep breath. It's coming back to her like inside the bar. Little by little.

'We argued because of Daniel's daughter,' she says. 'It was all about Cathy.'

She was eating an avocado, salsa and bean burrito sitting at a picnic table at Shoshone Point when Daniel told her. Her mouth had been full of food when he said the last thing that she was expecting him to say.

'I'm going back to Ireland.'

She had spluttered, spraying beans all over the picnic table.

'I'm sorry,' he said to her. 'We have to go back.'

She was choking with shock and her eyes were streaming. She gasped for breath. Daniel got up and smacked her back. She swallowed, took a breath. She felt the sting of his slap on her back.

'I don't understand,' she said once she could speak again. 'You told me you never wanted to go back to Ireland.'

'I don't *want* to, Maya. But I think it's the only thing to do.'

'Why?' Even as she asked him, she knew why. Deep down she had known this moment would come ever since the night in Prescott.

'Cathy,' he said, spreading his arms wide in explanation. 'She's losing her way here. We need to get her back home.'

'But that won't make any difference,' Maya protested. 'If she wants to behave badly, she'll do it just as well back in Ireland.'

'I can keep an eye on her back home,' he said to her. 'It's impossible to do that in Arizona.'

'But what about your job? Don't you love it?' Maya said to him.

She couldn't believe he was sacrificing everything he had built up in Arizona. 'And your house in Flagstaff?'

'Cathy is more important than any of that,' he said in a sad voice. 'I've arranged things with Constance's uncle. He's getting too old to run his farm. He's going to let me take over the management of it.'

She felt herself stiffen at the mention of Constance.

'You can't be serious?'

'I think it's the only way. There's no son to take the farm and I get on well with her uncle Jack. He always used to hint at me taking over from him.'

Jack. He was on first-name terms with his wife's uncle. Of course he was. He didn't even know her father's name, or if she even had an uncle. He never would.

'If we're living on the farm with Constance's uncle and

aunt,' Daniel continued, 'we'll all be able to keep an eye on Cathy.'

'You won't be able to control her, Daniel. It's a mistake,' she said to him.

'I don't know what else to do,' he said, in a desperate voice. 'I thought I'd fixed things.'

'But you did,' Maya tried to reassure him. 'You stopped her from seeing that creep.'

'But not until it was too late.'

He gave a bitter laugh.

'Cathy threw it in my face. She said that she had lost her virginity to him.'

He closed his eyes as if the thought of it was so horrific, he could even see it.

'Are you sure that's true?' Maya said as carefully as she could.

But Daniel wasn't listening to her.

'She's not even sixteen,' he declared, looking as if he was in pain.

'Yes, but her affair with that man is over now,' Maya said, as a flickering memory of the fair-haired cowboy and his wedding band surfaced in her mind.

'He had sex with my little girl,' Daniel said, his voice raw with agony. 'That's statutory rape.'

Maya didn't say any more. She knew otherwise. She also knew that Cathy was not irredeemably damaged from her relationship with that cowboy, but her father would never think that. His daughter had grown up too soon. And he hadn't protected her.

'She's at it again,' Daniel said to Maya. 'She's slipping out late at night. Or saying she's staying over at her friend Lisa's house. And I can't make a scene because then I would have to tell her mother about that guy, and what she is up to now.' He sighed. 'And then that would lead to telling Constance about you.'

'But you've been promising to tell Constance about us for weeks. You asked me to marry you nearly two months ago,' Maya said in a careful voice, putting down her half-eaten burrito upon the picnic table. She had completely lost her appetite. 'I think Cathy's mother should know what's going on. I think it's time your wife knew about us.'

'But then my daughter will hate me even more. It's not the right time.'

'Your daughter won't hate you, Daniel,' Maya said, putting her hand on his. 'It's better to live in the truth. One day she'll respect you for it.'

'Why does it have to be a choice?' he asked her with tortured eyes. 'Why do I have to choose between you and Cathy?'

'Of course you don't have to. Just talk to her. Spend more time with Cathy. Give her more attention and stay in Arizona with me, like we planned. She's nearly sixteen, before you know it, she'll be gone to college—'

'No,' Daniel interrupted. 'I need to act now. I need to get her away from this place.'

Maya pulled her hand away. She wasn't good enough for him. It was the same as before. She hadn't been good enough for her own father either, and he had left her too. Her rational mind knew that Daniel was doing the 'right' thing, but her heart was raging. How dare he propose to her, make her fall in love with him? How dare he just drop her, like this, with no chance of ever seeing him again?

'I can come back when she's left home,' he said in a small voice.

'And when would that be?' Maya asked, her tone icy.

'Two, three years maximum.'

'And what about Constance?' Maya gave him a penetrating

glare. 'What if you can fix things between you? Maybe you'll be so happy on your idyllic little farm that you'll forget all about me?'

'I could never forget you, Maya.' Daniel gave her a searching look. 'I love you with all my heart, but I don't expect you to wait for me.'

Maya felt a flash of anger, like a lightning bolt in her chest.

'Don't you dare!'

Daniel looked at her in confusion. She could see his eyes were wet and it made her even angrier.

'How can you say you love me and then make it my decision to leave you? How could you?'

'I don't want it be over, darling,' he said, in a shaky voice.

'Then don't let it happen to us! Cathy will be okay I promise.'

'No,' he said, avoiding her eyes. 'I owe it to her. And I owe it to Constance to keep our daughter safe.'

She felt like screaming at him, shaking his hunched shoulders. Maya stood up suddenly. She felt suffocated by the intensity of her feelings. She stormed away from where they had been sitting, marched down the trail towards the pine trees.

'Maya!' she heard Daniel calling her. 'Maya, please!'

She whipped around on the path. He was behind her, his face flushed red.

'Please don't make me feel worse than I do,' he pleaded with her. 'Let's just treasure the time we have together. '

'And how much time is that?' she asked him, her chest tight with fury.

He didn't answer her. They were blocking the path but she didn't care. A couple walked around them on their way out. She sensed their curious stares, but they kept on walking and soon they were out of sight.

'How much time?' She heard her voice hoarse with anxiety.

'Sunday,' he said. 'I booked flights for Sunday night out of Phoenix.'

Five days' time. She staggered back in shock.

'I haven't told Cathy or Constance yet. I haven't even told my brother. I wanted to tell you first.'

Her whole body was convulsing in shock. Five days. Was this going to be their last full day together? Ever?

'I'll come back,' he said again. 'I promise.'

Black waves of hate swept through her.

'How?' she shouted at him. 'You'll be knee deep in pig shit. And I can promise you I'm not decamping to some bog-filled miserable country just to be your bit on the side.'

'Maya.' Daniel stepped towards her, reaching out. 'You were never that.'

He said her name in the past tense. It was over. She knew it was.

'You always said you never wanted me to leave my wife and daughter for you.' He took her arm. 'Remember, you told me you're a free spirit?'

He tried to take her to him, but she was consumed with anger. How dare he denigrate her feelings, her love for him? She pushed him away.

He tried to catch hold of her again, but she kicked him hard on the shin. Daniel grabbed his leg in pain, looking at her with a mixture of hurt and confusion. She was no longer the soulful sensual Maya he had fallen in love with. She was a scorned woman full of fury.

'I hate you,' she screamed at him. 'Fuck off back to Ireland. I never want to see you again.'

This is what Maya believes must have happened although she cannot remember what she said and did after the moment she had told him to fuck off back to Ireland. This is because she had entered a black hole of despair and rage.

She must have driven off. Her pain rocking her as she put her foot to the pedal and sped away. Surely that is what she did?

'Was that the last time you saw him?' Katarina Nolan asks her as they drive through the black night.

Maya feels tears loading her eyes. She is dizzy and sick. Her anger at Daniel has long dissipated.

'It's all my fault Daniel is dead,' Maya says to Katarina. The ranger turns and glances at her. She can sense the hunger in her gaze to know more. A small voice inside Maya's head tells her to be careful, but the tequila has loosened her tongue. She can't help herself.

'I might have lost control,' she admits.

'What do you mean?' Katarina pushes.

'It's happened to me once before. Years ago. When I get really angry, it's like this red mist descends and I get violent, but I can't remember afterward.'

The park ranger doesn't reply, and Maya knows she should shut up, but she is wracked by guilt. Terrified this is all her fault.

'Maybe it happened again, because I can't remember how I got home. All I know is that one minute I was raging with him, and the next I was alone in my house. Maybe I killed Daniel?'

CHAPTER THIRTY-TWO

FOUR DAYS AFTER, SATURDAY

Constance has survived her first full day as a widow. Liam was on the phone all morning ringing family and friends back home while Stacey bustled around in the kitchen, cleaning the sink for the twentieth time, and making endless pots of coffee. Constance was completely wired. She doesn't often drink coffee and today she must have had at least five cups of strong black brew.

Her suggestion that Daniel's mistress had anything to do with his death was met with disbelief by both Liam and his wife. Stacey was aghast that Daniel had been cheating in the first place.

'Are you sure, Connie? He was so devoted to you and Cathy.'

'It was Cathy who saw them together,' Constance said in a flat voice.

'Christ almighty!' Liam said, shaking his head. 'Where *is* Cathy? Stacey thought she could take her out, you know, distract her.'

'Well that's why she's not here,' Constance said, feeling

pathetic that her daughter sought comfort elsewhere. 'She's at her friend's house. She said she couldn't bear to be home.'

'Poor darling,' Stacey said, her eyes filling with tears. 'When my daddy died, I was Cathy's age. It was just devastating... and he died of natural causes.'

Liam put his arm around his wife, pecked her on the cheek. *It's all show*, thought Constance. She had an overwhelming urge to tell Stacey that her husband was probably as much a cheater as his brother.

'If it wasn't an accident, maybe the mistress had something to do with it?' Constance said, trying to get a reaction out of them. She needed them to stop canoodling in front of her.

'But wouldn't there have been witnesses?' Stacey asked.

'He wasn't on a touristy part of the rim,' Constance said.

'Come on,' Liam said, looking at Constance as if she was unhinged. 'Why would she do such a thing? She's a hippy, an artist, not some crazed jealous woman.'

'How do you know she's an artist, Liam?' Stacey asked her husband, stepping away from him. 'Did you know about Daniel and this woman?'

'Well, I'm sorry, yes I did, baby,' Liam appealed to Stacey before turning to Constance, his eyes wide open with apology. 'I told him to stop, and I am sure it was just a fling you know...'

'He was cheating on Connie and you kept his dirty little secret.' Stacey looked furious.

'He's dead, Stacey, please don't talk about my brother like that now.'

Stacey crossed her arms and glared at her husband. 'I'm sorry, Connie, I knew nothing about it at all I swear.'

'It doesn't matter now,' Constance said.

She was worn out by their presence. She wished they would go, leave her in peace.

'Look I'm really tired. I need to sleep.'

'Would you like to come home with us?' Stacey offered. 'We can pick up Cathy on the way, look after you both.'

She thought of Liam and Stacey's boys, running around the house like maniacs. How Cathy would react to being in Scottsdale with Liam and Stacey.

'No,' she said too quickly, for she could see Stacey was affronted. 'We need to stay in Flagstaff.'

'But you don't want to be here. In this house all alone, surely?' Stacey looked horrified.

'Yes, I do. And Cathy will be staying here too,' Constance said with determination.

It dawned on Constance that she no longer had to pretend to like Daniel's brother and his wife. She had only put on an act for her husband, and now he was gone. She could just be herself. It felt like a weight had been lifted off her chest.

'I'd like you to go now,' she said firmly. 'I have to pick up Cathy.'

Liam looked happy to do so, but Stacey was clearly insulted. She opened her bag, and pulled out a small packet of pills, placing them on the counter.

'Here's some Xanax,' she said, a disapproving clip to her voice. 'They might help you sleep. Ring us if you need anything.' She paused. 'I really don't think you should be on your own.'

This time when she rolled up at Lisa's house, Constance accepted Julie's offer of coffee, although she was already wired. She couldn't help noticing that the other woman was not wearing a wedding ring. She remembered now Cathy speaking of Lisa's mam with admiration. She had raised her daughter all on her own, with no help from any man.

'The girls are both asleep,' Julie said apologetically. 'Cathy came round so early this morning. And we've been talking for hours. She's done in.'

Constance wanted to ask the other mother what it was Cathy had been saying for so many hours, but she was too embarrassed. She felt a twinge of jealousy.

They sat at a messy table, one end of which was stacked with books.

'I've gone back to college,' Julie explained, indicating the books. 'Never got the chance when Lisa was little.'

Constance nodded, took a big gulp of coffee.

'I'm sorry about Cathy landing on you like this,' she said.

'It's no trouble,' Julie said. 'Cathy's great to have over. I work late nights bartending, so I'm glad Lisa has the company.'

They sat in awkward silence. Constance found herself staring at one of the books. It was a huge tome on family law.

'How are you doing?' Julie spoke up. 'It must all be a terrible shock.'

'I can't believe it,' Constance said in a hollow whisper. 'It's like I'm in some kind of nightmare.'

Julie placed a hand on hers. Constance felt an overwhelming urge to scream. She had to get out of this woman's house.

'I think I want to get Cathy. Go back home,' she said, pulling her hand away and standing up.

'Are you sure? You can stay here,' Julie said, looking very concerned. 'I've taken the night off work.'

'Thanks. But no.'

Cathy and Lisa were fast asleep. Constance stood in the doorway of the bedroom staring down at the two girls curled up together on the bed. In slumber, years had been shed. They both looked so young. So vulnerable. The sun was close to setting, and it streaked through the blinds, illuminating Cathy's red hair, turning Lisa's dark hair glistening jet. She felt a deep tug in her belly. In sleep her daughter was no longer angry with her. She was an angel. Once she woke, her peace would shatter.

'Are you sure you want to wake them?' Julie was whispering to her.

She drove home on her own. Refusing to stay the night despite Julie offering again and again.

'You shouldn't be on your own.' She echoed Stacey's earlier advice.

But all Constance craved was solitude.

Now she is home, Constance lets the silence in the house seep into her body. She lies on top of her and Daniel's bed, her bones heavy, and her heart racing from all the coffee. She picks up his pillow and smells it. She imagines she can still detect his scent, but really all she can smell is laundry detergent. In fact, she has probably changed the sheets since he last slept in them.

She lies on her side and watches the last light from the setting sun out of their bedroom window. She can see the purple silhouette of Humphreys Peak behind the roof of Matt Lopez's house. The sun has sunk below it and turned the clouds above red and purple. It is resplendent. The kind of sunset that could never be captured in a photograph.

Daniel had gloried in these desert skies. The red earth and the red sun. The saguaro cacti that looked like they belonged in Road Runner cartoons from their childhood. Daniel told her he had loved this cowboy landscape because he had watched so many Westerns with his father. 'It's like being a boy again,' he had said. The first week that they had moved here, he had sent old black and white postcards to his sisters of the giant cowboy billboard on the way into Scottsdale: *Welcome to the Wild West.* It had amused him no end. 'We're pioneers,' he kept telling her and Cathy.

Daniel is gone. She closes her eyes. Now that she is all

alone, she can let herself cry. She can shout and wail and scream out her pain, and yet none of it comes. She is a wooden effigy, on top of the tomb of her bed. It is impossible to sleep. She looks at the Xanax Stacey had given her. She brought them upstairs along with a glass of water, but she doesn't reach out for them. She wants to remain clear-headed. Daniel is dead, but there is more to it than that. Daniel's life had been taken from him. She knows that is the truth of it.

She thinks about the past few months and all their arguments. She hunts for a time when they had been happy together. The best she can come up with is when he had met her and Cathy off the plane on the way back from Houston. He had been in great form that day. Constance wonders if that was when he had decided to book the tickets back home to Ireland.

Why did he do it? Without even telling her? Liam said they had huge debts back in Ireland. She feels sick with the ignorance of it. It seems that Daniel had deceived her about everything in their lives. Had there been anything true left between them?

A loud bang somewhere in the house wakes her up. It is near black. The crescent Moon faint, no street lighting. All she can see are the spinning stars in the indigo sky. There it is again. A banging, or a knocking sound. She has probably just left a window open... but then she's sure she hadn't.

Constance gets out of bed. Stands against her bedroom door, craning her neck to listen. Again, she hears a noise. It sounds as if it is coming from Cathy's room. Her daughter must have decided to come home, and Constance hadn't heard her. She glances at her alarm clock. It is only midnight.

She steps out into the hall and turns on the light.

'Cathy?' she calls out.

She hears a clatter in Cathy's room, but her daughter doesn't answer her.

Constance goes to open the door. She feels a knot of anxiety in her belly for some reason. An image of Maya D'Costa, her sweet, dimpled smile contorted into a maniac's grin appears in her head. She shakes it away. She is being ridiculous. She opens the door as her heartrate accelerates with anticipation.

The room is empty. But the window is wide open. The curtains billowing in the light spring breeze. Constance shivers. She most certainly had not left that window open. Had Cathy come and gone? But she has a key—why on earth would she climb through the window?

Constance walks across the room to close the window. As she picks her way through Cathy's mess of clothes and books, the room feels even more chaotic than usual. She turns slowly in a circle. It really doesn't feel right.

Has someone broken into their house through Cathy's window? And, if so, is it something to do with Daniel's death?

Suddenly, she senses someone watching her. She stares into the dark corners of the bedroom, but they are thick in shadow. She can feel a presence though. She runs out of the room, back into her bedroom, and slams the door closed. Turns the key. She is just being paranoid, surely? But what if Daniel's death at the Grand Canyon pushed Maya D'Costa over the edge? Should Constance ring the police? As she takes her phone off the bedside table, a card drops onto the floor. She picks it up. It's Matt Lopez's number.

It takes Special Agent Lopez just over five minutes to get to her house. She runs down the stairs to let him in. All the time she imagines the crazed mistress jumping out of Cathy's room to attack her.

'Okay, Mrs. Garvey, let's take a look,' Lopez assures her as soon as he steps over the threshold.

'I heard a noise. The bedroom window is open. I'm sure it was closed but I felt silly to call the cops. You said to ring you any time so...' she babbles.

'That's good. You did the right thing.'

She follows him as he checks out Cathy's room and examines the catch on the window.

'Yeah, it looks like someone did get into your house. I guess this window was the easiest one to break into,' he says to her.

'Do you think it's something to do with Daniel's death?'

'Likely it's a coincidence. Though we've had no break-ins around here for a long time. And it looks like nothing was taken. I should call it in. Get someone to come out from the Sheriff's Office.'

She is shaking all over.

'No, I don't want to make a fuss,' she says.

'But it could be important, Mrs. Garvey...'

'No,' she snaps. 'Please I don't want to see the police again tonight.'

He gives her a strange look, but nods all the same.

'Okay then, here,' he says, taking her arm. 'You're shivering. Let me make you coffee.'

'No,' she says, her teeth chattering. 'No more coffee.'

'Okay, well a glass of milk then?'

He leads her down the stairs and into her kitchen.

'There's beer,' she says. 'I could do with one.'

'Okay,' he says, opening her fridge as she flops onto a stool by the breakfast counter.

'Would you like one too?' she asks him.

'Sure,' he says, still watching her. 'I'm off duty now.'

He looks taller in her kitchen than when she had first met him. He is wearing a blue shirt covered in white stars, just like the sky outside. Close up he is even more attractive than from a distance in that bathroom mirror. She notices he hasn't shaved yet tonight.

He passes her a bottle of beer and slips onto the stool next to her at the kitchen counter.

'So how are you doing?' he asks her.

'Okay,' she sighs. 'Not too good.'

He is so close, she can smell him. His scent is citrusy, clean.

'Where's your daughter?'

'She's at a friend's.' Constance bites her lip. 'She didn't want to be here with me.'

'That's tough.'

She can see the compassion in his eyes and she feels ashamed that she isn't closer to Cathy. He must think she is a shit mother, and a shit wife for that matter if her husband was having an affair.

She takes a big slug of her beer. She normally doesn't drink beer. It was Daniel's.

'It's really hard for you,' Special Agent Lopez says to her. 'It's like a double shock when someone you love dies and then you find out all this stuff about them that you didn't know...'

She nods. 'A friend of mine, Frances, found out that her father had a whole second family in England at his funeral. She and her mam and sisters had no idea.'

'Wow,' Lopez says. 'That must have been heavy.'

'It was.' She glances at his face. He looks tough, as if he could survive out in that desert with one small canteen of water for days. And yet his eyes are tender brown, reassuring.

'But I knew about Maya D'Costa, so it wasn't such a shock,' she says in a small voice. 'I knew that Daniel was cheating on me.'

Lopez says nothing. He just keeps gazing at her with his limitless eyes.

'Our marriage was over,' she admits.

They don't speak for a while. She fixes her eyes on his beer bottle, watches his slender finger trailing through the condensation.

'I've seen you watching me,' Special Agent Lopez finally says.

She doesn't know how to respond. She takes another gulp of beer, perches on the end of her stool. She is ready to flee upstairs.

'I watched you too,' he says. She can feel his gaze upon her. She raises her eyes to his. 'I call you the woman in the window.'

'The woman in the window?' She gives a little laugh. 'It makes me sound like a prostitute.'

'Oh no...' He smiles back, and it transforms his face. 'Untouchable behind the glass. Beautiful.'

He has called her beautiful.

'Well if I'm the woman in the window, you're the man in the mirror,' she whispers, as she looks into his eyes. There is no denying the message within them. She feels her chest tightening. What exactly is happening here?

'You looked the saddest woman in the world, the most lonely.'

'I was. I am lonely,' she whispers.

He gets up from his stool. He bends down and to Constance's utter astonishment he kisses her. Quickly but softly upon the lips.

'I'm sorry,' he says, stepping back, and shaking himself as if from a dream. 'I've been wanting to do that for weeks. I must be out of my mind...'

To her amazement Constance is not shocked. In fact, it feels so natural that Special Agent Lopez has just kissed her. As if she knew it was going to happen all along. For the first time since she moved to Arizona, she feels a wave of pure energy. She grabs his hands and pulls him to her. She kisses him back.

Something is happening inside her. It is as if all that fear banging around inside her heart all day long has gone. Just like that. She feels a parting of her heart. It is like curtains being drawn aside to reveal who she really is. She has been surrounded by death. But this is a kiss of life.

CHAPTER THIRTY-THREE

SIXTEEN YEARS BEFORE, 27 JULY 2002

Maya is lying on a sun lounger on South Beach, next to her new stepmother, Celeste, the antithesis of her chaotic and emotional mother. A quiet, contained woman, Celeste has hardly spoken to Maya. But that's okay, she doesn't want to have to talk to her, or have to look at her pregnant belly as it bulges in her swimming costume. Maya looks out to sea and watches her father trying to surf. He is making a mess of it. He doesn't have a surfer's physique. He's fine boned with slim legs, not suited to the challenges of the sport but of course he refuses to give up. He tumbles into the water again and again, yet seems delighted with himself.

'You should go try it,' Celeste says, getting up and stretching. Her stomach domes above her and Maya looks away in disgust.

'No thanks,' she says sourly, flipping over the pages of her book.

'Why did you come, if all you're going to do is sulk?' Celeste asks her. 'Your father is trying, Maya, and you should make an effort.'

'I'm here, on the beach, with you, aren't I?'

'But you refuse to do anything fun with your father,' Celeste says to her. 'Do you think he really wants to surf on his own? He got the boards for you to do it together.' She sighs, dusting sand off her legs. 'I guess you're just like your mother. Holding onto resentment. It's sad.'

Celeste waddles off down the beach, waving to her father, before wading into the sea. Fury curls through Maya's body. How dare she talk to her about her mother like that? Celeste has no idea what it's like for Maya. She still can't get the image out of her head of her mother crying when she waved goodbye to her at Heathrow airport. She can't have fun in Miami with her father when her mother is on the other side of the world devastated and betrayed. But Celeste doesn't care about anyone but herself. She's the interloper. She stole her father from her.

Maya flings her book down, and springs up from the sun lounger. The sky is a strange color as if the sun is already setting, or a red mist is rolling in from the sea. She begins to run down the beach to the ocean, her heart black with rage, propelling her forwards. She hates Celeste. Hates her. She wishes her dead.

She plunges into the ocean. Her father is a little way over to her left, and for a moment she is vaguely aware of him waving and calling to her, but then the red mist descends and it's as if she has tunnel vision. Celeste is bobbing in the ocean in front of her. She has the audacity to smile at her. All Maya wants to do is push her pretty head under the water.

'Maya! Maya!'

Her father's face looms in front of her. His black hair is thick with sea spray, and his eyes are red and streaming. He slaps her face, and she cries out.

'Come back, Maya, come back.'

She is on the beach, gasping. How did she get here? What

just happened? The sky is a clear blue again, and the sun beats down upon her, but she is cold. She hugs her knees to her chest; she can't stop shaking. Now she remembers her last thought, and she is almost paralyzed with horror. She looks frantically around and to her relief she sees Celeste sitting on the beach, a towel around her shoulders. She is staring at Maya as if she is a dangerous animal.

'What just happened?' her father asks her.

'It was only horseplay,' Celeste says, still staring at Maya.

'But you were so rough! Pushing her under the water and holding her there too long,' her father accuses Maya. 'Celeste is pregnant, what were you thinking of?'

Her father is furious with her.

'I'm sorry,' she stutters but she still can't remember what happened.

'It's okay, Antonio, we were just having fun,' Celeste says.

Maya and Celeste lock eyes, and her stepmother regards her warily. She realizes the woman is afraid of her. But she is only sixteen, she has no power.

CHAPTER THIRTY-FOUR

FOUR DAYS AFTER, SATURDAY 6 APRIL 2019

Constance reaches over and flicks off the light. No need to make a show for all the neighbors.

They make love in the kitchen. It seems appropriate to be having sex with Special Agent Lopez while looking out of her kitchen window. Catching sight of a star shooting across the sky, right over the roof of his house opposite.

It is as if her body has awoken from a deep slumber. She never imagined that being touched, just the stroking and kissing, would have such a dramatic effect. It is as if her head is being filled up by thick mist blanketing all reason, making her act without any thought at all. She is intoxicated by sensation. Lopez's lips against hers, the feeling of his lean, strong body pressed against hers. He is a lot taller than Daniel and she likes it. He makes her feel small and precious. She is no longer too tall and clumsy, but sultry and desirable.

He backs her to the kitchen table. She is in her robe, just a T-shirt on underneath. All he has to do is untie the belt. Pull the T-shirt over her head.

'You're gorgeous,' he says.

She bathes in his praise and it makes her forward. As they kiss, she fumbles with his belt.

'Are you sure this is okay?'

'Yes,' she says to him, thinking how bright the whites of his eyes are in the dark. 'I haven't been made love to in so long.'

His hands cup her breasts. He bends down and kisses each nipple.

'Your husband must have been crazy,' he says to her.

It flashes into her head for a second. Daniel is dead. She has known for only one day, and she is fucking another man. So much for the grieving widow.

'I guess he didn't want to be unfaithful to his mistress,' she says, unable to hide the bitterness in her voice.

'Hey, shush.' Lopez presses his fingers to her lips before he kisses her again. The heat in her belly grows. She feels a deep ache inside her. She has never wanted sex so badly in her life before.

They are on the dining table. All she sees is the face of the special agent above her. She doesn't close her eyes, not like she used to with Daniel, and nor does he. As Lopez pushes inside her, they hold each other in their gaze.

Trust me.

The first time Constance spoke to this man was yesterday. They are not even on first-name terms. Yet she has been watching him for months. It feels as if she has known him for that long. His touch doesn't feel like a stranger's.

Something is happening to her body. It is a feeling she has never encountered before. He is deeper and deeper inside her. She has given herself plenty of orgasms, but this is different. He is tipping her in a place that her husband had never reached. She can't help gasping with the pleasure of it. She has never before made any noise when she and Daniel had sex.

She releases a sigh from so far inside herself, she is shocked by the sound of it.

She feels herself catapult against Lopez. Her whole body liberated from its very core. A second later he moans as he comes too.

The two of them lie entwined on her dining table.

I'll never be able to eat on this again without thinking of Special Agent Lopez.

He is still wearing his night sky shirt. It is soft against her skin, and it makes her feel safe.

'What just happened here?' Lopez speaks first. He sounds dazed, and he looks it too as he cradles her in his arms.

'I think you went beyond the line of duty,' she jokes weakly.

Her heart feels so much lighter. It is all wrong. She should be mourning her dead husband, and yet she feels like laughing so hard. Letting all the pain, the loneliness, and the anger that has built up over the last few years out.

'You must think I am some kind of whore,' she says, her voice more serious.

He strokes a strand of hair from her face.

'Not at all,' he says. 'He was cheating on you, Constance.'

It feels wonderful for him to say her name with such tenderness.

'But I guess you know I shouldn't have taken advantage of your vulnerability.' He slides off the table and pulls off his shirt. 'Here,' he says, taking her by the hand, and putting the shirt on over her head. There is that clean citrus smell again. She never wants to take his shirt off. She sits with her legs hanging over the edge of the table, fingering the buttons on his shirt. Her body is still trembling inside.

'Do you want another beer?' he asks her.

She drops off the table. The soles of her bare feet are warm against the marble floor.

For the first time in her life, she feels in charge.

'No, let's go upstairs,' Constance says, holding out her hand to Special Agent Lopez. 'I want more.'

CHAPTER THIRTY-FIVE

FIVE DAYS AFTER, SUNDAY 7 APRIL 2019

Her darling Daniel. Gone forever. Maya tries not to think of his last moments as he fell. How long did it take to drop all those hundreds of feet? Seconds, or a whole minute? Was he screaming? Or did he pass out with fear? Did he pray for an angel to swoop down and save him?

Maya finds herself shaking Katarina awake.

'What did he look like?' she asks her in a panic. 'After he fell, how did he look?'

'What?' The other woman jolts upright in bed.

Katarina looks at her in horror. She is very pale in the face, her eyes wide with fright, as if it is she who has been bereaved rather than Maya.

'Tell me, I need to know, were his eyes open?'

'No.' She shakes her head, looking a little sick. She closes her eyes. 'I don't want to think about it.'

She lies back on the bed and rolls over. Her shoulders hunched. Maya isn't sure if she's sleeping, but it's clear she doesn't want to talk to her.

Maya raises herself up on her elbows, looks around the small, neat trailer. Her head is pounding. She is searching for something. Anything that might distract her. The trailer is extremely clean, and smells of winter pine. She can see that the park ranger doesn't own much. There is one bookshelf, with a few paperback thrillers on it, and a framed photograph of the park ranger with a man. He is tall and broad, with fair hair and wearing the same park ranger hat and uniform as her.

She gets up on shaky legs and opens the door of the trailer. It is early; she can smell it in the air. The sun has just risen, and the rocks are blushed with its honeyed glow. She takes a step out and sits down on the top step. She is still in her dress from the day before.

What is she doing here in this woman's trailer in the middle of the Grand Canyon? What exactly had she said last night? She's no memory after the third shot of tequila in the bar.

At least she hadn't got so drunk that she stripped naked and had sex with the park ranger. Katarina is the kind of woman that Maya would have been attracted to in the past, but she has been so ashamed of what she did with Joe. It hasn't made her feel any better. By fucking Joe, she has desecrated her love for Daniel. She is despicable.

Across the trailer park, a tiny hummingbird is feeding off the top of a blooming barrel cactus. The bird's breast shimmers jade and electric blue, such vibrancy as it dips its tongue into the bright pink petals. Most hummingbirds live for less than a year. Her and Daniel's love had lasted the span of a humming-bird's life. Hummingbirds never mate for life. That is why she has a tattoo of one on her shoulder. She never told Daniel why she had the tattoo done. It had been a pledge Maya had made to herself when she was eighteen. She would never marry and try to possess another person as her mother had. She would be a hummingbird. And yet, Daniel had turned all her convictions upside down. She had wanted him so badly. She had wanted him forever.

Maya had known that the day Cathy Garvey had turned up

at the gallery in Sedona. She had been about to close up, when Daniel's daughter had come charging into the gallery space. She had been dressed in black this time. Could not have looked more different from the mini-skirted siren she had seen in the Bird Cage Saloon in Prescott the week before.

Maya had been lost for words when she had seen Cathy Garvey. The girl had walked in a calm, menacing circle around the gallery. Maya had almost expected her to whip out a knife and start slashing her paintings, but instead she had walked right up to her so that she was literally a couple of feet away. Her wan face had looked even paler close up. It was like the finest porcelain. Maya had fought an urge to touch its delicate texture.

'So listen, you can tell my dad to back off,' Cathy had said to her.

'Look, do you want to sit down and talk?' Maya had asked the girl. 'Have a cup of coffee?'

Cathy had looked at her as if she had two heads.

'Are you serious?' she had said. 'Why the fuck would I want to sit down and have a chit chat with my father's mistress?'

'Well, you're here...' Maya had begun to say.

'I came here to warn you,' the girl hissed at her. 'If you don't tell my dad to stop trying to control my life, then I will tell my mom about what you two have been up to.'

'Go ahead. Do it,' Maya heard herself say.

It had been a relief to get it out in the open. She had been waiting for this moment for months.

Cathy Garvey looked taken aback at her words. She had not expected Maya to say that.

'I will, you know. And my dad will drop you as if you're toxic, and go back to my mom. Like he did before.'

Maya had felt a hot stab of panic in her heart. What did Cathy mean when she said, *Like he did before*?

'Oh you didn't know, did you?'

Maya's face must have given her away.

'You see Dad makes a habit of cheating on Mom. But he will never leave her for you,' Cathy had said, pointing her finger at her. 'He's weak. Pathetic. And you're just a slut.'

The girl looked at her in disgust. Maya tried her best to ignore the abuse, even feel compassion for Cathy Garvey, but she seemed so hard. It was clear that her father loved her. Couldn't she see that?

'Daniel is a good man,' Maya had said. 'He's trying to look after you.'

Cathy had given a sharp, bitter laugh.

'You don't know him at all,' she had said. 'He doesn't care about me.'

'That's not true,' Maya had tried again. 'He's worried for you.'

'Just tell my dad to leave me alone,' Cathy had said, slamming her hand on the gallery desk so that the visitor book went flying. 'You tell him to butt out of my business.'

Maya had seen Cathy's lips wobbling. She was trying to appear tougher than she really was. Maya could sense she was close to tears.

'Cathy, please listen to me,' Maya had said as gently as she could. 'That cowboy you're seeing. He's too old for you. He's married.'

Cathy had put her hands on her hips and stepped back. Her face a mask of scorn.

'Are you for real?' She had looked at Maya wide-eyed. '*He's married*,' she had mocked. 'I don't think you're the best person to give me any kind of moral advice, now do you?'

'But it's different for me and Daniel. You're so young,' Maya had tried. 'Your dad's upset that you have been taken advantage of.'

'I was not taken advantage of. Let's get that straight. I knew exactly what I was doing.'

Maya had shaken her head. 'He shouldn't have slept with you...'

'I was no virgin!' Cathy had said hotly. 'I lost that when I was fourteen in my bedroom in our house in Galway. All the while my parents were having yet another huge argument in the *next* room.'

She had picked up the pen from the visitors' book, twirled it between her fingers.

'I brought Darren O'Reilly home with me to *study* together. We were both under no illusions what that entailed.' She had given Maya a piercing look. 'My parents were in the house all the time, so caught up in their own stupid fighting that they didn't even notice I was having sex for the first time.'

Cathy's confession had not shocked Maya. In fact it had made her feel so sorry for the girl. She had wanted to tell Cathy she knew how she had felt, but she held her tongue.

'You know it was the day after I first saw you with Dad at the Desert Botanical Garden that I started sneaking out at night,' Cathy had said. 'So in a way, it's your fault.'

Cathy dropped the pen suddenly on the visitor book. It rolled off it and onto the gallery floor. Maya stooped down to pick it up.

'I was so angry at him,' Cathy had said above her.

'So you did it to get your father's attention?' Maya suggested gently.

'No that wasn't it,' Cathy had said. 'I was having fun. I could forget about my parents and all that shit. But now I've been dumped because of what Dad did.'

'You're better off—' Maya had begun to say.

Her words had sparked Cathy again. The girl had swept her hands across the gallery reception desk in one wide dramatic movement so that the visitor book tumbled to the floor along with the pen.

'Well let's see how *you* like being dumped? Shall we?'

Cathy had swept out of the gallery, her long black dress billowing behind her, and her red hair flying into Maya's face as she turned on her heel.

Maya had not followed her. She had stood quite still for several minutes, letting the contents of the conversation sink in before she picked everything up. Finally she and Daniel's daughter had been able to speak face to face. But it had been a disaster. She could never see that girl accepting her.

Maya had felt a little dizzy, sick all of a sudden, and had sat down on a stool, clutching the visitor book to her chest. Trying to steady her breath. She was in it deep. Right up to her neck. She had decided to hold off ringing Daniel to tell him what had just happened.

In fact she had never told him about Cathy coming into the gallery. Maybe she had known in her heart that what it would come down to for Daniel was a choice between her and his daughter. One she lost.

'Here, drink this.'

Maya hadn't heard Katarina get up. She hands Maya a tall glass of iced tea. She has filled it with fresh mint, and slices of lemon.

The park ranger joins her on the step, with her own glass of iced tea.

'There's Alka-Seltzer in it,' she says to her.

Maya gratefully takes a sip. They drink in silence. The bubbling concoction settles her stomach, clears her head slightly.

'What day is it?' she asks.

'Sunday,' the park ranger tells her.

The day Daniel planned to return to Ireland with his wife and daughter. Maya would never have seen him again, anyway. She feels a wave of darkness pass through her. She pushes it away.

'So you're married right?' she asks Katarina, looking at the gold band on the ring finger of her left hand.

Katarina nods.

'Yeah,' she says. 'He's a park ranger too.'

'So where was he last night?'

'He's away.' She pauses. 'He's coming back tomorrow.'

Maya takes another sip of her iced tea. She wonders why this woman is being so kind to her. Maybe it's because she's not white either. Though their heritage couldn't be more different. But does Park Ranger Nolan feel as much an outsider as Maya does sometimes?

'With Daniel, I never thought about the fact that he was white, and I am Indian,' Maya says. 'It was never an issue. And yet with his wife and his daughter, it's the first thing I can think of. They are white. They are privileged.'

Katarina nods.

'Shane's family were mad with him for marrying me,' she said. 'They didn't want their pure American son marrying a Hispanic mongrel.'

'And yet what is pure American?' Maya asks her.

'It should be Native American,' Katarina says. 'But they have the least say.'

Maya thinks of Special Agent Lopez and his Native American ancestry. How hard has it been for him to get to where he is now?

'So in the end Daniel Garvey chose his wife. And she's white,' Katarina says to her. 'But he loved you, right?'

Maya looks at the park ranger in shock.

'Did I tell you that?'

'Yeah, last night. You told me what happened at Shoshone Point,' Katarina tells her. 'Well, all that you could remember.'

Maya frowns. It's coming back to her now. That desperate pain when Daniel told her he was going back to Ireland.

'What does his wife look like?' Katarina asks her.

'I don't know,' Maya admits.

'You've never looked her up on Facebook?'

Maya shakes her head.

'I don't do Facebook, or any of that stuff.'

The park ranger takes out her phone, begins punching in letters.

'Okay, here we go, Constance Garvey. Ireland. Oh she hasn't changed her profile yet...'

Maya stands up suddenly.

'I don't want to see,' she says in a tight voice.

Katarina waves the phone in front of her. She looks away.

'Are you sure? She's only got five friends. Now that's sad,' the park ranger mocks. '*And* one of them is her daughter! Cathy Garvey. Bet she's a right little daddy's girl.'

'Yeah actually she is,' Maya says despite herself.

'Can't stand daddy's girls,' Katarina comments. 'Always wanting to be rescued by the big man. Don't like it when I drop out of the chopper in my harness!'

'I don't want to see,' Maya tells Katarina. 'Please put it away.'

'Okay.' The ranger gives her a sympathetic smile, tucking her phone back into her pocket. 'If it makes you feel any better, you are way more good looking than his wife.'

'Stop,' Maya says. 'Please.'

They sit in silence for a while. Although they are surrounded by other trailers, no one else is up yet. Maya listens to the sounds of the Grand Canyon. The distant waves of wind weaving through the rocks like the roar of the sea rushing onto a beach.

'You know, I was the other woman once.' Katarina breaks the silence. 'My husband was married to someone else before me.'

'So he left her for you?'

'Yes.'

'Does he have kids?'

'No.' She shakes her head. 'He's never wanted kids.'

Maya sighs. 'I never meant to fall in love with a married man.'

Katarina puts her hand on hers. Her gesture surprises her, but she likes it. She feels the warm comfort of it penetrating her skin.

'Nor did I,' she says. 'It happens.'

CHAPTER THIRTY-SIX

FIVE DAYS AFTER, SUNDAY

The sun has barely risen when Special Agent Lopez gets out of her bed. They must only have slept a couple of hours, and yet Constance feels as if she has had the best sleep of her life.

'Can I get you some coffee?' she asks him. Her body feels lazy, and full. She stretches her legs, and points her toes, watching Lopez's muscled back as he pulls on his shirt.

'Hey you should go back to sleep, darling. It's six.'

To hear him call her darling makes her feel giddy. She is like a teenager all over again.

'But where are you going so early?' she asks him.

'I have to go to work.'

'On a Sunday?'

'Yeah. They wanted me to live on site, like the other rangers, but I insisted I had my time off. My own place outside of the park.' He pulls on his jeans. 'Downside is I can't complain when I have to do long shifts.'

He gives her a serious look. 'We shouldn't have done this,' he says. 'It was very unprofessional of me...' He stumbles over his words. 'I'm sorry.'

She feels the blood rush to her face.

'Stop,' she begs him. 'Don't apologize. Don't ruin it.'

He sits on the bed, picks up her hand. He seems to be examining every one of her fingers.

'I want you to know that I don't usually behave like this,' he says. 'But it's different with you.'

He looks up at her. She feels her heart take a sudden lurch at the power in his gaze.

'I know,' she says. 'I feel the same way.'

'We have been watching each other for so long,' he says. 'What happened felt inevitable.'

She nods.

'I know.'

'But it's wrong in the circumstances,' he continues.

'It doesn't feel wrong.'

Special Agent Lopez says nothing. He cradles her face in his hands, and he kisses her on the lips. She feels faint from his touch. Liquid beneath his strong fingers. He pulls away and she can feel his resistance to leave her. It makes her feel magnificent.

'Okay,' Special Agent Lopez says. 'I have to go. You should try to sleep.'

'It's to do with the investigation into Daniel's death, isn't it?' she asks.

He shrugs, looks away from her.

'I can't talk to you about it,' he says. 'I'm sorry.'

A ray of morning sun bursts through the slats in the blinds flooding the room with golden light, yet Constance suddenly feels very cold indeed.

'I should never have slept with you,' he says again.

'Please don't say that.'

'I don't regret it,' he says, squeezing her hand. 'This is something special, isn't it?'

She nods, biting back her tears.

'Okay well, just hang in there,' he says, reaching forward

and stroking the side of her face with such tenderness it twists Constance's heart even further.

'I'll get to the bottom of things. This will be over soon.'

'Before you go, I have to show you something,' Constance says, leaning over and pulling open Daniel's nightstand drawer. She reaches in for the flight itinerary. As she does so, a tiny voice inside her head taunts her.

If your husband was still alive, you'd be on your way home to Ireland by now.

If your husband was still alive, you would never have had sex with Special Agent Lopez.

'Daniel bought tickets for the three of us to go back to Ireland. He was leaving Maya D'Costa.'

'Could it have been just for the Easter holidays?' Lopez asks her, taking the sheet of paper from her and looking at it.

'They're one-way tickets,' Constance says. 'I think he intended for us to go back home. For good.'

Lopez reads the flight itinerary. He looks up at her, his brown eyes pensive.

'But he worked for his brother, right? Did he know he was going home?'

'No, I don't think so.' Constance frowns.

'Okay, well these flight tickets look like he didn't intend to kill himself at least.'

'I keep telling you that Daniel wouldn't do that.' She takes a tight breath. 'Don't you see? Maya D'Costa got mad when she found out Daniel was returning to Ireland with his family.' She can feel her head pounding with the rightness of her theory. 'I mean she was the last person with him at the Grand Canyon. They had a fight when he told her. She pushed him and because of his vertigo he lost balance and he fell...'

She can hardly breathe she is so agitated.

'Maya D'Costa killed my husband. You have to arrest her!'

'Hey, calm down, okay.' Lopez reaches over and puts his

hands on her shoulders. 'I have Park Ranger Nolan going through all the surveillance footage available. In the car parks and at the Canyon View Information Plaza. We're also interviewing any witnesses who were on Shoshone Point that morning. If she did it, I'll find out.'

'There's CCTV footage?' Constance hears herself asking in a small voice.

After Lopez has left, Constance can't go back to sleep. The ghosts of their night of passion are fading, replaced by a tight knot of anger in her belly. What will Park Ranger Nolan find out? She just can't wait. She pulls back the covers, and hurries into the bathroom.

Constance stands under the jet from the shower. She turns it on full, blasting herself with its force. Her husband has been murdered. She knows that is the truth. Yet this morning she feels less like a victim than she has ever done in her life. She is filled with new determination. She knows that now, finally, she can face the mistress. Being with Special Agent Lopez has infused her with new strength.

She dresses in a hurry, filled with a sense of urgency. In the sideboard downstairs, she pulls out the painting. She will get rid of it once and for all. She will show Maya D'Costa that she is no fool. She will smash her sublime watercolor up in front of the conceited artist. Show her how it feels to have something you own, you create, destroyed.

She is in the kitchen, wrapping newspaper around the picture so that she doesn't have to look at it when she hears the front door opening in the hallway.

'Cathy, is that you?' she calls out. There is no answer, but she can hear voices.

A minute later Cathy appears in the kitchen, her Virginia Woolf tote bag slung on her shoulder, Lisa by her side.

Constance feels a blast of annoyance that Cathy's friend is with her. Can she do nothing without the girl?

'What are you doing, Mom?'

'None of your business,' she hears herself snap, quickly concealing the picture with the rest of the newspaper.

Cathy looks surprised at her sharp rebuttal.

'I was going to come and get you later,' Constance says to her. 'I didn't expect you up so early.'

'I couldn't sleep,' Cathy says. 'Lisa suggested we come over. Pick up some stuff.'

Constance looks at Lisa. The girl possesses the same knowing sea glass eyes as her mother.

'I want you to stay here,' she says emphatically. 'You can't spend all your time at Lisa's.'

'My mom said it's fine,' Lisa jumps in.

'I don't care,' she says, trying to control her anger. 'I want you to stay with me. I'm your mother.'

'You can't make me,' Cathy says, looking furious. 'I don't want to be in this house. I can't stand it!'

Her daughter makes to storm out the room. Constance grabs her arm, tries to pull her back in but Cathy pushes her away.

'You're still a child. You're my responsibility.'

'That's bullshit!' Cathy rounds on her. 'You know nothing about me.'

She could make her stay. She looks at Lisa for some kind of support, but the girl is staring at the kitchen floor, clearly mortified by the scene. What would Daniel think of this? How can it be that so soon after finding out about his death, she and Cathy are fighting? They should be supporting each other.

'Okay,' she says, defeated. 'Go over to Lisa's again if you must. But you better be here when I get back.'

She picks up the picture in its newspaper wrapping, makes for the door.

'Where are you going, Mom?' Cathy asks.

But Constance doesn't reply. She wants to tell her daughter she is going to fix things. Make everything all better. So they can start over fresh. But of course that is impossible. Her father is gone forever. And Constance knows who is to blame.

As Constance gets in her SUV, slipping the keys into the ignition, she remembers something Daniel once said to her. The memory of it makes her laugh out loud like she has gone mad. But her husband never did know her. Not really.

Daniel had told her that he wanted to marry her because she was soft-natured and kind. 'You're so nurturing,' he said as if it were a compliment. 'You'll stick by me.'

He was wrong. That had just been her outer face. The real Constance is far from nurturing. She is tough, and she wants vengeance. She is going to drive out to Luna House, batter the door with that loathsome painting. She is going to have Maya D'Costa up against the wall and she is going to make her confess to killing Daniel.

LISTEN TO ME

Sometimes you remind me of my father. He always used to say that small actions can have big consequences. He claimed that the fact I told my mother about what I had seen destroyed not just their marriage, but her. He claimed that I would ultimately become the death of her.

He laid it all on me. Just like you did.

My father said that it was me, not my mother, who drove him away. He said he couldn't take my judgement. He claimed that she accepted his needs as a man.

'You'll understand one day,' he told me. 'It's harder for a man than a woman to be faithful.'

He made a little laugh. I think he thought he was being funny. We were sharing a rare moment of fatherly advice.

'Men are weaker than women,' he said as if that excused his behavior.

So you see, you weren't even sorry about what you'd done. Not really. When you made out that I even drove you to it because you said I was so controlling. It reminded me of my father. Well I found it hard to forgive you. But I did the first time.

It was only after I caught you out a second time that I knew I couldn't take any more of your lies. I wasn't sure really how many times you might have deceived me. When I confronted you, I could see you thought you could get round me again. You even said I made you do it.

'You're so cold,' you accused me. 'You never talk to me.'

What did you expect?

I couldn't trust you.

You broke me, and you weren't even sorry. You never really tried to make it up to me. You hurt me so much. I was in agony. Really. I loved you so much. But I wanted the pain to stop.

In the end it was you who pushed me to do it.

CHAPTER THIRTY-SEVEN

FIVE DAYS AFTER, SUNDAY

Maya is on her way back home. It is early still, the sky tender with morning light. She lifts her hand off the steering wheel and smells the inside of her wrist. The scent of rose and sandalwood envelops her. Her heart is in smithereens but even so, she feels a tiny seed of peace has taken root.

The ceremony this morning helped. After she had left Park Ranger Katarina's trailer, she had walked along the South Rim of the Grand Canyon. She had intended to go back to Shoshone Point where Daniel had fallen but she couldn't do it. Instead, she took the path that they had taken the first time she had brought Daniel to the Grand Canyon to the watchtower at Navajo Point on the eastern edge of the South Rim.

It was so early in the morning that there were no other visitors, and she was able to climb the watchtower on her own. The views from the top were possibly the most sublime. She never stopped being stunned by it. She gazed at the undulating formations of rock, so brutal in their beauty, the distant Colorado River, and she wished with all her heart that she could fly. Soar above the Grand Canyon and be free yet again.

But her grief refused to let her go. She had delved into her bag and brought out a candle scented with rose and sandal-wood, placing it on the very edge of the watchtower wall. She lit it and focused on the tiny flame. She tried to find words to say her goodbye, but all she could do was cry. She heard voices below. Others were climbing up the watchtower. Hastily she blew out the candle. With the wax still warm in her hand, she threw it out as far as she could and watched it fall into the canyon.

Maya had felt Daniel again, right by her side. She could feel his breath on the back of her neck, his arms around her waist. He was swaying with her to the rhythm of her keening. He had been right. They would meet again in another lifetime. A love like theirs doesn't just end.

She feels better driving home. Katarina said to take one day at a time. Maya will get through today. She isn't so sure about tomorrow. But she has to keep on living.

She has a sudden urge to paint. That's what she will do when she gets home. She will lock herself in her studio and she will paint her love for Daniel on all her canvases. She will not stop until she literally drops with exhaustion.

To her dismay, when she pulls up at Luna House, Joe's old banger is back. Not only that, it is parked diagonally in front of the house, blocking the path. He is clearly stoned or drunk. She has had enough of him. She doesn't want Joe pulling her back into his world. She needs to be alone. She needs to hold this new peace she has attained close to her chest. She thinks about turning her jeep around and driving away again, but Joe is already out the door, waving to her.

'So, baby, where were you last night?' he asks her as he puts a plate heaped with scrambled eggs in front of her.

She picks up the chipotle bottle and splatters her eggs with the hot sauce.

'It's not really any of your business, Joe.'

She could have easily told him she was at Park Ranger Nolan's trailer, but she is annoyed to find Joe making himself at home in her house. He has clearly slept there, and cooked a huge breakfast. She isn't even hungry.

'Well that's mighty rude of you, specially since I made your eggs just how you like them.' Joe sits down opposite her with his plate of eggs. He gives her a little nudge as he does so. He is pretending to be light, but she can sense he is annoyed at her.

'I thought you left yesterday,' Maya says to him. 'You'd gone when I woke up.'

'I told you, had to go to the recording studio in Phoenix. I said I'd be back.'

She frowns. She has no memory of Joe telling her that, but then she'd really been out of it.

'It's good of you to look out for me, Joe,' she says. 'I appreciate it but—'

He has his fork heaped with eggs. He holds it mid-air staring at her.

'But what?' he interrupts her. If she doesn't know any better there is an edge to his voice.

'But I need to be on my own.'

'Why, Maya?'

She looks at him in astonishment.

'I need time alone to grieve Daniel's passing.'

Joe stares at her. He looks genuinely surprised by what she has just said.

'I told you to forget the married guy,' he says.

'I can't just forget him, Joe. I loved him.'

'If you loved him so much, why did you fuck me then?'

She feels slapped down by his words. She can't believe he has just said that. He clearly has no comprehension of what she's going through. Joe puts his fork down, leans across the table and picks up her hand.

'Baby, he was no good for you. And now he's gone for good.' He brings her hand up to his lips, kisses it. 'I'm here, right in front of you and I love you.'

There is an unpleasant whine to his voice.

'We're just friends,' Maya says in as calm a voice as she can manage. 'You know that.'

'No, baby, you're The One. You've always been The One.'

She pulls her hand away, completely thrown by his declaration.

'Joe, you've got it all wrong. I don't feel the same way.'

Just like that, he changes. A sudden snap. He picks up his plate and throws it across the table. It smashes against the wall behind her. She watches the scrambled eggs run down her kitchen wall in stunned silence.

'I love you!' Joe is yelling at her. 'How could you treat me like this?' He throws his coffee cup after the eggs. 'You're breaking my fucking heart!'

She stands up. She has to stay calm, but she can feel anger stoking up inside her belly.

'Get out, Joe. Get out right now!'

But instead of leaving, Joe comes towards her. She backs across the room, until she is flat against the wall. He towers over her.

'I know you love me too,' he shouts before lunging at her.

She tries to turn her face away, but his mouth grinds against hers, his teeth are biting her lips and she can taste blood. He is pinning her with his body. He is lanky, but all sinew. She tries to push against him.

'Come on, baby,' he says pulling back, as he tears at her dress, pushing his hand between her legs.

'Stop it, Joe, I don't want to.'

'Yes you do, I know you do.'

He is forcing himself on her. She feels herself catch fire. She is aflame with rage. She can't move her arms, but she kicks out with her legs hard, and knees him in the groin. He staggers back, bent over. How dare Joe make these assumptions. How dare he try to possess her, touch her, force her feelings. Her anger is out of control. This man is the enemy, and she wants to destroy him. Black waves of fury fill her mind, and her body acts instinctively. She picks up the frying pan and raises it above her head.

CHAPTER THIRTY-EIGHT

FIVE DAYS AFTER, SUNDAY

The painting is tucked underneath Constance's arm, wrapped in the old piece of newspaper. She can't bear to even take one peek at it. It is the picture her husband's lover had painted for her. She had adored that painting. It almost feels like the worst betrayal of all. As if Maya D'Costa was a best friend who slept with her husband. She never wants to see the dripping green of those gallery forests ever again.

She walks towards Luna House, her head held high. As she climbs the porch steps, she can hear raised voices. Her intention had been to knock on the door immediately but through the glass porch doors, she can see that man Joe again. The one who had called Maya D'Costa his girl. The last thing Constance wants is to have to talk to him as well. She crouches down behind one of the porch stairs, and spies on them. The man Joe is in the kitchen area shouting at Maya, and his face is red and angry. To her shock she sees him push Maya D'Costa up against the wall, and Maya is wriggling beneath him. Constance looks on in horror. She begins to get up. This is a woman under attack and she has to rescue her, but then she stops. This woman was also Daniel's mistress. Just this morning Constance told Special

Agent Lopez that she believes Maya D'Costa is responsible for Daniel's death. She wants her to suffer. What does she care about her?

During her moment of hesitation, Constance sees Maya kick the man Joe with surprising force from a woman so small. She knees him in the groin and he falls back. Constance watches transfixed as Maya D'Costa picks up a frying pan and raises it over her head. She is going to smash it over him. She is going to try to destroy this man.

Constance looks at Maya D'Costa's face and the sweet pixie girl has disappeared. She looks demented, her eyes black and merciless. However, the man Joe is on his feet now. He grabs Maya's hand, begins shaking it so that the frying pan falls, clanging to the floor. He knocks her down. Maya falls flat on her back. Constance sees him straddle her as she struggles beneath him. He is ripping at her clothes, forcing himself on her.

CHAPTER THIRTY-NINE

FIVE DAYS AFTER, SUNDAY

Maya is not giving up. Daniel is beside her, urging her on. *Fight him, Maya, don't let him do this to you.* She screams and she kicks. Luna House is too far away from any of the other cabins for her to be heard, and yet she yells with all her might.

Joe's weight bears down upon her.

'Stop making such a fuss,' he hisses at her. 'It's not as if we haven't done this a thousand times.'

'I don't want to,' she pants. 'Stop it, Joe.'

But he is laughing.

'No chance. Nothing like getting kicked in the nuts to turn you on.' His voice is grim all of a sudden. 'I'm going to make you come, baby, I'm going to make you beg for it.'

She feels his hand inside her panties. She squirms to be free.

Daniel, she cries inside her head. *Daniel, save me.*

'Get off her right now!'

Joe suddenly freezes on top of her.

'I said get off her!'

Joe slides off her, leaving Maya stranded on the floor. As he stands up, she sees a woman in her kitchen. She is pointing an old pistol at Joe.

'What the fuck are *you* doing here?' Joe says. He takes a step towards the stranger. 'Is that my gun?'

How does Joe know this woman? Moreover, since when did Joe have a gun?

'Yes, it is your gun,' the woman says. 'I found it in your car.'

'Well, lady, put it down for fuck's sake. We're just having a bit of fun here.'

'It didn't look like fun to me,' the woman says.

She isn't looking at Maya, as if she can't bear to. There's something about her voice. Something familiar. A certain lilt to the accent. She isn't American, that's for sure.

Maya pulls her dress down and stands up shakily. She licks her lips. There is blood on them.

'You do know who this mad bitch is don't you?' Joe says, though he doesn't turn around. Maya wants to scratch his eyes out. She wants this woman to shoot him she is so mad with him. She doesn't reply.

'It's the dead guy's wife, that's who it is.' Joe gives a short nervous laugh. 'So she just might shoot us both.'

Constant Constance.

Maya stares at the woman holding the gun in astonishment. Constance Garvey is not how she pictured her. She imagined that Daniel's wife would be plainer, older. This woman is none of those things. She is tall, with short fair hair, womanly curves, and sun-kissed skin.

'The cops are on their way,' Constance Garvey says. 'They'll be here any minute.'

Constance begins to rotate slowly on her heels. All of a sudden she swings the gun towards Maya. Her eyes are brilliant green and she looks at Maya with pure, undiluted hatred. Joe takes a step forward. Constance switches back and points the gun at him again.

'One of you is responsible for Daniel's death,' she says, her voice in high staccato, the gun now shaking in her hand. 'I want to know which one of you.' She takes a breath, steadies her voice. 'One of you has to confess.'

CHAPTER FORTY

FIVE DAYS AFTER, SUNDAY

Katerina feels her eyes dropping as she stares at the screen. She takes another slug of her coffee, makes herself sit up in her chair. She knows it's crucial that she goes through every scrap of surveillance and webcam footage meticulously. She has already seen images of Maya and Daniel at the information plaza.

Katarina is exhausted from the night before. It's not that she has a hangover. She had been very careful to not actually drink more than one shot of tequila with Maya D'Costa, but she had been forced to stay up for hours listening to the hippy girl going on and on about Daniel Garvey and how it had been true love. Who was she kidding? Katarina had held back so many times. She had wanted to shake some sense into the girl.

He's just another cheating husband, darling, she had wanted to tell her. *He would have discarded you as soon as he got bored with you.*

Why are so many women so naive? She bites her lips as she tries to concentrate on the grainy images in front of her. Katarina made sure she appeared sympathetic to Maya. But deep down she despised her. Maya D'Costa had tried to take another woman's man. Katarina had lied to her about her own life, just to get her to open up. There had been no ex-wife. She was Shane's one and only wife.

But at least she got her to talk about what she and Daniel had argued about. Maya more or less confessed to killing Daniel, although she couldn't remember what exactly had happened. But hopefully if she keeps combing through the surveillance footage, she'll find evidence to present to Special Agent Lopez.

It was clear that Maya D'Costa had an issue with the daughter. So Daniel Garvey planned to go back to the wife all along. Play happy families. What a farce! The damage had clearly already been done. The wife knew about the mistress. Moreover, according to Maya, so did the daughter. That girl was twisted already. Torn between her bitter parents. But Katarina doesn't feel sorry for Cathy Garvey. Her father had put her first. She had all the comfort and privileges that Katarina had never had as a child.

At last Maya D'Costa had collapsed on her bed. Although she was tiny, she seemed to take up the whole thing. Katarina had been unable to sleep. So she did what she always did when she couldn't sleep at night.

She got in her truck, and she drove out of the Grand Canyon. She drove into the dark night, and she pulled over in some random spot. She phoned Shane.

'Come back,' she begged, her voice cracking with despair. 'Please come back.'

But he would not answer her.

And after she'd done that, she started driving around again. She didn't stop driving until the sun was rising, and only then did she feel tiredness creeping into her bones. She headed back to the Grand Canyon, and their little trailer home.

.   .   .

Katarina drains her coffee mug. She is just about to get a refill, when she sees something quite unexpected on the traffic camera at the South Entrance Station. She presses pause. Rewinds the film. And plays it again. She zooms in.

Her heart begins to accelerate.

She reaches over for her laptop, to double check. Is she mistaken? There are so many doppelgangers out there. She does a search on Google, finds their Facebook page and stares at the profile picture then back again to the webcam footage.

It is her.

She looks at the time on the image.

Zooms in further. Takes a good look at the face again. There is no doubt in her mind.

She has her now.

CHAPTER FORTY-ONE

SIX DAYS AFTER, MONDAY

Constance looks out the window, across the backyards to her own house. So, this is how it looks from the other side. She can see the detail of her kitchen quite clearly. The pristine white wall cupboards, the pale blue walls, and the stainless-steel fridge. She sees the ghost of herself, looking out of the kitchen window, staring with longing into the big blue sky.

She presses her hands together. She can still feel the cold hard metal of the gun indented in her palms. She had wanted to shoot her.

Was it because she blames Maya D'Costa for her husband's death, or was it simply because she was the other woman? Could Constance have pulled the trigger? She had only ever held a gun once before. She had gone clay pigeon shooting in Ireland with Frances to celebrate her fortieth. She had been surprisingly good at it. Once she got the hang of the recoil. But those had been rifles. Yesterday, it was a pistol of some kind.

It had been one second of absolute eternity when Constance Garvey stood with her finger on the trigger, staring into the pleading eyes of Maya D'Costa. She had witnessed the fury that had ripped through that woman's body when the man

Joe had attacked her. Constance had detected what Maya D'Costa was capable of. The manic rage that possessed this young woman. The hard gun had been pressed into Constance's hot soft palm, her fingers sticky on the trigger. She possessed ultimate power. She could kill.

Constance had been aware of Joe taking a step toward her so she had turned the gun on him again. He stopped in his tracks. Right at that moment, the cops showed up, and she had snapped out of it. Dropped the gun in shock at the intention that had possessed her.

After she had made a statement with Deputy Peters, Constance called Cathy straight away. She had to call Cathy's phone twice before her daughter answered.

'Are you back home?' she had asked.

She didn't want to tell Cathy anything over the phone. She wasn't even sure what was going to happen now. Both Joe and Maya had been detained at Flagstaff Sheriff's Office, and Deputy Peters had showed up to interview them. Lopez hadn't been with her. Would Maya D'Costa be charged with Daniel's murder? If that's what it was.

'I'm in Phoenix, with Lisa and her mom. We're staying over.'

'What are you doing in Phoenix? I didn't say you could go.'

'It's my birthday weekend. I wanted to go.'

Constance tried to ignore the hurt. She'd suggested the day out in Phoenix for Cathy's birthday, and her daughter had rejected her. Picked Lisa, and cool mam Julie as her replacement.

'I need you to come home, Cathy.'

There was a sullen pause.

'Put me on to Lisa's mother.'

'No,' Cathy said, sounding panicked. 'Please, don't embarrass me.'

'But, Cathy, we should be together.'

'I'm not ready to come back. I don't want to face all the stuff on the net.' Cathy's voice cracked. 'I saw a paper. It had about Dad on the front of it. They said it looked like suicide.'

Constance's throat went dry. She had forgotten about all the media attention there would be over Daniel's death.

'It's not suicide, Cathy. Daddy didn't kill himself.'

'What do you mean?' Cathy's voice sounded harsh, angry.

'Look, love, we can't talk about this on the phone. I'll drive to Phoenix tonight. Pick you up.'

'No, no, please!' Cathy sounded desperate. 'Don't come. I don't want you to...'

'But, Cathy, I'm your mother. This isn't right.'

'I said don't come. I'll be back tomorrow. I just want to forget about it right now.'

'I need you with me,' Constance said in exasperation. 'I'm worried about you.'

'Just leave me alone.'

Her daughter didn't want her. Cathy was only sixteen but she sounded so grown up and in command of her own life.

She should have had another child. But Constance hadn't wanted to, had she? And now she had been abandoned by Daniel *and* Cathy.

Constance hadn't driven straight home from the Sheriff's Office. Instead, she had headed south, towards Phoenix. She was going to get Cathy back, whether her daughter liked it or not. But at Cottonwood she had changed her mind. Cathy had been so adamant. She had to get control of things again. Get Cathy on side. But much as she hated to admit it, after meeting Julie, she knew her daughter was in good hands.

Constance took a turn following the road that ran alongside the Verde River. At the bridge on the way to Camp Verde she pulled in and got out of her car. The sun was sinking, behind the willow trees on the other side of the water, as mist settled on the surface of the river. She walked through the high grasses, the cattails, and yellow wildflowers reminiscent of primroses back home. She needed to be by water. She would have preferred the sea, but she was far, far away from her beloved Atlantic Ocean. She crouched down and dipped her hand in the river. It was shockingly cold, considering the warmth of the spring day still lingering in the air.

She searched for that familiar feeling of her longing to be home. It wasn't there. She thought of their stone house by the sea, and the surf as it pounded on the beach. The memory felt like a fragment from another life. It dawned on her that she didn't want it back now. Unwillingly her mind turned to Special Agent Lopez. An image surfaced in her mind of the two of them in a dugout canoe gliding down the Verde River. He was taking her somewhere new. She wanted to go. She wasn't afraid.

By the time Constance got back to the house in Flagstaff it had been dark. She walked around the whole house, checking each room. Lopez had fixed the lock on Cathy's bedroom window, but she pulled on it to make sure. The incident at Maya D'Costa's house had unsettled her. If either Joe or Maya were released, might they come looking for her next?

On her way out of her daughter's room, Constance tripped over Cathy's Virginia Woolf book bag, spilling the contents all over the floor. She crouched down to scoop the stuff back into the bag. She had expected it to be full of books from the library, but to her surprise, there was just one book. It was a hardback edition of *Middlemarch* by George Eliot. It was as if her daughter had placed this big book on the top of the bag to conceal what lay beneath. Clothes. Nothing so unusual about that. But for Cathy these clothes were strange. Her daughter dressed entirely in black, and all the time. The clothes that had

spilled out of the bag were all the colors of the rainbow. Apart
from the red, purple, blue, and orange that surrounded her,
what disturbed Constance even more was the type of clothing.
Her daughter dressed in big T-shirts, jeans, and body-covering,
billowing shirts and long tunic dresses. These clothes looked
like they belonged to a Barbie doll. A tiny PVC mini skirt in
scarlet. Spiky pink stilettos. A bright blue silky camisole. Cut-
off denim shorts, and a tiny white T-shirt with a pink heart
printed on it. This was fashion that her daughter regularly
mocked. There was underwear too. A red lacy thong and a tiny
red satin bra. This stuff couldn't be Cathy's. It must belong to
Lisa and her daughter was looking after it for her friend. She'd
have to talk to Julie about it, or should she? Was this any of her
business at all?

As Constance was deliberating, something else caught her
eye in the seam of the book bag. A silver foil square, with the
word Trojan printed on it. She felt slammed in the chest. She
pulled it out, and examined the condom packet. Her heart was
accelerating in panic and fury. She tried to persuade herself that
all this stuff was Lisa's, but deep down she knew it must belong
to Cathy because why would she be carrying around Lisa's
condoms? What other secrets had her daughter been keeping
from her?

Constance laid the stuff out on Cathy's bed. That was it.
They were going to have it out as soon as she got her daughter
home. Her shock and concern turned to fury. She slammed the
room of the door and stormed downstairs to the kitchen. She
had been a big fool. Her husband had been behaving badly and
so had her daughter. All she had done was try to please them
both.

Constance poured herself a big glass of red wine. If she
didn't know who her husband had been or who her daughter
was anymore, well then who exactly was she?

She turned the light on by the window and stood looking

out at Special Agent Lopez's house. A light went on in his kitchen. She could see him standing at his porch doors, and she knew he was watching her too. His presence across the yard calmed her. She took in his height and breadth, and her stomach did a small flip. They stared at each other across their parched Arizona grass, his orange trees, and her swimming pool. The sky was jammed with stars. She felt their distant motion. The celestial fire and heat blazing in her heart. She finished her glass of wine, and rinsed it out, before turning it upside down on the draining board. She listened to her instincts, shut down her rational mind. She opened her back door, and locked it behind her.

At the old wooden fence, her view of Lopez was now blocked, but she knew he was waiting for her, in his house. She pushed against the wooden boards and two flipped up. She was glad now that Daniel had never fixed it. She crawled through the hole in the fence, and proceeded across Lopez's back yard. His orange trees were in full bloom, the scent enveloping her. She could see four orange orbs hanging in them. She reached up, shook a branch and an orange fell out of the tree.

He opened the porch door and she stepped through into his cool house. The light glowed over the stove. She felt bold for the first time in her life. She offered him the orange.

'Shall we share it?'

'Sure,' he said, watching her peel the orange.

He took the orange from her and bit into it, and then he kissed her. His mouth was full of sweetness and salt. All she wanted was this man. Her need was primal, and she could resist it no longer.

Constance has stayed the whole night in Lopez's bed. She is now standing at his bedroom window, in one of his shirts, and staring at her own house. Listening to the street stir, as her neighbors get up to go to work.

'Come back to bed,' Lopez calls to her.

He gets up and pulls her back and in next to him. She wraps her arms around his lean back. She wants to hide forever in Special Agent Lopez's bed. She dreads what this day will bring. Is Maya D'Costa going to be charged with Daniel's murder? And then there's Cathy. What has her daughter been up to? On top of it all, no doubt Liam and Stacey will be harassing Constance. At least Frances is due to arrive this evening.

She tries to push her worries away, focus on Lopez and the fact he is kissing her again, but just as she begins to let go, his phone rings.

'I'm sorry, I've got to take the call,' he says.

He gets out of bed, picks his jeans up off the floor and pulls his phone out.

'Lopez here.' He walks away from her to the other side of the room.

'Yeah. Okay go ahead.'

He turns to look at her, gives her a half smile before disappearing out of the room. Constance can hear him talking but not what he's saying. It must be something to do with Daniel, surely? She sneaks across the room, presses her head against the door but hears nothing but murmuring. He has gone downstairs.

She opens the bedroom door and surveys the landing. The house is smaller than their place. Lopez likes art too. Hanging on the wall over the stairs is a large Haida print, circular with strident lines in red and black. She can make out eyes, and a hooked beak. She takes a step closer. It's an eagle, she guesses, but it is split with two faces, and in its tail is a humanoid face. The whole image makes her tremble. It is so controlled within its geometry, yet brimming with raw vigor. She turns around and on the walls of the landing are a series of old sepia-toned photographs of Native American people. She looks at their faces and she feels such a deep sadness. They had their homes taken from them. They had been deceived, butchered, forced to live in reservations. She remembers her mother telling her that in 1847 the Choctaw people sent $170 to help the Irish during the potato famine. It was such a powerful gesture of solidarity. Lopez told her that he is Navajo and had grown up in the Grand Canyon, although he'd been away for years. She knows so little about his heritage, she feels unworthy of him, but she is drunk on their lovemaking. Having lived without sex for so long, she craves it now, endlessly.

She is a complete idiot. Her husband has just been killed. Moreover, the man she is sleeping with is investigating his death. She needs to sober up and think of her daughter. She needs to gather up her dignity.

She scurries back into the bedroom, tearing off Lopez's shirt and pulling on her dress. Just as she is doing up the last button, Lopez comes back into the room. He is still holding the phone in his hand. He takes her in, dressed, hunting around for her sandals.

'Are you leaving?' He is giving her a strange look. She stops what she is doing.

'What's happened?'

He looks so stern that she knows it is something serious. Her heart is fluttering with anticipation. 'Has Maya D'Costa been charged?'

The conversation is surreal. A few days ago, she was an ordinary Irish housewife, living in suburban America. Today she is the widow of a murder victim. And she has a lover. But Lopez really is looking at her funny. Her heart is hammering inside her chest.

'No,' he said. 'I was talking to Park Ranger Nolan. She's been going through all the surveillance footage.'

Constance looks into Lopez's eyes. A few hours ago they had been full of desire for her, but now it is as if he has shuttered his feelings. A cold chill snakes down her back; dread mushrooms in the pit of her belly.

'Maya D'Costa was seen leaving in her vehicle. After she left, your husband was spotted by witnesses at Shoshone Point.'

'What about the man Joe? Did he do it? Kill Daniel because he wanted Maya D'Costa for himself?'

'No,' Lopez says. 'I checked him out last night. He has an alibi. He was in Austin, in Texas when Daniel fell off the Grand Canyon.'

Constance takes a step back. Why had Lopez not told her that last night? Her mouth is dry.

'Constance, why didn't you tell me that you were at the Grand Canyon the day your husband disappeared?'

Suddenly the whole world goes quite still. She can feel a rare rush of blood to her cheeks.

'It didn't seem so important...' she begins to say.

'Of course it's important.' He looks at her in astonishment. 'You were there, in the Grand Canyon. There's an image of you on the traffic camera at the South Entrance Station. What were you doing there? Why didn't you tell me?'

She looks down at her bare feet. Her nail varnish is chipped. She doesn't like the color anyway. It is whore red.

'I was embarrassed,' she says in a small voice.

He says nothing. She feels his presence towering over her.

'I was following Daniel. I don't know why, I mean I knew all about them and I did nothing, said nothing...' Her voice peters out.

She is pathetic. All her strength seeps away. She is the stalking, jealous wife. That's who Lopez sees now.

He takes a breath.

'What happened?'

'I went home. I followed Daniel to the Grand Canyon, but I

lost him as soon as I got to the car park.' She steals a look at Lopez. He is frowning at her.

'I walked around for a bit, feeling like a fool. And then I drove home. I didn't see Daniel again, I promise. I never even saw Maya D'Costa. I had no idea they went to Shoshone Point. I'm sorry, I should have said...'

'Do you not realize what you've done?' he says to her. 'Park Ranger Nolan saw you on the footage. She's sending the material to Deputy Peters. You *lied* to her.'

Constance looks in horror at Lopez.

'Furthermore, she's uncovered that you had flights booked for you and Cathy for tomorrow. Don't you see you're under suspicion now?'

'But I booked those flights ages ago, I was planning to leave Daniel, but I didn't do anything,' she says, though even as she says it, she knows she must look guilty.

'In cases like this, usually it's the wronged spouse who is the prime suspect,' Lopez says in a formal tone. He looks furious. 'You had motive. You were there.'

'But you saw the tickets Daniel booked for Ireland. Daniel wasn't going to leave me. He was taking us back home.'

Constance begins to shake as the position she is in dawns on her.

'Besides, it's not even certain that someone killed him,' she says tearfully.

She is terrified. Only last week she read the case of a woman on death row in Arizona for twenty years. Accused of killing her child, when all along she had been innocent.

'I didn't do anything, Matt,' she pleads with him.

'Hey, I know,' he says, his tone softening. 'Of course you didn't.'

He tugs his hand through his hair. She can see a lone white strand in the darkest black. 'But I'm compromised now. We shouldn't see each other.'

'Of course.' She nods, wiping away her tears with the back of her hand. She is even more frightened now. Lopez believes her. She needs him on her side. 'I don't think Deputy Peters likes me.'

'That's just her way. No one thinks that Peters likes them.'

Lopez gives her a rueful smile.

Her thoughts bounce around crazily. 'I'm scared.' She starts shaking all over. 'I mean who broke into my house the other night?'

He pulls her into his arms, holds her tight. 'It's going to be okay. I promise.'

He kisses her on the lips.

'I don't know why Peters is being so insistent anyway,' Lopez says. 'To me what happened to your husband really does look like a terrible accident.'

He kisses her again. His touch soothes her. She finds herself kissing him back again.

'We shouldn't do this,' she whispers.

'I know,' he says, backing her all the way to the bed.

She pulls him to her. To be with this man feels like the most essential thing right now.

Special Agent Lopez will save her. She trusts him.

CHAPTER FORTY-TWO

SIX DAYS AFTER, MONDAY

Disappointed by Special Agent Lopez's reaction to her discovery, Katarina sits at the little table in her trailer, staring out its small back window. She looks at the ribbon of sky above the rocks. At a raven that is sweeping with vigor in the currents of the canyon wind. Her eyes ache from looking at a screen for so long.

She is tired. Exhausted.

Katarina has spent the past twelve hours trawling through surveillance footage. She was the one who spotted the wife driving through the entrance of the South Rim of the Grand Canyon.

Yet when she rang Special Agent Lopez with the information, he hadn't even thanked her, or praised her for great detective work. Indeed, he kept questioning her.

'Are you sure it was her, Ranger Nolan?'

'Yes, of course, I sent the information to Deputy Peters, and she's checked the car registration.'

'The Sheriff's Office knows?'

'Yes, I rang Peters straight away. They're taking a more serious look at the possibility the death was suspicious.'

'Great,' Lopez said, but didn't sound like it was great. In fact, he sounded pissed off.

She was going to tell him about what she had found as well. But something made her hold back. If she did tell him, she was really going to get pulled into this investigation. And she wasn't sure that she wanted to stick around.

Katarina is beginning to feel confused about what is right and what is wrong.

Maya D'Costa told her that she had no memory of the last moments she spent with Daniel Garvey, and that she's frightened she might have killed him. But Katarina knows the mistress is innocent. She had been witnessed leaving the park before there was the last sighting of Daniel Garvey at Shoshone Point.

Katarina would have liked to have blamed the irresponsible hippy girl. She despises Maya's sense of entitlement. Her privilege. They might both have dark skin, but they could not have been from two more different backgrounds. Maya D'Costa is the kind of woman that goes sailing through life wrecking marriages, and breaking hearts all under the banner of a free spirit. Katarina calls it selfishness.

These are the worst kind of women. There are so many of them out there, willing to steal other women's men away.

She puts her hand in her pocket and fingers the small metal object. She feels the contours of the tiny silver pendant. Pushes the links in the chain into the soft pads of her fingertips. She pulls the necklace out, and holds it dangling in the dusty light that fills her trailer. It is a plain silver chain, with a silver letter hanging off the end of it. It is a C.

Katarina could present this to Special Agent Lopez as a crucial piece of evidence, found under a small ledge of rock on Shoshone Point. How could he have missed it? But Katarina would tell him that she had seen it shimmering in the sunlight when she had gone back on her own. Checked yet again for signs of what might have happened to the Irishman. This pendant is identifying, is it not? C for Constance.

It proves that the wife has lied all along. Constance Garvey must have been with her husband moments before he fell into the Grand Canyon. Did she actually push him?

CHAPTER FORTY-THREE

SIX DAYS AFTER, MONDAY

Back at Luna House, Maya hears a low rumble. She opens her eyes to see a flash of lightning in the distance. The sky is loaded with dark thunder clouds. She rubs her eyes; they always itch before a storm. Again, a rumble of thunder, this time much louder. The storm is approaching. A flash of lightning and the rain is released. It comes down in a torrent, battering the porch.

She pulls open the porch door and goes outside. Collects up all the cushions and brings them in. She watches the rain for a moment. She loves the sudden violence of these rare Arizona rainstorms. She runs back outside again, and down the steps of the porch. She lets the rain wash over her. Drenching her clothes and pouring down her face. She wants to be cleansed of all this darkness.

She doesn't understand the violence of humanity. Her mother believes in evil. But Maya has never let herself think such a thing. People do bad things because they are damaged. So what had made Joe want to hurt her? How had he been damaged? She knows the reason that Cathy abused her that time in the gallery was because she had been damaged by her parents' unhappy marriage. She had fixated on Maya because she needed to blame someone. Maya had tried to explain to Daniel that he wasn't helping his daughter by keeping his family together. He was destroying her.

And what about Constance Garvey? Is Daniel's wife so damaged that she wanted to kill her husband, rather than let him go?

Maya spins in a circle. The dry dirt in her back yard turning to mud within moments. She pushes her toes into its thick warmth, and listens to the creek as it swells and rushes down the canyon. The rain roars like a lion, and she roars back. She is angry about what has been taken from her. Her father. And Daniel. She is not giving up anything else.

The rain stops as suddenly as it came. Everything shines around her with new fresh sunshine as if it has been washed clean. She makes her way back up the porch and that is when she sees it. Lying on its side, the glass and frame broken. She bends down and picks it up. The rain has destroyed the painting, but she recognizes it as one of her own. She can see the faint tracings of pencil marks as the layers of green paint run into each other. It is her painting. The picture that Daniel had bought for his wife all those months ago. So, that was why she had come to the house last night. Constance Garvey had wanted closure, not to kill her.

CHAPTER FORTY-FOUR

SIX DAYS AFTER, MONDAY

Constance feels more alive today than she has ever felt her whole life. It is as if this whole time in Arizona, in her heart she had been living in her stone house in Galway. She had placed herself inside her own prison.

Though the threat of what might happen now frightens her, at the same time it exhilarates her. Special Agent Lopez will prove her innocent. She is sure of it because of what has happened between them. It is more than a fling. It means something. Constance has flung wide open the window of her life. She is not looking out, watching others living. She is part of life at last. She is a protagonist, no longer a voyeur.

She walks briskly away from Special Agent Lopez's place, down his street and round the corner to her own house. He has already driven off. He is going to talk to Deputy Peters. See where they are at with the investigation.

'Come out to the Grand Canyon this afternoon as soon as you're ready,' he said.

'I have to pick up Cathy.'

'Do that first, then come on over. We need to take your

statement. I'm sure plenty of witnesses saw you leave when you said you did.'

He squeezes her hand before pulling her into an embrace and kissing her.

'Don't worry, Constance. I've got your back.'

She trusts Special Agent Lopez, even though a week ago he was merely a stranger that she watched from her kitchen window. Today, she is sure of his protection.

Be careful, Constance. He could be playing a game with you, a voice warns inside her head.

Constance's phone rings just as she is opening her front door. Cathy. She is surprised that her daughter is the first to make contact.

'Can you come and get me?'

Constance is suddenly reminded of her daughter's wardrobe of slutty clothes. She had tipped them all over her bed the day before. She bites back the temptation to launch into an inquisition. It is better to have that talk face to face.

'Of course. Are you back from Phoenix already?'

'Yeah, we got up early.'

'Okay well, I'm just having a shower, and then I'll come.'

'Mom?'

'Yes?'

'I'm sorry.'

Her daughter's words surprise her. Tears spring in her eyes. There is hope at last, that she can bring her daughter back to her.

'Hey, love, there's no need to be sorry. I'll be over soon as I can.'

In the shower, Constance turns the jet on full. The water pummels her back, reminds her of Lopez's hands massaging her shoulders.

She puts on a dress. It is for Lopez, of course. A blue silky dress, with a plunging neckline. She has never worn it before because she always felt too fat for it. Now she feels sultry. The dress hangs off her perfectly.

Constance is at the top of the stairs, about to leave, when she remembers Cathy's bedroom. She retraces her steps and crosses the landing into Cathy's room. Her daughter's trampy wardrobe and the packet of condoms are still spread out on the bed as if they are on exhibition. Waiting for the fight she is going to have with her. She can't help thinking how devastated Daniel would be to find out what Cathy might have been up to all those times she had told them she was in the library studying. At least he was spared that. She can't bear to look at the awful clothes on display any longer and pushes them all back into the bag before hurling it into a corner of the room.

On her way to Lisa's house, Constance's phone rings. She pulls in, but it has already gone to voicemail.

'*Hello this is Park Ranger Nolan. Special Agent Lopez asked me to call you. We have some new information for you. Can you please meet us at the car park at Shoshone Point?*'

Constance tries calling the number back, but it rings out. She calls Lopez's number but it's busy.

'Hi, Matt, I'm on my way, but why do you want me to meet you where Daniel fell?' She pauses. Licks her lips. 'Call me.'

She doesn't want to go back to the scene of Daniel's end. What new information is Park Ranger Nolan talking about? Maybe it's a good thing. Evidence that puts her in the clear once and for all. She feels a flutter of nerves. Park Ranger Nolan is the one who had found Daniel. Maybe she somehow knows the truth.

CHAPTER FORTY-FIVE

SIX DAYS AFTER, MONDAY

Katarina spins the silver necklace in her trailer. She watches the light reflections bouncing off the faded yellow walls. It strikes her that she really hates this trailer. It is nothing like a home. With Shane it had been their love nest, but on her own, it has become more like a cage. She longs to return to the plains and forests of Montana. Away from everyone.

Lopez doesn't believe her. In fact, there is something altogether off about Special Agent Lopez. It is suddenly quite clear to Katarina that he has no interest in her, or in helping her to advance her career in the park service. As soon as she realizes this, something snaps inside her. She is done. She loved the Grand Canyon but she misses her husband more. She is done waiting for Shane to come back. She is going to go to him. She has made up her mind, and she isn't going to change it.

But before she leaves, she has to set things right. That is why she contacted Constance Garvey and asked her to meet her at Shoshone Point where Daniel Garvey had fallen. It is time to hear her confession.

She's not sure how she will manage this, but she does have faith in her ability to get to the truth of the whole tragic business. It is a risk. Sure. But Katarina feels she has nothing left to lose.

As she stands up, she hears a clap of thunder. The sky fills with storm clouds to the darkest shade of gray possible. She can smell the power of the storm approaching and it makes her fidgety and excited. She pulls open the knife drawer and takes out her pistol. Strapping on her gun belt, before putting on a waterproof over the top. The sky cracks and roars across the roof of her trailer, as a jagged splinter of electric light splits the sky above the canyon. She pushes open the door of the trailer and steps out into the first downpour. She lifts her face to the sky and breathes in. Lets the water baptize her. She is calm now. Ready. Soon she will be with Shane, and she can forget about the Garveys and Maya D'Costa forever. A part of her will always be in the Grand Canyon. And yet she is content to leave it all behind. Nothing is worth more than true love.

CHAPTER FORTY-SIX

SIX DAYS AFTER, MONDAY

Maya puts her hands on her stomach, pushes down with her palms. Feels a stirring within her. She is filled with such longing, and such regret.

The reason she had fallen in love with Daniel was precisely the reason their affair had been doomed.

He was a good father. He put his daughter first.

After the incident in the Bird Cage Saloon in Prescott, he had talked about his concerns over Cathy several times.

'We used to be so close,' he had said. 'She looked up to me.'

'What happened?' she had probed.

He shook his head.

'I don't know,' he said. 'I guess she grew up.'

'It might not look like it, but Cathy does need you, Daniel,' Maya had tried to reassure him.

It had only been a few days before that conversation that Cathy had stormed into the gallery in Sedona, demanding that Maya tell Daniel to 'butt out of her business.'

'We used to have such fun,' Daniel told Maya. 'She was a real tomboy when she was younger. We'd go to Gaelic football matches together.'

He had picked up Maya's hand, laced his fingers through hers.

'I remember when we went to Majorca, we had such an adventure,' Daniel said to her, his eyes shining with the memory. 'Constance got some kind of food poisoning so it was just me and Cathy. We decided to go exploring. So we took off on a magical mystery tour of the island.' He smiled. 'That's what we called it. We were like two mates, not a father and daughter. Taking buses all over the island. We got lost. By the time we got back to the apartment, Constance was in a complete lather.'

Maya tried to picture it. The family on their holidays in Majorca. Daniel and Cathy, a little girl then, hanging onto her daddy all day. She would have had his complete attention. Maya had been surprised by a twinge of jealousy.

'We never told Constance how we ended up in some stranger's house having dinner with them in the middle of nowhere. And they drove us all the way back to the resort. She would have gone spare.'

Daniel had asked Maya where he had gone wrong with Cathy. Despite the fact that he had warned that cowboy off, he had not stopped Cathy from behaving badly.

'She wants your attention,' Maya had told him.

'Well she has it now!' he had said angrily, raging around her cabin, shattering the serenity of their love nest.

Now, Maya is listening to Eva Cassidy singing 'Over the Rainbow'. It is her favorite Eva Cassidy track. She turns on her side. Imagines Daniel facing her. She summons his face to her. Those jewel blue eyes, the faint blush to his face when he touched her. She wants to feel him making love to her, but Daniel is talking to her now. He keeps asking her again and again.

Who pushed me, Maya?

Who took me away from you?

Who?

Without warning, a face flashes in her head. Maya sits bolt upright in bed. She blinks. The face is still there. Crystal clear in her mind. Frozen in time. The cold eyes. A soul with no morals.

Maya re-traces the last few days, collecting all the visual fragments together. She begins to tremble with comprehension. Someone *had* been watching her and Daniel. That person had followed them all the way to Shoshone Point.

She had passed them on her way back to the car park. Sure, she had been running, almost blind with fury, and she had averted her head. But still Maya had seen enough.

If Daniel had been pushed off the edge of the Grand Canyon, Maya knows who did it. She can't quite believe it. But her instincts are screaming at her that she is right.

CHAPTER FORTY-SEVEN

SIX DAYS AFTER, MONDAY

Watching her daughter get into the car, Constance feels nervous of her own child yet again. She had tried to lay down the law yesterday, but it hadn't worked. Cathy had done exactly what she had wanted to, irrespective of her mother's wishes. Constance is afraid that if she pushes too hard, she might lose her for good.

Their last phone conversation had given her hope. Cathy had said sorry, but Constance knows instinctively she should tread carefully.

Her daughter pulls her seat belt across her slender frame.

'Are you okay?' Constance asks her.

Cathy nods. But she looks so tired. Constance feels sudden shock at her appearance. How has she not noticed just how wan her daughter has become?

'I have to drive out to the Grand Canyon, to go over some details with the authorities,' Constance says.

She is not ready yet to tell her daughter that she had been at the Grand Canyon the day her father died. She can't face the questions from her. The humiliating admission that she was stalking him and his mistress.

'I want to come with you. It's the last place Dad was,' Cathy says.

It gives Constance a sudden pain in her chest to think of Daniel. Her errant husband. He had cheated on her in their old life in Ireland, and he had cheated on her in their new life in Arizona. But she can't hate him for it. In fact, she forgives him. And if she can forgive her husband, she has to forgive Maya D'Costa too. It is a bitter pill to swallow. Her husband had chosen a younger, more beautiful woman than her. But what hurt her the most is that Maya D'Costa is an artist. She is successful and talented, in a world that Constance secretly desires to be a part of. But Constance had never been good enough.

Still, she will not pollute Cathy against her father, especially now he is dead.

They drive north. Cathy puts on some music. A girl's voice. Ethereal, with a lightness to it that lifts Constance's mood. She is singing about running with the wolves. It makes Constance want to drive even faster. She imagines herself and Cathy as part of a pack. Not driving, but running forwards, towards the wilderness of the Grand Canyon. The answers to their lives.

'Whose music is it?' she asks her daughter.

'Aurora. She's Norwegian,' Cathy answers.

Despite the fact it isn't even noon, Constance feels as if she is driving into the night. The sky is heavy and brooding, loaded with storm clouds. There is a line of white between the vast desert horizon and the black sky. She sees a fork of lightning in the distance.

'Can you see the lightning?' Cathy asks her. 'It's getting closer.'

Constance grips her hands around the steering wheel and when the heavens open, she doesn't even pull over. Thunder crashes overhead, and they are deluged by rain. The sound of it drowning out Aurora's singing. It is as violent as it is sudden, almost blinding her, but she keeps on driving. She is exhilarated by the storm. She has missed rain so much.

'Mom, pull over,' Cathy asks, sounding subdued.

'It's fine,' she assures her, but when she glances at her daughter, she is curled up in the passenger seat, her face white and stricken.

'I can't stop, Cathy. There's nowhere to pull in here.'

A jagged flash of lightning. She counts under her breath. A roll of thunder but it is more distant now. She can sense the rain abating. She drives on, her heart throbbing.

She glances at Cathy again. She looks so lost. So young. What has happened to her little girl? So full of secrets. She has to try to reach her. She leans over and turns the music down.

'Cathy, if you open up my bag, you'll find a black box,' Constance tells Cathy. 'It's your birthday present.'

She takes another sideways look as Cathy pulls out the box. With her eyes back on the road, slippery and washed out by torrents of storm water, she hears her daughter's pained gasp.

'Oh Mom!' she says. 'I love it.'

'Your father chose it for you. He bought it before...'

Constance can't continue. She can feel her whole mouth wobbling, her eyes filling with tears again. She bites her lip. Tries to concentrate on the road swimming in front of her.

Cathy says nothing, but Constance hears her sniffing. When she looks again, her daughter is crying. Quietly. Tears streaming down her face as she clutches the little blue hummingbird necklace.

Now Constance pulls in off the highway. The sky is clearing. The last traces of storm dissipating in the high dry desert air.

'I'm sorry, love. That was badly done, I should have prepared you.'

'It's okay, Mom,' Cathy says, wiping her eyes with the back of her arm. 'I just feel so guilty. I was horrible to Dad.'

'He knew you loved him, Cathy.'

'He was always buying me necklaces,' Cathy says, looking a little less upset.

'Yes, that was his thing, wasn't it, darling?'

'I still have them all. Every single one.'

'I know,' Constance says, reaching across, and taking the hummingbird necklace out of Cathy's hand.

'Come on, let me put it on you.'

Her daughter twists in her seat, and Constance slips the pendant around her slender neck. Cathy faces her again. The blue hummingbird is the same shade as Cathy's eyes.

'It suits you,' Constance says, looking away, and blinking back tears. 'You know, your father was planning on bringing us back to Ireland.'

'For Easter?'

'I think for good, Cathy. I found one-way tickets in his bedroom drawer.' Constance looks Cathy in the eyes. Her daughter has gone a little pale again. 'Have you any idea why he would do that? I thought he loved Arizona.'

'No,' Cathy says, blinking at her. Her voice is tight and high.

An instinct stirs inside Constance. Her daughter is lying.

'Are you sure you've no idea why he did that, Cathy?' she pushes.

Cathy shakes her head, but she won't meet her eyes.

'Last night, I was in your room, and I knocked over your book bag.' Constance tries to keep her voice calm, and gentle. Cathy jerks up her head. 'Those clothes, Cathy. When do you wear them?'

'They're not mine,' Cathy says.

'But whose are they? Are they Lisa's?' she asks incredulously.

As much as she cannot picture her own daughter in the skimpy prostitute clothes, she cannot imagine Lisa, with her baggy hoodies and boyfriend jeans, in them either.

'It's none of your business,' Cathy snaps.

'But why do you have them...' she tries to push.

'I told you. They're not mine,' Cathy insists.

'Well who do they belong to then?'

Cathy doesn't reply. Constance stares out the windscreen at the wet road ahead. It looks like a long streak of brilliant black in the new sunlight.

'I found condoms too.' She takes a breath. 'Cathy, what's going on?'

But her daughter won't answer her. She crosses her arms, and stares out the passenger side of the car, the back of her head turned to her.

'Just drive, Mom,' Cathy says. Her voice sounds strangled.

'Please, Cathy, talk to me.'

'Not now.' Her daughter turns up the music again.

She wants to switch it off. Scream at Cathy to tell her the truth, but instead Constance starts up the engine again. Breathing out slow and steady, she takes off towards the Grand Canyon. The voice of Aurora fills the car with just one word: *Home*.

She wishes more than ever that she and Cathy could be home again. Together. A week ago, Constance believed she was going to bring them back home to Ireland. But now there is the question of a suspicious death. And now there is Special Agent Lopez. She doesn't want to let him go. Not yet.

As Constance drives the long straight road through the desert, it feels as if she and Cathy are the only people in movement. There are no other cars, no buildings. There is no sign of the storm that has just passed. The rocky land looks as parched as before, the cardboard cut-out cacti appearing freeze-framed like a scene from an old Western. It is her and her daughter. Driving. Amid scrubland and desert rocks, upon the black road with the yellow line down the middle. And yet they are exactly where they are meant to be.

The car park at Shoshone Point is empty. It has taken Constance a while to find it, driving up and down Desert View until she saw the unmarked turn-off. As she pulls in she can see Park Ranger Nolan leaning against her truck on the other side of the car park. The ranger has her back to her, and she seems to be staring at the trail before them, and a sparse pine forest. There is no sign of Special Agent Lopez. Maybe the storm has delayed him.

She wishes that they were not the only vehicles here. As she switches off the engine she has a strange sense of foreboding. It is ridiculous. Other hikers are bound to turn up any minute. She is in one of the most popular tourist attractions in the whole world. And yet not even its popularity can tame the Grand Canyon. It is at its heart pure wilderness.

Constance looks down at her hands. She realizes that her nails are digging into the leather of the steering wheel. She isn't sure she wants to get out of the car.

Where is Lopez? He is from this place too. He has more right to be here than her, or Daniel or Maya D'Costa. His vast Navajo reservation is state-sized. How does Matt feel here, in the Grand Canyon? Does he feel like he belongs here, as she feels she belongs on the west coast of Ireland?

'Can I come with you?'

Constance had almost forgotten Cathy is still in the car beside her, she has been so quiet.

'No,' Constance says too quickly. She doesn't want Special Agent Lopez questioning her daughter. Not yet. She needs to tell Cathy herself about why she followed Daniel to the Grand Canyon.

'I'll talk to the park ranger, and then I'll come back.' She takes a deep breath. 'We'll go to the place where your daddy fell. Together. Say a prayer for him. Okay?'

'Okay,' Cathy says, her eyes bright, her expression solemn. 'Can I borrow your phone, my battery's gone.'

'Well I might need it...'

'Please, I want to send Lisa a picture of the necklace Daddy gave me.'

'Okay,' she says, handing the phone over.

As she gets out of the car, Constance turns to her daughter. 'Everything is going to be alright,' she says. 'I promise.'

'How do you know?' Cathy asks her, giving her a searching look. It reminds her of all the times Cathy would question her when she was little. How her curious mind had been constantly seeking answers. How Cathy had made her feel the center of her daughter's world.

'Because I will make sure of it, Cathy.'

Park Ranger Nolan's hat is tipped low over her brow so that it is hard to see her eyes.

'Where's Special Agent Lopez?' Constance asks her.

'He's waiting for us at Shoshone Point,' Park Ranger Nolan says.

'But where's his car?'

'He came with me, decided to walk on ahead.'

The park ranger pushes the brim of her hat up. Constance can see her eyes now. They are a penetrating dark brown.

'It's at the spot where your husband fell,' she says pointedly.

Constance is slapped by her directness.

'What's the new information? Why do I have to meet him there?'

She is annoyed now that she doesn't have her phone on her. At least she could ring Matt and ask him to come back and meet them in the car park. She considers running back to the car to take it off Cathy, but Park Ranger Nolan is eyeballing her. She feels as if she is judging her. As if she can read her mind.

'Why did you lie?' the woman asks her.

LISTEN TO ME

You were surprised to see me again, but you still smiled at me. You had no idea of my intentions.

'I want to take a photograph of you,' I said. 'You look so good.'

You were so vain that you fell for the bait. Wanted me to take the picture with your phone. You stood there, posing against the iconic backdrop of the Grand Canyon. I wasn't lying. You did look good. I savored my last image of you. Drank every inch of you in. I memorized the color of your eyes, the shape of your lips, the light stubble on your chin. I memorized your lean, manly silhouette dark against the brilliance of the Arizonan sky. I burned your image forever inside my head so that I still see you smiling at me when I close my eyes. I saw no guilt. No shame in your expression. You were willing to destroy me to satisfy your desires.

My act was one of self-preservation. The only way my pain would stop was if I could make you stop breathing.

'Well?' you asked, getting impatient as you waited for me to take the photo.

'Can you step back a little further? I can't get you all in.'

You looked around your shoulder. Took a tentative step back. A little more.

'It's very close to the edge,' you said.

'You're perfectly safe,' I said. 'Trust me.'

You took a small step backwards. You were right on the edge.

'Come on,' you said, shoving your hands in your pockets. I knew you did that to stop me from seeing them shake. You were scared being up so high, but you didn't want to show me.

I stepped up to you.

'Your hair, it's in your face,' I said.

I stared into your eyes. I could see no true love for me in them. All I could see was that you were a liar. You would go on lying to me. Your deceptions would never end, and you would break my heart again and again. It had to stop.

It would have been perfect if she was standing next to you, then I could have pushed you both off the Grand Canyon. The happy couple. Pretending it was all about love, when all you were doing was acting like animals. Just like my father had done.

I hated you all.

It was easy in the end. I tucked that stray

hair behind your ear, and with my other hand on your chest I gave you a good shove. Your eyes opened wide in astonishment as you lost your balance. You reached out to me. I could have helped you, yet. Saved your life. But I was a cold killer now. Dead inside. As dead as you would be.

I stepped back.

Heard your cry peal out. A long, silent free fall.

I had pushed my husband off the edge of the Grand Canyon. Into the abyss you fell. I hoped never to be found again.

CHAPTER FORTY-EIGHT

SIX DAYS AFTER, MONDAY

Maya puts her foot on the pedal as her jeep picks up speed. She is possessed by instinct. A voice inside her is screaming at her to hurry up. She has no idea why she feels such a sense of urgency, but she knows something bad is about to happen. She feels it in the nausea that sweeps through her in black waves.

All Daniel had done was try to protect his daughter. Now he is gone, she has to do this for him. She owes him that, at least.

She could have picked up a phone and called the cops but she no longer trusts the police. Deputy Peters just doesn't seem to care enough about what happened to Daniel. She tried calling Special Agent Lopez, but he hadn't answered. She didn't want to leave a voicemail or a message because she can't trust any of the other rangers, clearly. It is best she looks into his eyes and knows that he believes her.

The storm has cleared, and the road is already dry again, but there is a freshness in the air. As if the land has been washed through by pure rain, and is glistening with new energy. She can hear the desert humming around her, the cacti twitching in the growing warmth as the last of the moisture is absorbed into their thick skins. The road is straight and long, and she imagines Daniel the last time he drove it. On his way to meet her.

She feels his presence again, beside her in the jeep.

I will always be with you.

She pushes her foot down even harder, speeds forwards.

'Come back!' she screams. 'I want you back!'

She pulls off the road onto the dusty shoulder, the tires losing grip and swerving. She slams on the brakes and the jeep shudders to a halt. She falls out of the jeep onto the hot earth, pitches over and vomits into the desert.

Maya sits back on her heels, her whole body trembling in shock. She is weak and dizzy, but she knows she must pick herself back up again. She has to get to the Grand Canyon and tell Lopez what she thinks happened. She has to protect Daniel's daughter, Cathy.

And his wife.

This sort of thing never happens. Someone like Maya never works out what happens to murdered people. And yet it seems she has found too many connections for it to be a coincidence.

There is no doubt in her mind that she has recalled the same person.

The posed smile, the thinning fair hair, and narrow high cheekbones were the same as the man in the picture frame in Park Ranger Nolan's trailer. He had looked cleaner, and more wholesome in the photograph than he had done in the bar in Prescott. But it was the same man, she was sure of it, who had been Cathy's cowboy. Shane Nolan. The older married man, whom Daniel had warned away from his daughter. And he was the husband of Park Ranger Katarina Nolan.

Daniel had been obsessed with him.

Two days after that incident in the bar, he had made Maya

stake out Cathy's friend's house with him. Maya hadn't wanted to spy on her lover's teenage daughter.

'You need to talk to her again,' she had said to him as they sat in her jeep, drinking coffee.

'She just lies to me,' Daniel had said. 'Says she's stopped seeing him.'

'Then you have to talk to her mother.'

'No,' Daniel snapped. 'I can't. Because if I do that Cathy will tell her about us.'

About time! Maya had wanted to scream at him. But she said nothing. Took another slurp of her coffee. A part of her had wanted to protect Cathy Garvey, but another part of her had been furious with her. No one had cared what Maya had got up to when she was Cathy's age.

'Honey, how much longer do we have to sit here?' she had moaned.

'Wait,' he had whispered. 'She's coming out.'

They had watched Cathy climbing out of her friend's bedroom window, and creeping across the front lawn. The light on her phone came on as she raised it to her ear, illuminating the side of her pale face.

'God almighty, look what's wearing,' Daniel had gasped.

Cathy had been tottering along the sidewalk. As she passed by a streetlight, Maya could see she was wearing very high-heeled ankle boots, a scarlet mini skirt, and a blue denim jacket. Granted, she had looked a bit cheap, but Maya remembered how she used to dress at that age. Just because a girl likes to dress provocatively, it doesn't mean she's a slut.

'Why don't we go get her now? Bring her home?' she suggested to Daniel.

'No, wait,' Daniel said. 'I want to get a hold of him. The only way I can stop this is by threatening that man.'

'But with what?'

'Statutory rape. Cathy is only fifteen. I'll ruin the bastard.'

'But you don't know who he is.'

'He doesn't know that. Besides, we can take down the car reg. Give it to the cops.'

As Daniel had spoken, Maya had seen car lights approaching. A pick-up truck. It slowed down, and stopped right by Cathy. Maya saw Cathy get in.

'Okay let's follow them,' Daniel had instructed her.

Maya had turned her jeep around and trailed the pick-up. They had followed it into downtown Flagstaff. She had driven past as it parked in the Monte Vista hotel car park.

'Drop me here,' Daniel had said.

'What are you going to do?' Maya had asked.

'I'm going in there and I'm going to get Cathy. End this for good.'

'Should I come with you? Wait here?'

'No, go home, Maya. I'll get a taxi with Cathy.'

'Are you sure this is a good idea, Daniel?' She had put her hand on his arm.

'She's my daughter,' Daniel had said, pulling away from her.

He had got out of the jeep, leaned in, and put his hand on hers on the steering wheel.

'I'm sorry, darling,' he had said, his voice tender. 'You understand, don't you?'

'Of course,' she had said. 'But, Daniel, be careful. You might never know the repercussions if you threaten that man.'

She had been worried that the big butch cowboy would have laid into Daniel. Hurt him. Or even had a gun. You had to be careful who you wound up in Arizona. And she had been right. There had been repercussions from that night.

Daniel's actions had broken up his daughter's relations with that cowboy. As Cathy had told her just one week later when she had stormed into her gallery in Sedona. Daniel's daughter had been dumped by the older man. But the story clearly hadn't ended there. Daniel had threatened him with statutory rape. He could have ruined Park Ranger Shane Nolan's career and marriage if he had wanted to.

Her darling Daniel had been pushed off the Grand Canyon. A brutal, horrific end. But it hadn't been Maya's fault.

Maya closes her eyes and summons Daniel before her. She sees him on their last day. Those awful final moments she will never forget just before she stormed off. The heartache in Daniel's blue eyes. She knows he loved her with all his soul.

It had been a love like no other, and she would never know it again. She had turned away. She had run away from him. Pine trees flashing past her, the dusty path pitching up toward her, as she pushed through a cluster of hikers, passing a park ranger.

The park ranger.

Maya gasps. Despite the heat of the day, she feels as if she has been submerged in icy water, her heart about to explode from shock.

Park Ranger Katerina Nolan had been following Daniel.

CHAPTER FORTY-NINE

SIX DAYS AFTER, MONDAY

They've been walking for over half an hour uphill through a sparse pine forest. Constance thinks of Cathy waiting for her in the car. She should ring her and tell her where she's going. But she can't of course because she has given Cathy her phone.

Eventually Park Ranger Nolan leads her out of the trees where the trail opens up. Her sandals keep nearly losing their grip on the sandy ground. She is hot, and she is anxious.

'Okay so here we are,' the park ranger says. She stops and takes off her Stetson. Wipes her brow with a small red handkerchief.

Constance looks around for Lopez. There are some picnic tables, a barbecue pit, and a small building that looks like it houses toilets. There is no sign of the special agent. Maybe he is using the facilities? They look locked up.

'Lopez said to go out onto the promontory.' Park Ranger Nolan indicates a ledge of rock that juts out over the canyon. There is a standing stone at its end, with a couple of prickly bushes, and not much else.

Constance's heart tightens in her chest. She looks with terror at the precipice of land jutting out over the Grand Canyon.

Unwillingly, she follows Park Ranger Nolan to its tip. The view is stomach clenching. Swathes of multi-colored rock slashed into vast gorges and tiny crags. A drop to eternity. She can't even look at it. Instead, she looks up at the sky and its serene blue contours.

'Where is Special Agent Lopez?' she asks Park Ranger Nolan.

'He's coming. I am sure he is on his way,' the ranger says, passing her a bottle of water.

Constance takes a big slug of water. Her legs feel shaky. She doesn't want to be standing here at all. It's dangerous.

'But you told me he was already here. Why did you bring me to this place if Lopez isn't here? I don't understand. Where is he?'

'He's on his way back from the Flagstaff Sheriff's Office where you were supposed to meet him this afternoon.'

Constance turns to Park Ranger Nolan in confusion.

'He told me to call you, but I gave you the wrong message,' she admits. 'You see there's no need for you to make a statement now. I know what happened.'

Constance stares at Katarina Nolan. She has taken her hat off again. She holds it in her hand. She notices it is shaking. The hard dark look in her eyes is gone. She looks down at the earth and then she speaks in such a low voice that Constance can hardly hear her.

'It was an accident,' she says to Constance. 'I was trying to catch him.'

The whole world begins to tilt. The vast vista of the yawning canyon before her tipping on its side. She struggles to maintain focus.

'We were arguing, and he stepped too far back,' Nolan says. 'He lost his balance and I tried to reach him but...'

Constance stares at the park ranger in horror. This woman killed her husband, and now Constance is all on her own with her. She steps back from the edge instinctively. Is she in danger too?

'I tried to save him,' the park ranger says desperately, looking up at her, her eyes swimming with tears.

'I don't understand. Why were you arguing with Daniel?' Constance's voice sounds calm, outside of herself. She takes another shaky step back away from the edge of the rim.

'You know nothing about it do you, Mrs. Garvey?'

'About what?'

'You and I are not so different.' A little color comes back to Park Ranger Nolan's cheeks. 'Both our husbands cheated on us. Deceived us.'

Constance stares at Park Ranger Nolan. She doesn't understand what she's saying.

'Were you having an affair with my husband?' she asks, her voice hoarse with dread.

Ranger Nolan gives out a short harsh bark of laughter.

'No, not me. I fucking loved my husband.' Her eyes grow dark. 'I would *never* have cheated on him. I'm talking about your daughter.'

Nolan licks her lips, her eyes almost black with bitterness. 'Your daughter and *my* husband.'

What on earth is Ranger Nolan talking about?

Constance takes another shaky step backwards. She is almost in one of the bushes at this stage. She needs to put distance between herself and this woman.

'Your husband knew. But he didn't tell you, did he? Maybe if he had, you could have persuaded him to drop the whole thing.'

'Are you talking about my daughter, Cathy?' Constance says in a hollow whisper.

'Well yes, you only have one daughter, Cathy Garvey, don't you?' Katarina Nolan's tone has completely changed. Her humble confession replaced by hard accusation. 'She was screwing my husband.'

The violence of her words makes Constance flinch in horror.

'No, I don't believe it.'

'Yes, she was,' Nolan says in a nasty voice. 'It wasn't a proper affair. Because your daughter makes a habit of sleeping with older men...'

'No!' Constance interrupts her. 'My daughter is just sixteen. She would never do that.'

Park Ranger Nolan takes a step toward her. She is pointing her finger at her.

'Yes, not quite sweet sixteen, and underage in the State of Arizona. So, your husband decided he was going to prosecute my husband with statutory rape.' Nolan puts her hands on her hips.

'I couldn't let that happen. Shane would have lost his job as a park ranger. The scandal would have ruined any chance I had. We would have had to leave the Parks. I love my job. The Grand Canyon is *my life*.'

'So you killed my husband?' Constance accuses in a trembling voice.

'No, I already told you that was an accident,' Nolan says emphatically. 'When Shane told me, I went to your husband and I begged him to stop proceedings but he refused. So I had to take matters into my own hands.'

Nolan takes a deep breath.

'When I saw your husband at the Grand Canyon on Tuesday, I just wanted to tell him that what his daughter did meant I had lost *my* husband for good. The little bitch,' she hisses.

'It's not true.' Constance leaps to Cathy's defense. 'My daughter would never do what you are saying.'

'You know how it feels, of all women, Mrs. Garvey,' Park Ranger Nolan says. 'I met Maya D'Costa. She is very beautiful.

Young. I would hate my husband for cheating on me with her. I would want to kill him...'

'But I didn't.' Constance feels fury growing inside her. '*You* did.'

'It was an accident!' Katarina Nolan almost screams at her. 'I told him that your daughter, and his threats, had ruined my marriage and he didn't care. But I didn't kill *your* husband, Mrs. Garvey. He fell.'

'Why are you telling me this now?' Constance's voice is trembling in fright.

'Because I am not a bad person,' Katarina Nolan says, dropping her ranger's hat on the ground as if in defeat. 'After it happened, I couldn't sleep. I thought of your husband's body lying out in the Grand Canyon for three nights. I felt guilty. So I went and found him.'

Park Ranger Nolan closes her eyes, presses her fingers into her forehead.

'I thought everyone would assume it was an accident or suicide as usual. I didn't count on Lopez investigating. So then I thought I could blame Maya D'Costa or even your daughter. Those girls should pay for the damage they have caused.'

Constance shakes her head. She can't believe what this woman is saying of Cathy. Her daughter is still a child. She is not at all like Maya D'Costa.

Katarina Nolan opens her eyes. 'I broke into your house and I took a necklace that belonged to your daughter. I was going to give it to Lopez. Say I found it here, where your husband fell.'

Katarina Nolan takes a chain from her pocket and throws it at Constance. She sees the small silver C pendant land on the earth in front of her.

'It was a dumb idea,' the park ranger says. 'Lopez had already checked the place thoroughly. He would have known I was lying.'

Constance picks up her daughter's necklace. Slips it in her

pocket. She remembers Cathy's delighted face when she had put on the hummingbird necklace in the car. Her daughter's heartache for her father. Her innocence. She can't believe what this woman is telling her.

'I really loved my husband, Mrs. Garvey,' Katarina Nolan says. 'He was my whole world. Your daughter took him away from me.'

There is more. Constance can sense it in the other woman's tone.

'This has nothing to do with my daughter,' Constance says, firm in her denial of Cathy's involvement. But even as she says the words, she can see all those dreadful clothes spilling out of her daughter's book bag. The lacy thong. The Trojan condoms. She is sick in her belly. How had she failed her own child to such an extent? She had been so lost in her own misery as a spurned wife that she had ignored her own daughter's trauma.

Katarina Nolan clasps her hands and closes her eyes. She looks as if she is seeking divine intervention.

'I didn't kill *your* husband,' she says, her voice breaking. 'But I killed *my* own husband.'

Constance freezes in horror as Park Ranger Nolan opens her eyes. Looking at her almost calmly now, the park ranger takes a gun out of her belt.

'I pushed Shane off a ledge out there in the middle of nowhere,' she says, waving the gun around. 'No one will ever find his body. The Grand Canyon has taken him.'

It is as if there is no air left in the world. As if a door has slammed shut in the Grand Canyon and she is trapped in a hot suffocating room. Constance shakes her head in terror but Katarina Nolan is not pointing the gun at her. She has put it to her own head.

'No, stop!'

'I can't live without Shane,' Katarina Nolan says to her. 'I thought the pain would end when I killed him. But it's worse than ever now.'

'Why are you doing this to me?' Constance screams at her. 'Stop it now!'

'Because you need to know the truth,' Nolan spits at her. 'You and your husband created your daughter. I see it in her. She does not love, she hates. She is a destroyer of love.'

'No, that's not Cathy.'

'You thought she was with her friend last night? Not at all, she was in downtown Flagstaff, picking up someone else's husband, and fucking him in the Hotel Monte Vista...'

Constance puts her hands over her ears. An image comes to her of Cathy as a small child, picking bog cotton, crouched in the purple heathers of the western bog with the blue Atlantic Ocean framing her red hair.

'No that's not my daughter.'

'Yes it is.'

Constance spins around to see Cathy walking towards them along Shoshone Point. For a moment she almost doesn't recognize her daughter. Even though she has been with her less than an hour ago, Cathy's face appears narrower, her eyes a brighter shade of blue, and her hair almost bronze in the glaring light.

'It's true.'

Constance feels as if she has been knocked to the ground, but she is standing still, somehow.

'You shouldn't have brought her.'

To her horror, Constance turns around to see Park Ranger Nolan has pulled the gun away from her own head and is pointing it at Cathy. She is framed by the tombstone of rock, like a dark, avenging angel.

'You destroyed my life,' Katarina Nolan accuses Cathy. 'You took my husband away from me.'

'You're a murderer,' Cathy shouts at Katarina Nolan in fury. 'You killed Shane.'

'It's *your* fault my husband is dead,' Katarina counters. 'You little whore!'

The woman almost doesn't look human anymore. Her teeth are bared, a dog about to attack.

'She's just a child...' Constance beseeches her.

'You killed my father.' Cathy hurls the words at Katarina Nolan, storming toward her as if she is daring the park ranger to shoot her.

'Don't you think the world would be better off without girls like Maya D'Costa and Cathy Garvey?' Katarina Nolan turns to Constance, her voice low and steady, her eyes glittering with venom, all the while the gun still pointed at her daughter. 'Cheap sluts that steal away our husbands?'

Constance isn't listening anymore. All she can see is that gun pointing at her daughter. All she can feel is raw primal fury.

'Don't you touch her!'

It is as if she has wings. As wide as those big black condors that are sweeping the sky above. Constance flies to her daughter. She throws herself upon her. Cathy's red hair is in her face, her fragile limbs banging against the hard earth beneath her as Constance hears a noise like a firework and then pain. Intense pain in her side.

'Mammy! Mammy!'

The Grand Canyon is spinning and spinning. Her mouth is full of dirt, and her body is screaming in agony. She rolls over. As she does so, she sees Lopez running towards her from the trail. And she sees Katarina Nolan running away. Past the tombstone. Right over the edge of Shoshone Point. No scream. Just a splattering of small rocks following her and then silence.

Cathy is crying. 'Mammy, please, Mammy.'

Her daughter's pale face swims before her. Finally, she is calling her 'Mammy' again.

She tries to speak. To tell her girl she is okay, but her mouth is full of something. It tastes like metal. Lopez is by her side. His hands are covered in blood. *You're bleeding*, she wants to tell him but then she realizes that he is holding his hands to her side. It is her blood. And though she should have been looking at her daughter, it is Lopez's warm brown eyes she seeks comfort in.

'I've got you,' he says to her. 'I've got you,' he keeps repeating.

There is someone else behind Lopez. A shadow. The scent of rose and sandalwood. Maya D'Costa. Constance wants to tell her, *It's not your fault*. But all she can do is close her eyes.

Daniel is there.

As he used to be. He is in his tux. He is holding out his hand to her. She looks down to see she is wearing her green Debs dress, with its bodice of sparkling sequins. Daniel is smiling at her. 'Let's dance,' he says.

She sees the young love in his eyes. It is how it was on their first date. The flutter of anticipation in her stomach. The growing excitement as she realizes this boy really likes her.

She takes his hand, and they are dancing. It is an old-style waltz. Up and down, round, and round. As they dance, she realizes they are upon the sea. Tiny frothy waves are lifting them up and down. They are buoyed upon the water. It is a miracle. She is back home in her beloved Ireland with the old Daniel. The boy she had first fallen in love with. They spin upon the misty sea within the chasms of the Grand Canyon, and the condors are dancing with them.

Daniel lets her hand go. She is sinking into the sea. Wet. She is soaked through. But he is spinning above her. His eyes gleam with regret. His lips curl a goodbye.

The sea swells. A big wave crashes over him. And then Daniel is gone from her forever.

LISTEN TO ME

I have called you up night after night.
Stacked your voicemail with messages you will
never hear. I have spoken into the silence of
your dead phone. Begging you to come back.

Pls, I text. *Pls 4give me.*

You see it was only after you were gone, I
began loving you again. None of your cheating
mattered anymore because I missed you so much.
I thought I could live without you, but I
understood that, in the end, I could not. We
belong to each other, Shane. In this life, and
the next.

The first time I laid eyes on the sheer
splendor of the Grand Canyon it was at Mather
Point. The futility of my existence, the
sublime immensity of the vista hit me full
force. It made me want to jump even then. I
always knew this would be my end.

I seek forgiveness in the Grand Canyon. My
shattered bones, my torn flesh becomes as

fragile as a tiny shell. I lay myself upon her rocky bed, and wish to become one with the earth.

Down there, way down deep, I will find you again. And maybe if I look hard enough I will find my parents too. At a time when they loved me, before they began to hate each other. Before they took me over to the other side of love when my shame turned into violence.

CHAPTER FIFTY

FOUR YEARS LATER, THURSDAY 12 JANUARY 2023

Maya waits. The space is teeming with people. She has not stopped talking since she arrived and yet the whole time, she has kept one eye on the door.

It is dark outside. She can see the inky contours of a New York winter evening pressing in on the glass front of the gallery. The hazy lights of cars and cabs. The glowing stores on the other side of the street. The glimmers of pale-faced commuters hurrying home. It is beyond cold. Outside, the freezing air bites the skin, claws to penetrate clothing. Everyone is complaining that it is too cold. Yet Maya takes a strange delight in its extremity. Just as she once loved the soaring heat of Arizona, she likes to pit herself against the frozen streets of her new home in Brooklyn. The snow banked up and graying, the roads slippery with ice, the air tight with the promise of yet another snowstorm.

The door of the gallery opens. She feels herself stiffen with anticipation, but it is only Bernie, her agent. She flings her long black coat onto the chair behind reception, and weaves through the crowd towards her.

'Sorry I'm late,' Bernie says, hugging Maya.

Maya can still feel the chill of the arctic night off her. She shivers involuntarily as Bernie's dark curls, which are stiff with cold, brush against her cheek.

Her agent steps back and surveys the exhibition. 'It looks great, Maya,' she says. 'The colors are so rich. I feel like they are warming me up.' She laughs, her eyes flitting over the crowd.

'So is he here?' Bernie asks as she takes a glass of prosecco from a passing waiter.

'Yes,' Maya says, pointing to a small throng grouped around a slight yet distinguished-looking Indian man. Her father, Antonio D'Costa. Only last month described in the *New York Times* as one of the twenty-first century's most significant abstract expressionists.

'It's so great he's opening your show,' Bernie enthuses. 'It's getting your work the attention it deserves.'

Maya is only half-listening. The gallery door opens, and a young woman walks in. Long red hair. That Irish creamy skin. She looks at her face. But it is not her. She feels a mixture of relief and disappointment.

What kind of miracle is she expecting? The likelihood of Cathy Garvey turning up at her exhibition in New York is beyond remote.

Maya had sent an invitation just one week ago. She had found Cathy quite easily on Facebook a month ago. Had seen she was a student at Columbia. She had been in two minds about doing it, but last week she had taken the plunge and sent the invitation via Cathy's college. She had put a photograph in the envelope.

Maya needs to see Cathy Garvey.

Maybe then the nightmares might stop. Again and again, she has dreamed of that moment on Shoshone Point four years ago. Running through those woods to the edge of the Grand Canyon. She and Special Agent Lopez tearing through the trail one after the other. Lopez went straight to Constance Garvey on the ground. Cathy was screaming by her mother's side. The girl's hands had been covered in blood.

Maya had looked around for Katarina Nolan but all she could see was the park ranger's Stetson lying on its side in the dusty earth.

Her instinct had been to calm Cathy while Lopez tried to save her mother, but the girl was hysterical. Beating Maya's chest with her bloody fists. Incoherent with rage. Abusing her.

She let her hit her. She had wept with shame. She wanted to tell Cathy that she knew how she felt. But she hadn't been able to. In her dreams she tries to tell her, but just as she is about to, Maya wakes up. She has never got to explain.

That is why Maya had contacted her own stepmother. After everything that had happened in the Grand Canyon, she wanted to see her father more than anything. But it was Celeste she had rung up first.

'Can I come?' she had whispered down the phone.

'Sure,' Celeste had said right away. No questions.

Her stepmother, along with her half brother and sister, are back at the apartment in Brooklyn, minding her little boy, Danny. Cathy Garvey's little brother. This is why she needs Daniel's daughter's forgiveness. It is for her son's sake.

'So who is "The Woman in the Window"?' Her father has joined her side. He hooks his arm through hers. Bernie is the other side of the gallery now. It is just the two of them. Her father smiles at her, and she sees something like pride in his eyes. And it shocks her. All these years she thought she could live without her father's approval. But it isn't true. She has missed him.

'No one really,' she says.

'Not your mother?' Antonio D'Costa pushes tentatively.

'No,' Maya sighs, feeling sad. Since she has made friends with her stepmother, her mother now refuses to talk to her.

Maya takes a step forward, moving away from her father.

She looks at her own paintings. She knows exactly who 'The Woman in the Window' is. But she wants only one person to know that too. It would be their secret.

On the pure white gallery walls is a series of views of the Grand Canyon, and the back of a woman looking at them through a window. The landscape filtering in through the window frame. The wings of a condor. The branches of a piñon tree. The lesions, gorges, and chasms of ancient rock. The rushing river. The flaming sunset. The tombstone at Shoshone Point.

The woman in the painting has short blond hair, and is wearing the same blue dress Maya last saw on her. Lying on the ground, a fan of crimson spreading across the shimmering blue silk.

She does not know why she has painted all these portraits of Constance Garvey in the Grand Canyon. All she knows is that she had to.

Maya turns her back on the exhibition. The work is done now, and she has no desire to see any one of these paintings ever again.

It has begun to snow outside. She stands at the gallery window and watches the swirling flakes spiraling slowly in the streetlights. She thinks of Daniel.

She had come to live in New York hoping it might help her move on. But every time she looks into her boy's blue eyes, she is reminded of his father. Daniel is everywhere. As much in the intricate and transient beauty of a snowflake in New York City as in the eternal resilience of the red boulders of Sedona. He will never leave her side. And as she thinks this, she sees a figure on the other side of the street looking at her. A girl with long red hair. Dressed in a green coat. A face she could never forget.

Terrified, and hopeful at the same time, Maya waits for Cathy Garvey to cross the street, and enter the art gallery. But the girl continues to stare at her through the falling snow. All the bustle and noise around Maya fades to a hum. All she can see is the figure looking in at her. Still and focused, steam pluming from her breath, her eyes burning through the spinning ice.

Cathy Garvey moves. But she doesn't cross the street. She pushes her hands deeper into her pockets, as another girl approaches her. They kiss, and then turn away and walk towards the subway station arm in arm, disappearing down the steps. A part of Maya wants to run after them. But she knows better not to. She has to wait until Cathy Garvey returns. She hopes she will one day.

CHAPTER FIFTY-ONE

FOUR YEARS LATER, 17 MAY 2023

Already her daughter has changed. It has only been a few months since Cathy and Lisa were with them at Christmas and yet she looks so much older as she walks towards her in the arrivals hall at Phoenix Airport. It always gives Constance a jolt seeing Cathy because it brings Daniel back in a little way. The same shade of stark red hair. The ivory skin, and uncompromising blue eyes. Yet Cathy is herself too. Different. She has filled out a touch, still pale, but strong. Constance can see that.

Her daughter has shed her signature black, and become a devotee of New York vintage stores. Today she is wearing a green tea dress, covered in tiny blue buds the same shade as her eyes. Constance wonders if she is wearing green to please her.

Cathy sees her. Constance can feel herself smiling back. She is dying to embrace her, but she knows by now that her daughter is not keen on public displays of affection.

She takes Cathy for brunch to a classy bistro in Scottsdale. There is the usual awkwardness between them. Cathy says little as she picks at her sweet crêpe. Constance is struggling with her grilled asparagus. The food is delicious, it is just that she is nervous. She is not sure how Cathy is going to react to her news.

'So how's college?' she probes, taking a sip of her glass of water.

'Good.' Cathy nods.

'And Lisa?'

'Good, she says hi.'

Her daughter seems preoccupied as she cuts into her crêpe.

'Everything okay?'

'Yep,' she says succinctly, but her eyes will not meet hers.

Constance quells the annoyance, takes a deep breath. She knows now that it's best to say nothing rather than rile Cathy.

'*Just give her time.*' That's what Matt had told her.

She is itching to talk to him. She might even go to the restrooms and call him up. Just to hear his voice. Know that he loves her. Wants her. Some days it is hard to believe. But she is not going to run away from her daughter. It was hiding things that destroyed her family before.

She puts down her knife and fork. Prepares to speak. They are sitting outside, surrounded by the scent of orange blossom. It is spring again in Arizona. She has come to love this place. Four years ago, she never would have believed it, but through her feelings for Matt, and her new friendships with Julie, and Stacey of all people, she has looked at Arizona with new eyes.

Matt has taken her deep into the wild spaces of this landscape, and shared his desert world with her. Her heart has opened to the vast skies, as wide and blue as oceans. This ancient land of boulders, and red rocks. Together they have stood in silence watching the magnificence of a Grand Canyon setting sun. Its long fingers of gold penetrating her grief. She has lost herself among wildflowers. Smelt the fervor of the spring blooms and returned to life again. She has even learned to admire cacti for their true grit. It has been a revelation for her.

While she's still close to Frances back home, Lisa's mam, Julie, has become a true friend as well. It was Julie who helped her fix up her CV and get a job in an art gallery in Sedona. But it's Stacey who has been the real surprise. About a year after Daniel died, her sister-in-law had walked out on Liam after she discovered he was having an affair with another realtor. She has reinvented herself as a yoga teacher and reiki guide and has spent hours helping Constance heal from her injuries. Often Constance feels overwhelmed by Stacey's generosity, and guilty of how she had once judged her. Her life is so rich in Arizona now, she knows that she will not go back to Ireland—maybe never again. This is where she belongs.

'I've something to tell you,' Constance says to Cathy.

Her daughter stops eating. She says nothing. But the look in her eyes is wary. Constance has no idea how she will react.

'I'll just say it right out then,' Constance says, looking straight into Cathy's unwavering blue eyes. 'Matt and I. We want to get married.'

Cathy's eyes widen, but still she does not speak.

'And I want to check it's okay with you...'

'But it's not up to me. It's your life. What does it matter if I care?' Her daughter's voice is steady. Her cheeks are flushed, but she doesn't sound angry.

'Because you come first, Cathy. You know that don't you?'

All of a sudden, Cathy leans forward in her seat, picks up Constance's hand across the table and squeezes it.

'Of course I know that. Mam, you saved my life.'

Constance cannot answer for a moment, she is so surprised. Cathy has never spoken of that day before. She feels her daughter's fingers laced within hers. Her chest is tight with the emotion of it.

'I did what any mother would have done—' she begins to say.

'But it's my fault you did it,' Cathy interrupts.

'No of course it's not,' Constance says. 'That park ranger. Katarina Nolan...'

'Listen to me. You know it's true. It's my fault that Daddy is dead.'

Constance looks at her daughter in alarm. Is this what she has been thinking for the past four years?

'No, Cathy, it's not—'

But her daughter interrupts her again. She is squeezing her hand so tight her fingers feel like they might snap. But she doesn't let go.

'If I hadn't been seeing Shane Nolan then none of it would have happened. Katarina Nolan would never have killed Daddy.'

'She said it was an accident. Your father fell...'

Cathy shakes her head vehemently. 'I could see the mad look in her eyes.' Her voice trembles. 'When she was about to shoot me. She pushed him. I know it.'

Cathy closes her eyes. Takes a shaky breath. Constance is afraid to speak. She waits. At last her daughter is talking.

'If I hadn't followed you to Shoshone Point, Katarina Nolan wouldn't have tried to shoot me too.' Cathy opens her eyes again. A flash of furious blue. 'And you wouldn't have taken the bullet for me.'

Constance does not know what to say. The strange thing is she has no memory of being shot. The moment is a hot blank inside her. A place of terror she has no wish to remember. Instead, she holds her daughter's hands tight, looks at the tears welling in her eyes.

'I'm sorry, Mam. I blamed you. I thought you were weak. But you're not. You're braver than anyone.'

'I don't feel I was brave,' Constance protests. 'It wasn't a choice for me. It was instinct.'

They hold hands, neither of them speaking. A humming-bird hovers in front of the agave blossoms beside them.

Constance watches it dip its bill into the blossom to lap the nectar out with its long tongue. She turns to Cathy again. Her daughter is staring at the hummingbird, but her eyes look faraway. Constance notices Cathy is wearing the blue hummingbird necklace Daniel had bought for her birthday just before he died.

'Sometimes I think Daddy has just gone on a journey. And one day he will return,' Cathy announces.

'Me too,' Constance whispers back.

They take a walk through the Art District of Scottsdale, and into the old part of town. Something has shifted between them. Constance can feel it.

Outside the Old Adobe Mission church, Cathy stops walking.

'Let's go inside,' she asks her mother. 'Light a candle for Dad.'

They walk towards the white-washed church, gleaming in the afternoon sun, and enter its thick walls into the dim coolness of its interior. It is over four years since Daniel was lost. Constance remembers him telling her about this old church. How it had been hand built by Mexicans who had settled in Scottsdale in the first decade of the twentieth century. They had carried and placed by hand each one of the 14,000 adobe bricks. Daniel had admired their industry, and the purity of its architecture. Told her how he wanted one day to live in a house made with thick adobe walls. She had not really listened to him. At the time all she had wanted was to be back home in Ireland. And yet now she lives, with her lover, in her own adobe house. While Matt is out fulfilling his duties for the Grand Canyon National Park, she stays out of the heat of the day, working at her own desk. With the soles of her feet pressed against those cool clay walls, she calls up clients and contacts artists. Art books piled on either side of her like her own personal towers of discovery.

They light a candle for Daniel, but they do not kneel down and pray. Instead, they walk a circumference around the old church, arm in arm, admiring the stained-glass windows, and pausing by the main altar to look at the photograph of the statue of Our Lady of Perpetual Help, no longer standing in its original place. Being in this church reminds Constance of her own mother, and her rigid Catholicism. Had she failed as much as her in the end?

'I'm sorry that you had to witness all those fights,' Constance confesses. 'I should have left Daniel a long time before.'

Her daughter turns to her. Looks surprised.

'I'm sorry I was not a better mother to you.'

'Mammy, stop.' Cathy has put her hand to Constance's mouth, silenced her. 'You *are* a good mother.'

There is a feeling in this old church, or maybe it is the energy between herself and Cathy, but she has a sensation of stepping out of her reality. As if she is looking down at the two of them.

'I want to show you something,' Cathy says, opening her bag. Her daughter takes a photograph out of the inside pocket. Hands it to her.

Constance cannot help but gasp. She is looking at a little boy. With bright red hair, blue eyes. A smile that would soften the hardest heart. It doesn't need explaining but Cathy speaks all the same.

'He's called Danny. My half-brother.'

Constance looks up. 'Have you met him?'

'Not yet.' Cathy shakes her head.

'But how did you get the picture?'

'She sent it to me.'

She. Maya D'Costa. The other woman that Constance will never be able to forget.

'I don't know how she found out where I was, but she sent me an invite to an exhibition she was having in New York just after Christmas.'

Cathy takes the picture from Constance's limp hand.

'Did you go?' Constance asks. She can feel an ache in her side, right where the scar from the gunshot wound is. She puts her hand to it.

'I was going to.' Cathy pauses. 'I went all the way there. But when I saw her in the gallery, surrounded by all those people, and all the buzz about her art... I just couldn't do it. I called Lisa, and she came and got me.'

Cathy looks down at the photograph of her baby brother.

'It felt like I would be disloyal to you if I went in,' she says.

'But he's your brother,' Constance murmurs.

'Yes but you're family, not him.'

It is hard for Constance to say the words she does next, but she knows she must for her daughter's sake.

'Cathy, you don't need my permission to see your brother.'

'Sure.' Cathy shrugs, avoiding her eye.

Constance looks at the candle they lit for Daniel. The fighting tiny flame flickering within the cool peace of the old church.

'She called him Danny,' Constance says, her voice fading into faint echoes.

'I know,' Cathy spits out.

Constance sees the twist in her daughter's mouth. The fight not to cry as she puts the photograph back in her bag. Carefully tucking it into the zip compartment.

'So she's living in New York now?' Constance asks her.

'Yes,' Cathy says, looking up.

Constance can see it in her daughter's eyes. One day she

will seek out her little brother. Even sit down with Maya D'Costa and talk about Daniel. She knows it will be a good thing for Cathy, but still the thought of it hurts her. She presses her hand on her side, feels the throb beneath her skin.

Constance has gone to Luna House once since Daniel died. She had not known she was going there until she found herself driving through Oak Creek Canyon one afternoon six months after everything had happened. She had still been in pain from her injuries. A sore nagging stab in her side, as she got out of her car, and walked towards her husband's old love nest. She knew immediately that Maya D'Costa was gone. No wind chimes, or blanket-strewn chairs. Constance had peered in through the windows. The rooms were empty. The kachina dolls removed. The color and life of the artist dismantled. And with her the last shred of Daniel.

Constance had sat down by the little brook that tumbled through the undergrowth of the garden, and she had wept for her lost husband.

Afterward, she had felt lighter. As if the weight of her guilt had lifted. She had got back in her car and driven away. The next week she had moved in with Matt into their adobe house.

Constance and Cathy walk back out into the light. It is time to get going. They have a long drive back to Flagstaff, and Matt is waiting for them.

'So you're okay about the wedding?' she asks Cathy again, realizing her daughter still hasn't given her blessing.

Cathy turns to her. Her daughter is taller than her now. To her surprise she leans forward, takes a stray strand of Constance's blond hair, and tucks it behind her ear. It is an unexpected gesture. One a mother might make. It makes Constance feel as if she is protected by her own child.

'Of course it's fine. You deserve to be loved.' Cathy smiles.

At last Cathy has returned. The years of her daughter's difficult adolescence fall away, and Constance can see her little girl again. In the transformation of her face. The sweetness of her smile. The warmth in her eyes. And yet, this creature before her is so much more than her daughter. She is a young woman too. Full of grace. Forgiving.

A LETTER FROM NOELLE

I want to say a huge thank you for choosing to read *The Man I Can't Forgive*. If you did enjoy it, and want to keep up to date with all my latest releases, just sign up at the following link. Your email address will never be shared and you can unsubscribe at any time.

www.bookouture.com/noelle-harrison

Relationships are complex, especially marriages. I wanted to write a story which challenges society's romanticisation of marriage as well as our judgements upon infidelity and the 'other' woman. It was my aim to create a wronged wife and an abandoned mistress both flawed, both empathic, tied to a man who betrays them. How is it that such great love can turn to intense hatred? What actions might we take to find peace from our raging emotions?

It was against the dramatic backdrop of the Grand Canyon in Arizona that these characters surfaced, and I drew inspiration. The extreme beauty, and the dangers of its harsh climate, provided the perfect backdrop to my tale of passion and vengeance.

But this story has another one bubbling beneath its surface. It is about the toxic fallout of a bad marriage. It is about the children caught in the crossfire of their parents' arguments, unable to flourish in an atmosphere of disharmony. This book asks: is it *really* better to stay together for the sake of the kids? Ultimately, though it is called *The Man I Can't Forgive*, this story is in truth all about forgiveness—most of all about forgiveness between a mother and a daughter. No one can be the perfect parent.

I hope you loved *The Man I Can't Forgive*, and if you did, I would be very grateful if you could write a review. I'd love to hear what you think, and it makes such a difference helping new readers to discover one of my books for the first time.

I love hearing from my readers—you can get in touch through social media or my website.

Warmest wishes,

Noelle Harrison

www.noelleharrison.com

 facebook.com/NoelleCBHarrison

 x.com/NoelleHarrison

 instagram.com/noelle.harrison5

ACKNOWLEDGEMENTS

Thank you to my wonderful agent, Marianne Gunn O'Connor, and my fabulous editor, Lydia Vassar-Smith, and the great team at Bookouture. Thank you also to Alison Walsh, who provided invaluable insights on early drafts of this novel.

Thank you to the gorgeous Bespoke Inn in Scottsdale who hosted me on one of my research trips to Arizona; to Jo Southall, who first brought me to the Grand Canyon, and Barry Ansley, who brought me back.

I am also grateful to my friends and family who have supported me as a writer and believed in me. Thank you to Ila Moldenhauer for her insight on Matt Lopez's heritage, and the rest of the gang in Norway for their constant book club support: Tracey-Ann Skjæråsen, Nina Rolland, Marianne Mølholm, Sidsel Humberset, Joan Mikkelsen and Elisa Bjersand. Thank you to all my dear friends especially Kate Bootle, Donna Ansley, Becky Sweeney, Bex Hunt, Lizzie McGhee, El Lam, Monica McInerney, Sinead Moriarty, Page Allen, Sandra Ireland, Charley Drover, Caroline Byrne, Cora Cummins, and Bernie McGrath for their constant and enriching friendships. Special thanks to my son, Corey, and my daughter, Helena, and all my cherished family, my siblings, Fintan, Jane and Paul, my cousins, my aunt Joyce and to my mother-in-law, Mary Ansley. Finally, dear reader, thank you for taking the time to immerse yourself in my story. I hope it took you on a journey worth taking.

PUBLISHING TEAM

Turning a manuscript into a book requires the efforts of many people. The publishing team at Bookouture would like to acknowledge everyone who contributed to this publication.

Commercial
Lauren Morrissette
Hannah Richmond
Imogen Allport

Contracts
Peta Nightingale

Cover design
Jo Thomson

Data and analysis
Mark Alder
Mohamed Bussuri

Editorial
Lydia Vassar-Smith
Lizzie Brien

Copyeditor
Natasha Hodgson

Made in the USA
Monee, IL
21 July 2024

62402957R00198